KING'S REIGN

BRADLEY WRIGHT

ALSO BY BRADLEY WRIGHT

The Xander King Series

Whiskey & Roses

Vanquish

King's Ransom

Vendetta (prequel novella)

KING'S REIGN

Bradley Wright/King's Ransom Books
www.bradleywrightauthor.com

Cover Design by DDD, Deranged Doctor Designs
King's Reign/ Bradley Wright. -- 1st ed.
ISBN - 978-0-9973926-3-0

For Heather and Haley Jo
Two of the greatest girls in all the world

I survived because the fire inside me burned brighter than the fire around me.

— JOSHUA GRAHAM

In any moment of decision, the best thing you can do is the right thing, the next best thing is the wrong thing, and the worst thing you can do is nothing.

— THEODORE ROOSEVELT

KING'S REIGN

1

The Itch

The slow dance between day and night had begun its twirl out over the Pacific Ocean. As the waves rolled gently ashore, the tangerine sky above Cabo San Lucas, Mexico, continued its fight against the black of night. A warm breeze whispered through the palm trees, rustling the leaves: a tropical lullaby. Out in the distance, storm clouds gathered, the threat of a tropical storm looming.

The Resort at Pedregal looked out over that ocean, many of its rooms embedded in the side of a cliff. It had a large patio area with sweeping views of the Pacific, and the lagoon-style infinity pool looked as if it emptied right out into it. A circular tiki bar—thatch roof and all—was half swim-up from the pool and half bar stools on the other side. Xander King sat at one of those stools, taking in the view. As he was considering which of the views to be more breathtaking, the auburn sky or the woman relaxing at the pool's infinity edge, he struck a match, lighting a Davidoff 702 Reserve cigar. After a couple of puffs, the clouds of smoke scented the air with cocoa, almonds, and cream. Xander sat back in his chair, and with a deep, relaxing breath, the woman who was now stepping out of the pool made the decision easy for him.

It was her.

If he didn't know better, he'd swear it was J.Lo who stood toweling off just twenty feet from him. Xander took a sip of his Don Julio Blanco tequila—on the rocks with a lime—and wasn't at all shy about letting his eyes linger. When the woman noticed him noticing her, she wasn't shy about flashing him a smile, acknowledging their mutual attraction. Xander moved his attention back toward the ocean. Every time he saw a breathtaking woman, he thought of Natalie Rockwell. And every time he thought of Natalie, it nearly ruined his evening. While it wasn't that he hadn't been with another woman since he last saw her in Paris almost five months ago in June, because sexually he had, but his heart still belonged to Natalie. They'd spoken several times on the phone and chatted briefly via text messages, but it was clear Natalie still didn't believe that Xander could stay away from the fight. She kept saying it was just a matter of time before he couldn't resist scratching that itch. "You can't fight who you really are, Xander," she would say. But he had resisted the itch over the last five months. The CIA had called for him several times, and several times he declined. The only question he kept asking himself was whether he was declining because he wanted to, or if it was for her.

Bob Marley kept telling him not to worry about a thing over the speakers fixed to the underside of the bar's thatch roof. He said don't worry, because every little thing was gonna be all right. But it wasn't. Things were very different. His best friend, Kyle, had taken over the day-to-day operations of Xander's company, King's Ransom Bourbon. And Sam, Xander's longtime partner in the fight to find his parents' killer, well, she'd grown bored of watching Xander, in her words, "deny his true calling." His "calling" to her was defined as continuing to rid the world of bad guys.

But after all that happened in Syria, Moscow, and Paris, it seemed to Xander that he had lost his motivation to give a damn about the bad guys and what they were doing. His giving such a damn about them had lost him the chance of a life with Natalie. Sam said he was moping around like a little bitch. Her version of tough love. So while Xander "moped" around, she had been consulting for the director of the CIA, Mary Hartsfield, in her spare time.

Xander didn't consider what he was doing to be "moping," however. He considered it healing. Taking time away from every-thing—healing his body, *and* his mind. It was something he needed to do. And just because the last few weeks he'd been having dreams of running down gunmen, jumping out of planes, and pulling the trigger on his Glock 19 didn't mean he was missing it. And just because he had started back doing the highly intense Murph workout every morning again didn't mean he was preparing himself to jump back into the fray.

Did it?

Xander took a drag from his cigar and followed it with a sip of tequila.

He heard a woman's voice beside him: "I'll have what he's having." *Her* voice. She was even more beautiful now that she was closer. Her skin was the color of caramel; her long, wet dark hair fell down the back of her white tight-fitting, gauze-like cover-up dress.

Yum.

Xander smiled. "Aren't you going to buy me a drink? I saw the way you were ogling me from the pool."

She turned from the bartender toward him and smiled back. Wow, what a smile.

"I don't think my boyfriend would like that."

Xander made a point to search all around the bar, comically exaggerating the turn of his head and body; then when he turned back to her, he shrugged his shoulders and gave a considering look. "I don't see any boyfriends."

3

She held up two fingers to the bartender as she laughed at Xander's playful remark. When she turned to him, he noticed the most beautiful chocolate-brown eyes. They seemed kind, with a heavy side portion of sexy. "And *I* don't see any girlfriends." She looked him up and down. "What's a tall, dark, and handsome man such as yourself doing out here in paradise, drinking alone?"

"Waiting on nature to take its course." Xander didn't hesitate.

The bartender handed the woman two drinks, and she slid Xander's over to him.

"And he's charming."

"Just wait till you see what I can do in the kitchen."

Xander didn't cook, but it sounded good.

She held out her hand. "Well, Mister Perfect, I'm Gabriela Cisneros."

He took her hand. "Alexander King, my friends call me Xander. You have a beautiful name . . . is it Spanish?"

"Si, señor." She took a sip of her drink. As she did, Xander pulled out a bar stool for her. "A southern gentleman, I see?" She took the seat.

"Si, hermosa."

Xander didn't know Spanish, but he'd heard a man at the airport say that word about Xander's G6 private jet. His pilot Bob told him it meant beautiful.

"Lexington, Kentucky."

"Ah," she said, "home of the beautiful horses."

"You got it."

Xander reached his glass toward hers, and she clanked her glass against it.

"Salud."

"Salud," Xander said. "How 'bout you?"

"Scottsdale originally. LA now, well, when I'm not in Mexico with Antonio."

"So there really is a boyfriend."

Gabriela gave a faltering smile. "There really is. And I should really go before he gets back."

Xander shifted in his seat and set his cigar down on the ashtray. "I don't like the sound of that. Jealous type, is he?"

"You have no idea."

"Hmm." Xander contemplated.

"Hmm? What do you mean by that?"

Gabriela shifted toward him and recrossed her legs. The long, tan legs that were on another level.

"It's nothing. You just don't seem like the type of woman who would let a man tell her who she can and can't talk to."

"Yeah? What type do I seem like?"

"Unicorn."

Gabriela laughed. "Don't hold back now."

Xander smiled. "You really are a beautiful woman."

She sipped her drink. "Those blue eyes of yours are trouble. I bet there is a trail of broken hearts left in your wake, Alexander."

Hearing her call him by his full name sent a zing through him. That was Natalie's thing.

"You're safe with me."

"He says with such confidence." She brushed a few strands of hair back behind her ear. "Listen, this has been fun, but I really do have to get going—"

"Gabriela?" a man called from somewhere behind the two of them.

Immediately, Xander could see a shift in Gabriela. So much so that he became concerned. She was clearly afraid of whoever just called her name.

"Shit," she said in a panicked whisper as she stepped down from her bar stool. "Whatever you do, please don't antagonize him."

Now Xander was really worried about her. This could get interesting really quickly. Xander hadn't even seen this man, but he knew he already didn't like him. And just the slightest trickle of anticipatory adrenaline leaked into his nervous system. He hadn't had that feeling in a while. Xander had no idea what it was like to be hooked on drugs, but he felt as if that little shot of adrenaline had to be what it was like when a junkie got his fix.

"What the hell are you doing, Gabriela?"

Xander turned to find a man walking toward them. A man who was every drug-dealing cliché in the book. He was a Mexican man with a thick accent. White blazer with a white dress shirt under-neath, tucked into white pants, finishing with some of the tackiest white patent leather loafers on the planet. If all of that weren't bad enough, his jet-black hair was slicked back, Pat Riley style, and he was wearing enough gold chains and bracelets to make Mr. T jeal-ous. He wasn't very tall, but he was in good shape, and he stood like a peacock, chest jutted out in front of him.

Xander answered for Gabriela. "I was trying to buy the pretty lady a drink, but she said her boyfriend wouldn't much like that. Can't win 'em all, I guess."

He could see the appreciation in Gabriela's eyes when she glanced at him.

The man bowed up even more. "Of course she said no. Like she would want attention from a gringo like you when she has me."

Xander would let that one slide.

"Well, you're a lucky man." Xander played nice. "Xander," he reached out his hand.

The man looked at his hand with disdain and didn't so much as attempt to shake it. "Go back to your miserable life in America."

Xander wanted to leave it alone. He really did. But despite Sam's assessment that no longer going after the bad guys was Xander denying who he really was, not making a sarcastic comment would have much further gone the way of denying his true self.

"Charming." Xander glanced at Gabriela. "I totally get what you see in him." He looked back to Antonio. "You know you're not supposed to wear white after labor day. Or a bunch of gold rope chains after . . . well . . . ever really."

Damn it.

Antonio turned to face Xander. "The hell did you just say to me? Do you know who you are talking to?"

Xander could feel the itch burning inside him. *Scratch me . . . scratch me!*

"Um, not sure, but if your phone rings, it's 1980s Miami calling, and they want their look back."

Xander was ready to scratch. He knew it was going to feel *so* good.

Antonio lunged at Xander—Xander didn't flinch—and Gabriela stepped in and pushed him back. "Don't, Xander, please! Just go. You don't want to do this. He will hurt you."

Another drip of adrenaline seeped into Xander's bloodstream. It was like a smoker taking his first inhale after days without a cigarette.

Xander stepped down from his chair. He towered over the shorter Antonio. And Xander's bulk was more than twice that of the Mexican man. Antonio watched Xander step off the bar stool, and his eyes widened at the thought of this American having the audacity to challenge him. Xander could see by the look in his eyes that this didn't happen very often. Antonio had the false confidence of a powerful man. A man who was used to people jumping to fulfill his wishes.

Antonio then turned his attention to Gabriela who was still holding him back. "You are warning him? You are trying to help him? How dare you disrespect me!" Then he took her by the shoulders and tossed her to the side. She landed in a thud on the concrete below her, and the rest of the adrenaline that had been waiting for months to greet Xander released completely, surging through to his taut muscles. He slowly began to roll up the sleeves on his button-up shirt, and his breath became heavier with excitement. Sam was right, Natalie was right, everyone else who had tried to bring him back to battle were all correct: he lived for this shit.

"Don't, Xander. Please! Let it go! He'll kill you!"

Much to Xander's liking, Antonio stepped forward.

It was time to scratch that itch.

2

Not Your Ordinary Beach Bum

Antonio swung a wild left-right combination at Xander's head. Xander easily shifted his head from left to right, dodging both punches. He could see Antonio instantly recognize that Xander was no stranger to a fistfight.

Antonio stepped back and removed his shirt, revealing a lot of ripped muscles, but they were all tiny muscles. "So you are fighter, eh, gringo?"

Xander moved his eyes from Antonio's and gave the man's upper body a once-over. "That supposed to impress me? If you're not careful, I'm going to embarrass you in front of your friends, and your girlfriend." He motioned toward Gabriela. "You see, she won't hit you back, but if you try putting your hands on me again, I'll hit you for her." The feeling inside Xander was one he had truly missed. His body was begging him to teach this little shit a lesson.

Gabriela stepped back in. "No one is hitting anyone. Xander, I

9

don't need your help. Antonio, I couldn't care less about this man. I was just being polite. Let's go back and enjoy a nice dinner."

Xander couldn't help it. "You should listen to her, Antonio. Don't spoil your dinner."

Antonio's body jerked at Xander's taunts. The three other men with him moved toward Xander, but Antonio waved them off.

"Brave man," Xander prodded.

"I'll show you brave, esé."

Antonio moved forward, and once again Gabriela caught him. This time he made sure she wouldn't interrupt again, pushing her aside, then slapping her in the face. Xander rushed forward and caught her in his right arm, keeping her from falling. Antonio tried to take advantage and took a swing at Xander. Still holding Gabriela, Xander caught Antonio's wrist with his left hand and simultaneously drove his forehead forward and shattered Antonio's nose. Antonio shuffled back a few steps, grabbing at his face.

"My nose. My nose!" He checked his hands; there was blood everywhere. "You broke my nose!"

Xander looked at Gabriela. "I'm gonna need just a sec."

She took a step away from him. "I'm begging you, don't! You don't know who you're dealing with!"

Antonio moved his hands from his nose into fight position. "That's right, white boy, you don't know who you're dealing with."

Xander smiled.

"Is that right?"

Antonio lunged forward again, swinging a wide right hook. Xander moved his head back an inch, and the punch went sailing by. Xander opened his hand and slapped Antonio across the face. "You like slap fights, right? That's why you slapped Gabriela? I'll slap fight with you."

Xander slapped him again. Toying with him. Antonio was furious, and he took three more wild swings. The last right-hook threw him so far off balance that after Xander moved to the side, it took only a light smack on the back of the head to send Antonio down to the ground.

"No, Xander!" Gabriela screamed.

Xander's adrenaline was at full throttle. If Antonio couldn't give him a good fight, he was praying that one of his mountainous, bald-headed bodyguards would give him more of a challenge. Xander let Antonio get back to his feet, but when Antonio reached back toward the back of his belt line, Xander knew the fun and games were over.

"He's got a gun!" the bartender shouted.

"Antonio, don't!" Gabriela screamed.

Xander stepped toward him, and as Antonio brought the gun forward, Xander wielded a Thai kick to Antonio's bicep, and the jarring of the kick sent the gun clacking down on the ground. Antonio quickly bent over to pick it up, and Xander brought the same kick around and landed it to Antonio's chest. As Antonio desperately tried to suck in a breath, Xander picked up the gun and turned toward the three bodyguards who were closing in on him. They all froze when the gun was trained on them.

"Take out your guns and toss them in the pool. Now!"

There was a wildness in Xander's eyes. And he could feel that wildness palpitating all the way to his core. For the first time in five months, he felt alive.

And it felt good.

The three men took out their pistols and tossed them into the pool.

"Xander, please," Gabriela begged. "Drop the gun and run. I'm begging you! Don't do this!"

"But if I just let them go, how will they ever learn?"

The three men stood back, anger on their faces, but their hands were in the air.

That was when Xander shocked everyone around the bar, everyone around the pool, and especially Antonio and his thugs. He ejected the pistol's magazine, tossed it in the pool, then racked the slide to eject the round in the chamber and tossed it in the pool as well.

Xander gave a sweeping glance, looking each one of the Mexican men in the eye.

"You ready for that lesson?"

By the looks on their faces, you would have thought Xander was a piece of raw meat, and they were pit bulls about to come after it. But Xander knew it was absolutely the other way around. When they made their move, it was as if Xander had taken no time off at all. The first man—Thug One—all 250 pounds of him—lowered his head and dove for Xander's legs in an attempt to get him to the ground. There aren't a lot of rules to follow when taking on multiple attackers, but the number one rule, no matter what, is never let them get you on the ground. As the big man wrapped his arms around Xander's waist, Xander sprawled, simultaneously kicking his legs out behind him and forcing his hips down on the man's shoulders, landing on top of him. A second man—Thug Two—not quite as big, came at Xander, and Xander popped up to his feet just in time to catch the kick that was meant for his head. While he held Thug Two's leg, Xander violently kicked the big man's planted leg with the force of an axe, and just like a chopped trunk, Thug Two fell to the ground like a tree.

"Get him!" Antonio shouted to the third bodyguard.

Xander knew that before Thug Three made it to him, he had to do some damage to Thugs One and Two to level the playing field. As Thug One began to get back to his feet, Xander took the back of the man's neck in his hands and pulled downward as he drove his knee up into his forehead. The big man went limp, unconscious. Thug Two was just getting to his feet, and after delivering the knee to Thug One, Xander spun, whipping his leg around his body, and the heel of his suede loafer connected with Thug Two's jaw. The sound of his jaw breaking could be heard all the way to the beach.

That was when Xander felt Thug Three's arms wrap around

him before he could turn around. The man lifted Xander up in the air and began to walk him over to the bar, the most solid thing he could slam Xander down onto. In the eight-foot walk, Xander managed to turn into the man, and when he did get slammed, at least it was on his back. Xander's body being smashed into the bar top made a terrible crashing sound, and as the air was driven from his lungs, he managed to keep his head and searched for a weapon. Xander bit back the pain that encompassed every inch of his back. The bartender was standing five feet from him, his jaw agape, a bottle of rum in his hand. As Thug Three began to lift Xander back into the air, Xander took a deep breath and signaled the bartender by holding up his hand, a gesture to throw him the bottle. The bartender glanced at his own hand, then quickly tossed the bottle to him, and as soon as Xander caught it, he turned it in his hand and slashed it down on Thug Three's head as hard as he possibly could. The force of the blow shattered the bottle, and Thug Three let go of Xander as he fell to the floor.

Xander bounced off the bar top and landed on his feet. He glanced at the bartender, and through labored breath and a painful wince he managed to say, "Just put it on my tab."

Xander couldn't believe how much fun he was having.

By that time, Antonio was moving toward Xander, but his peacock chest wasn't sticking out quite as much as it had been before. He grabbed a nearby chair, took two momentum-building steps, and tossed it at Xander's head. Xander ducked, and the chair crashed against the bottles sitting on the middle shelf behind the bar. Xander was about to tell the bartender to put that on Antonio's tab when Antonio ran at him, and Xander caught his little pencil neck in his right hand. These guys had no business being in a fight with a certified, US military–trained killer. Any Navy SEAL would have broken them, but for a legendary ex-soldier like Xander, it was as easy as breathing. They were just small-time thugs, probably just as terrible with their guns as they were with their hands. They looked mean enough that Xander figured most people didn't mess with them. But as Xander squeezed Antonio's neck like a vise, and after dispatching all three bodyguards with relative ease, he knew they were all thinking what he was thinking: looks can be deceiving. That thought was more evident on Gabriela's face than anyone's. She was not expecting to see what just happened.

"Call off your dogs or I'll put them down for good," Xander told Antonio.

The sarcasm was gone.

Antonio looked over at his men as they all got back to their feet, then back to Xander. Xander could see in his eyes that he didn't want to be embarrassed. The three men stepped closer, and Xander squeezed and shook the much smaller Antonio. "Call them off!"

Antonio glanced at them once more, then swung his fist and hit Xander in the side of the head. Anger surged through Xander. As Antonio reared back to swing again, Xander lifted him off his feet, took two steps, then flung him through the air and into the pool. He immediately pulled his Marfione Halo IV OTF knife from his shorts pocket, pressed the action button, and the blade ejected from the handle.

"Don't just stand there," Xander said to the three thugs. "Let's get this over with."

The three bodyguards, unarmed and already humiliated, looked at each other, then to their boss. Antonio was out of the water, sopping wet, his arm hurrying Gabriela back toward the hotel. Xander took a step toward the three thugs, and they immediately followed Antonio's cue and began to shuffle off toward the hotel behind him.

As he walked away, Antonio shouted, "Stick around, white boy. You may have won this one, but stay here and see the hell I bring down on you."

Xander retracted his knife and put it away as he taunted back, "Says the little man as he runs away."

Gabriela shouted, "Don't be a fool, Xander! Get out of Mexico!"

"But Kyle will be here soon!" he shouted back, more just to amuse himself. He knew full well she had no idea what that meant. Xander was full of himself in that moment. Invincible. It had been far too long since his system had felt all the wonderful feelings that come with besting a man . . . or four. He realized if he did hang around in Mexico, there in fact would be consequences. And it was in that very moment that he knew beyond a shadow of a doubt that he wanted back in.

All in.

Because in that moment he was hoping against hope that those consequences would indeed come. His body and his mind welcomed the challenge.

The question that had been running through his mind, nonstop for five long months, had finally been answered. If the itch came back, would he scratch it?

He scratched it.

And damn it felt good.

3

All In

"Xander, are you drunk? You sound funny," Sam told him.

For five minutes, Sam listened to Xander rant and rave about getting in some bar brawl in Cabo San Lucas. Sam was Xander's partner in crime. For the last several years, she and Xander had been fighting together against the evil of the world. Up until five months ago, she had also been relentlessly helping him hunt down the men responsible for murdering his parents. She was ex-MI6 from London and a certified badass. There was no one Xander trusted more with his life, and the lives of his loved ones, more than her.

"What?" Xander sounded confused. "Drunk? No, I'm just . . . You were right. I'm ready to get back in the game."

Sam brushed away at her long dark hair, and as she stared into the mirror, she couldn't help but smile. She knew this call would come. She knew Xander couldn't wander aimlessly for long. But it had taken him far longer than she thought it would.

Since Xander was so excited, she decided to have a little fun with him.

"Back in the game?" She played dumb. "You mean the bourbon company? I thought you wanted Kyle to run that to help keep him out of trouble."

Xander was flabbergasted.

"What? My bourbon company? Are you listening to anything I'm saying, Sam?"

Sam's smile grew wider as she put her hair in a ponytail.

"Yes, of course I'm listening. You want back in the game. The horse racing then? I thought there was a new pony that had some potential."

Xander let out a sigh. "I hate you."

Sam laughed. "Well, I don't know what you want from me, Xander. It's past midnight here and I am trying to get to sleep. I suggest you do the same. Sounds like you've had enough fun and games for one night."

"Bullshit, Sam. You know exactly what I mean. Call Director Hartsfield in the morning and tell her I want to take her up on her offer."

Sam continued to play dumb. "Offer? What offer?

"Stop it."

"You mean the offer for me and you to run our own top secret division within the CIA of the United States of America? The offer you turned down flat some five months ago?"

"Yes, smart-ass, that offer. I want it, and I want to have free rein exactly as she stated we could. They give us the target or the mission and we see it to its end, as we see fit. Period."

"One little spat with some drunken frat boys and you're ready to work with the US government again? What do they put in their margaritas down there?" Sam was enjoying ribbing Xander.

"Are you finished? Listen, I've got some business to tend to here tonight. Call Director Hartsfield, then call the team. I want everyone in San Diego for dinner—no, hell with that—I want everyone on the yacht in Saint Thomas for dinner tomorrow evening. And I want our first target."

Sam finally let Xander off the hook. "I must admit, Xander, it's good to hear you have some cheer back in your voice. I'll make the calls, and I'll make sure the yacht is stocked with all the goodies Marv and the CIA will send us."

"Can you feel that, Sam?" Xander played.

"Now what are you going on about?"

"I know you feel it. You're excited. You've been bored as hell waiting for me to come around."

"It is about time, Xander. So, business to tend to tonight, you say? In Cabo? What's her name?"

"Oh, this is much better than a woman, Sam. I wish you could be here. Some local thugs are hopefully going to retaliate tonight. Can't you just feel the electricity?" Xander was overjoyed.

"I think they call it being snockered, but if you say it's electricity, it's electricity. Don't pull a muscle."

"Love you, Sam."

Sam rolled her eyes, yet she couldn't help but smile. She would never tell Xander this, but she missed her partner in crime. She could feel that same electricity he was feeling. She was also glad she hadn't let her skills slip over the last five months. She had been training religiously in anticipation of that very phone call. She was as sharp as ever and more than ready to get back to what the two of them did best.

"All right then, Xander. See you in Saint Thomas tomorrow."

Sam ended the call. As she laid her head on the pillow and stared up at the ceiling, she was grateful. As much as she knew Xander had needed the time away, she was happy it was over. The last five months had felt like five years. When your weekly routine is adrenaline-filled chaos, followed by the satisfaction of making your enemy pay, days filled with looking at random photos and maps and merely getting to offer an opinion of how to catch the bad guy were like entire days spent watching paint dry.

Samantha Harrison had conditioned herself over the years to be a machine that runs on the thrills of the next dangerous adventure. Her tank had been on empty for months. But hearing Xander excited once again about getting back to it, her tank began to fill again. By the time she pulled the team together and all of them were going over the particulars of the next target on that yacht tomorrow, she had a feeling that tank would be full.

4

Payback's a Bitch

Thugs One through Three, along with Antonio, made their way up the concrete steps that were cut out of the side of the cliff at the Resort at Pedregal. They were headed toward Xander King's suite. The four of them were moving much more slowly than they normally would, due to the battered state that Xander had left their bodies. However, the reason for the swift attempt at vengeance was because it had been their egos that had been the most bruised.

Antonio wasn't used to getting bested. Mostly because his men were usually there to form a protective barrier around him, ensuring that the man who paid their bills was never harmed. Antonio was determined to prove to the American who was the *real* man. Even though it would be four on one.

Antonio had connections all throughout Cabo, so it was easy for him to get a key to Xander's room. He wouldn't have minded kicking in the door, but he did enjoy the thought of sneaking up on Xander as he slept. He couldn't believe the stupidity of this brazen gringo. No one stepped to Antonio. And if they did, they sure as hell weren't dumb enough to stick around for the consequences. When the maids had informed him that in fact Xander had not fled from the resort, Antonio's blood was sent straight to boil. He didn't know what it was about this man that made him want to be so personally involved. He usually didn't get his own hands dirty. That is what he paid people for. Maybe it was the way he looked at Gabriela. Maybe it was the way there was absolutely no fear in the man when Antonio confronted him. Either way, he needed to be taught a lesson.

Behind the four men moving slowly up the outdoor stairway, a yellow three-quarter moon floated out over the ocean. The breeze was warm, and in the distance seagulls were settling into their homes, cooing to their babies as they fed them a snack. The midnight hour had come, and as Antonio approached the gate to the front patio of Xander's suite, he considered it to be a perfect night for revenge.

"Now listen," he whispered to his men. "We have a lot riding on this week, so we can't afford to have police investigating us for murder. So don't kill him. But once we have him subdued, we will bring him right to the brink of death. You understand?"

His men nodded.

Antonio fit a set of brass knuckles over the fingers of his right hand. Thug One readied his baseball bat, Thug Two a tire iron, and Thug Three would have to settle for his bare knuckles. Normally all these weak weapons would be guns instead, but the last thing Antonio needed right now was heat. And nothing brought heat like a dead body. Especially a dead American body. He knew there was still a strong chance that they would have to kill him. In the event that happened, he had a plan for that too. But he honestly wanted him to remember this night for the rest of his life. The night he crossed the baddest man in Mexico and paid dearly for it.

The hotel suite was completely dark. Not even the light of the moon penetrated the blackout curtains that were closed over the windows. Most vacationers staying at the resort were either out partying by the water or fast asleep in their beds. Either way, there wasn't a sound to be heard outside of the faint rush of the ocean greeting the sand at the bottom of the cliff.

The electronic key lock clicked—someone was opening the door. Yellow light from the moon, along with a rush of warm tropical air, poured in through the opening. After only a couple of moments, the light disappeared as whoever had come in the hotel room closed the door behind them, and it shut harder than they had meant for it to.

A lamp clicked on by the bed in the open room, and a dark-haired man sat straight up in bed, a frightened look on his face, as the four Mexican men stared back at him.

"You're not Xander King," Antonio said to the dark-haired man.

The man smiled at him as he scooted out of the bed and rose to his feet. Then he pointed behind the four of them.

"No, but he is."

"What took you all so long?" Xander said from behind them while snatching the baseball bat from the grip of the man closest to him.

The other three men turned just in time to see Xander smash Thug One in the stomach with his own bat. The man dropped to his knees, and Xander followed it up with a knee to his forehead.

One thug down.

"Get him!" Antonio shouted to his men, ordering them after Xander. Then he turned his attention back to the man in the bed. "You picked the wrong room to hang out in." He clenched his fist, squeezing the brass knuckles in his grasp.

"I'm pretty sure you are the one who picked the wrong room. I'm Kyle, by the way."

Kyle Hamilton held out his hand, as if Antonio would actually shake it. Instead, clearly not a fan of his sarcasm, he took a swing at Kyle's outstretched hand. Kyle managed to pull his arm back just in time to avoid being struck.

"I was just trying to be polite."

Antonio swung at Kyle again, this time at his head. Kyle jerked his head back out of the way, then stepped into a strong jab to Antonio's chin. It was immediately evident that what Xander said about them not being well trained was true.

On the other side of the room, Xander squared up into a fighting stance, opposite Thug Two and Thug Three. "You sure you all want to do this again?"

Thug Two answered with action. He stepped forward, swinging the tire iron down toward Xander's head. Xander managed to get both ends of the bat in his hands, thrusted it vertically, and it collided with the tire iron. Chips of the wooden bat flew into the air—better the bat than Xander's head. Thug Two reloaded before Xander could adjust and brought the tire iron back toward the bat. This time it went straight through the wood and broke the bat in half. Xander took a step back, glanced at the separated pieces he held in his hands, and just as Thug Two brought the tire iron back for another swing, Xander stepped forward and front-kicked him in the gut, pushing him back a couple of feet. He then planted the left leg he'd kicked with, spun his body around it like a top, and the heel of his right foot whipped with him, striking Thug Three square on the right side of his jaw.

Back by the bed, Kyle followed the left jab he'd landed with a right hand, but Antonio weaved left just as Kyle's fist whizzed by. Since Kyle wasn't expecting to miss, his balance was thrown, and Antonio took advantage. He moved forward, wrapping his arms around Kyle's midsection, and pushed him down onto the bed. His momentum carried him forward, and he landed on top of Kyle.

"X!" Kyle shouted. "Shit's getting weird over here!" Poking fun at the fact that Antonio was on top of him, in bed.

Antonio was unfazed, and he postured up, cocking his right arm back, ready to deliver a punch.

Xander had heard Kyle's announcement just as his foot hit the floor after knocking Thug Three unconscious. He looked toward the bed and in a continuous motion tossed the heavy end of his broken bat, which landed in a thud against Antonio's hip. Thug Two once again swung the tire iron, taking advantage of Kyle's distraction. Xander weaved but still took a glancing blow to his right shoulder. Pain swelled at the point of impact, and he stumbled forward. Thug Two swung again, and Xander quickly reversed course back to his right. As the tire iron narrowly missed his head, he threw a quick right hook to the big man's ribs, then a right hook to his forehead that stood him back up. He staggered back, dropped the tire iron, then dropped to the floor after Xander smashed his chin with an overhand right.

The man's hard head was like granite, and Xander shook out the pain in his knuckles as he turned back toward the bed. Antonio had moved back away from the bed after being hit by the piece of the bat, and Kyle had back-rolled to the opposite side of it, now on his feet as well. Antonio turned away from Kyle and looked over his three men who lay unconscious at his feet. Then he looked up at Xander.

Xander said, "Not the way you saw things going?"

"You have no idea who I am, do you?"

"Yeah." Xander gave a mocking expression and said, "Obviously. You're Antonio. Don't you remember me from throwing you in the pool earlier?"

Kyle smiled at Antonio and followed Xander's lead. "Wait, you mean he threw you in the pool earlier? Ouch, I bet that was embarrassing. I hope your girl wasn't watching."

Of course Kyle knew full well, from Xander's recounting of the story earlier, that Gabriela was indeed watching.

Antonio was turning maroon with anger.

Before he could speak, Xander piled it on. "Hey, bright side, at least she isn't here to see this. You can tell her you beat me up. I don't mind."

"You had better kill me, Xander King. Anything less and both of you will be dead men soon."

Xander walked over toward the door and opened it. "Tell you what, Tony, me and Kyle here don't want to end up dead soon, so we're gonna go." Xander picked up his duffel bag and threw the strap over his shoulder. Kyle pulled the extending handle on his rolling suitcase and comically exaggerated weaving his bag around the unconscious bodies on the floor.

"Just promise me you'll consider one thing," Xander continued. "Try to find some ex-military guys as your bodyguards. At least they'll have a little training. Your men are a reflection of their leader, and I gotta tell ya. . ." He paused and shook his head, disappointed.

"You have a big mouth, American," Antonio said. "And it is going to get you killed."

Xander looked over at Kyle, his best friend for almost twenty years. "You know, Sam says that same thing to me all the time."

Kyle rolled his bag in between Antonio and Xander and right through the open door. "The only thing Antonio there should concern himself with about your mouth is the fact that you've been nice enough not to use it on his woman."

Xander shrugged his shoulders at Antonio, as if to say, "He does have a point."

Antonio finally lost it and did exactly what Xander had wanted: he ran at him. Xander moved forward to meet him and lowered his shoulder like a linebacker, smacking into the much smaller man. The force knocked Antonio back a couple of feet, and Xander pressed forward, then with two hands pushed Antonio onto his back on the bed. Xander reached down, grabbed the lapels of his white silk sport coat, and pulled him back to his feet.

"You've made a lot of threats today, Antonio, yet here you are, at my mercy."

"I'll find you, and you *will* pay for this," Antonio spat.

"Get in line, my friend. But for your sake, I hope that day never comes."

Then Xander tossed Antonio so hard against the back wall that his body indention was left in the plaster after he fell to the floor.

"Tell Gabriela I'm thinking about her. This has been a real treat, but I've got some tequila that needs drinking. Know of any good bars?"

Xander stood over Antonio for a moment waiting for a response. When none came, Xander shrugged and walked out the door, shutting it behind him. When he made his way outside the gate, Kyle was waiting, a massive grin on his face.

"You missed it, didn't you?"

Xander sighed. "You have no idea."

"Does this mean we're back? Should I call Sam?"

The two of them started up the stairs to the hotel lobby.

"Already done."

"Finally!" Kyle was excited. He had been bored as well.

"Our first mission starts tomorrow. But for now we celebrate."

Xander put his arm around his friend, and the two of them headed off to find a little trouble of a different kind.

5

Old Friends and New Beginnings

A few hours on Xander's G6 private jet, and he and Kyle landed at Cyril E. King International Airport in Saint Thomas, US Virgin Islands. The small landing strip jutted out directly into the magnificent turquoise waters, and hugged tightly to the mountain just on the other side. It was easily one of Xander's favorite places to fly into. Of course, it didn't hurt that most of the year he kept his yacht here, which unquestionably rated higher than any of the resorts on the island.

After just a few minutes' cab ride down Long Bay Road, the two of them exited the vehicle at the Marina at Yacht Haven Grande. The name wasn't subtle, as it described the marina's exact function, a haven for yachts. The marina sat on Long Bay, the private docking area of Saint Thomas. Most of the boats were docked all together, clustered in the middle of the marina. However, Xander and Kyle had to walk all the way to the far outer dock, as that was the only spot in the marina that could accommodate his 250-foot yacht.

Rich people problems.

As the two of them walked toward Xander's floating hotel, he couldn't help but give Kyle fair warning.

"Listen, our new stewardess is what you would call a smoke show. Absolutely stunning. But you've got to do me a favor and let her alone while we're aboard the boat. I know it will be hard, but please, we can't afford to lose another good stewardess."

Xander was expecting Kyle to protest profusely. Instead, Kyle just wiped the sweat from his brow and agreed.

"Okay, I think I can manage."

Xander stopped in his tracks and turned to Kyle. "What? That's it?"

Kyle shaded his eyes from the sun as he looked to Xander. "Yeah, man. You don't want me to chase her, I won't. I respect that."

Xander reached up and held the back of his hand to Kyle's forehead.

"Doesn't feel like you have a temperature. You still hungover from last night? What's wrong with you?"

Kyle started walking. "Nothing man, just want to respect your wishes. Let's get out of the sun. Don't worry about me. I can keep my hands to myself."

Xander watched Kyle walk away for a second. What he was saying wasn't computing. Normally if you put Kyle within a two-mile radius of a beautiful woman, he would be falling all over himself to get to her. Even more so being confined to the same general quarters. Something was definitely off.

When Kyle noticed Xander wasn't walking beside him, he stopped and looked back. "What?"

Xander shook his head in disbelief.

"Nothing. You're just acting strange."

They both shrugged it off and walked toward the yacht.

"Well, if it ain't the King himself," an older man in a cowboy hat shouted down from the rail of the long, white monstrosity of a boat. "You put on some weight while you've been island hoppin'?"

Xander looked up.

"Jack! You ugly son of a bitch! You wish I got fat, then you might have a chance at keeping up. Good to see you, old man!"

They boarded the boat and the ex-CIA, real-life cowboy, Jack Bronson, greeted them both with a hug.

"Damn, it's good to see you boys too. I was gettin' tired of watchin' old *Mash* reruns and shootin' beer cans off the fence post."

Xander had grown to respect Jack as much as any man he'd ever met. He had shown up in Paris and Moscow in a way that Xander would never have expected a stranger to. His sniper skills saved Sam's and Xander's asses more than once in France.

"You haven't let your skills falter, have you, cowboy?" Xander asked.

"Don't you worry your pretty little head about me. I can still shoot a pimple off a whore's ass from a thousand yards."

"That's what I like to hear," Xander laughed.

Jack grabbed Xander's bicep and gave it a squeeze. "I was worried all this time off would make ya soft, but you still look like that Hemsworth fella that plays Thor, ya asshole." He turned and looked at Kyle. "Some guys have all the luck, I guess."

Kyle smiled and nodded. "You know, now that Thor cut his hair, I do see the resemblance. Where is everyone else?"

"They's all in there havin' lunch. I just stepped out for a smoke."

"Xander!" A red-haired woman with a Russian accent walked out onto the walkway from inside the cabin.

"Hey, Zhanna, long time no see."

She greeted him and Kyle with a hug. Zhanna was the daughter of the now-deceased—by Xander's hand—Vitalii Dragov. The largest crime boss in Russia and quite possibly the world. Of the many mistakes the fat crime lord made, estranging his daughter, was probably his biggest. That and crossing Xander King. Zhanna almost single-handedly saved the life of the president of the United States's daughter in Paris. Her time in the former KGB left her highly skilled. Her appreciation for Xander ridding the world of her evil father left her forever ready to fight by his side.

Zhanna pulled back and smiled, her accent thick. "It has been too long. I am glad to see you are back to old self." Zhanna's smiling face went solemn for a moment. "I am sorry to hear about Sarah. We will miss her."

Xander's stomach dropped.

Sarah Gilbright was the CIA beauty who came in and distracted Xander while Natalie was filming in Paris. Sarah looked like Barbie but kicked ass like Sam. Without her, more of this oddball little family would certainly be dead. Xander included.

"Sarah? What happened to Sarah?"

Sam walked outside at that moment.

Xander looked past Zhanna. "Sam? What the hell happened to Sarah?"

"Well, hello to you to, Xander."

"Sam."

"What?" Sam's British accent was sharp. "Don't get your knickers in a knot. Nothing happened. She is just on a different assignment with the CIA and couldn't be a part of our little top secret team."

Xander's shoulders fell and he exhaled.

"Jesus, Zhanna, don't scare a man like that."

"Sorry. I thought you knew."

Sam moved in for a hug. "You boys stay out of trouble last night?" she said as she looked over Kyle and Xander.

"We did," Xander answered, then motioned toward Kyle. "Take his temperature, would you?"

"Why's that?"

"I don't know, something's wrong with him. I told him how he'd be stuck on this boat with a gorgeous young stewardess and he hardly even cared."

Sam put the back of her hand to Kyle's forehead, just the way Xander had. Kyle moved her hand and scoffed at the two of them. "I'm not just a walking hard-on, you know."

Even Kyle couldn't help but laugh with the rest of them, as his reputation preceded him.

Xander changed the subject. "Well, I hate that Sarah can't be here. What about Viktor?"

Viktor was the crazy son of a bitch who flew in on his daddy's helicopter and saved Xander from certain death. He then almost got him killed a couple of times, but there was just something about that nut job Ukrainian that Xander loved.

Kyle fielded this one. "We kind of started a new business."

"Okay . . . and just what does that have to do with Viktor? Please tell me he's supervised, and whatever he's doing, please tell me there is at least a billion-dollar liability insurance policy in his name."

Sam said, "There is indeed a large liability policy. I told you he is crazy, but you insisted we find him a job. We couldn't, so we made one up."

"Bob kind of took a liking to Viktor," Kyle said. Bob was Xander's veteran jet pilot. "Said he always wanted a touring business. So Bob convinced us to open a Southern California helicopter tours business—"

"And you're letting Viktor fly the helicopter? Good God, you all are crazier than he is," Xander said.

Sam motioned them all inside, and they followed behind her. "Well, it's the only skill he's got, Xander. Other than video games and driving me mad. You said you wanted to keep him around, so Bob found a way to keep him around."

"Yeah, but I never meant put innocent lives of strangers in jeopardy. Why didn't Bob tell me about this?"

"'Cause he probably thought you'd fire him," Jack said.

Xander stepped inside the salon of the yacht. The floor was a dark hardwood, the walls were white, sprinkled with a few colorful paintings, and the chairs and couches followed the clean white look all the way to the oversized reclaimed-wood dining table.

"So this is it? This is the new team?"

"Don't forget me, X-man." A skinny, salt-and-pepper-haired man stepped into the salon, pushing his black-rimmed glasses back up the bridge of his nose.

"Marv!" Xander said. "Finally, someone with some brains around here."

Marvin—Marv—Cameron was the best with electronics in the entire CIA. His brains were also useful when running down clues on the web, and there wasn't a soul on earth he couldn't find, given enough time.

"You're going to make me blush." Marv smiled.

They shared a quick hug, then Xander got straight to it.

"Well, now that we're all here, let's get down to business. I have to say, this time off has given me a lot of perspective, and all of that perspective came to a head last night when a little bit of trouble went a long way in letting me know what I really wanted. Who I really am. And I have to say, all of you were right . . . Sam, we need a new bad guy."

Sam folded her arms and smiled.

"I've come prepared."

6

Coming Together

The sun was beginning to fade over Long Bay, but the fun the team was having on the top deck was not. Kyle passed the pitcher of margaritas to Zhanna, Sam passed the tray of pizza to Xander, and Jack was cracking off redneck wisdom like it was his job. Earlier, they had pulled the yacht out and anchored down so they could look back over the beautiful island. The look of it reminded Xander of a mini Hawaii.

The stewardess—Karen—whom Xander had warned Kyle to steer clear of, was once again up on the deck delivering another tray of pizza. And once again, Kyle didn't so much as look up from his plate. Something was definitely wrong with his friend, and then it hit him.

"Who is she?" Xander said to Kyle as he knocked his knee against Kyle's leg.

Kyle finished his bite.

"What? Who is who?"

"You sound like owl, Kyle." Zhanna laughed. She didn't joke much, so the margaritas must have been working. Kyle flashed her a fake and annoyed smile, then looked back to Xander.

"The woman you're seeing," Xander said. "Who is she? Why didn't you tell me about her?"

"What?"

"Don't play dumb, K. One of the best looking women we've ever had on this boat has been up here several times, and not once have you looked her way. And don't give me this BS about how I asked you not to. You and I both know that would only make you want her more. So who is she?"

"I was wonderin' the same thing," Jack chimed in. "The Kyle I know'd already have her snuck over in the pantry or somethin'. What gives?"

"Damn, you all, can't a man grow up a little without it being a federal case?"

Xander gave a sweeping look to all at the table. Everyone attempted to hold it in, but they couldn't contain their laughter, and all of them busted out at his expense.

After a couple of unsuccessful attempts at catching his breath, Xander finally calmed enough to answer.

"No."

"Whatever, X."

"There is no way this is about you 'growing up.' Come on, brother. I know you better than I know myself, but if you don't want to tell me who she is in front of everyone, that's fine. Just at least admit there is someone."

Kyle was over it. "Can we just talk about the mission? Marv, can you show us some cool gadgets you brought with you? Something?"

"He's right," Sam said. "We really do need to start to drill down on this thing. We had a few options for targets, but one very special opportunity came up, Xander, and I don't think you are going to want to miss it."

Xander's excitement to get back into the bad-guy business flooded back through, and he forgot all about the games that Kyle was playing.

"Okay, you've got my attention. But I want to hear all of the options."

"That won't be necessary, I assure you."

"Then lay it on us."

"Javier Romero."

Xander set down his glass. "This better be good. I've had my fill of Mexican thugs already this week."

"He is one of the largest drug lords in Mexico. Responsible for more than half of the narcotics that have made their way into Southern California over the last twenty-five years."

"Nope. Pass. Pasadena. Come on, Sam, you know drug dealers don't do it for me."

Sam sat up. "Are you quite through? Let me finish, yeah?"

Xander held up both hands as if to say, "Geez, okay, go on then."

"I knew the drugs wouldn't be your fancy, but over the past year his men have been linked to one of the fastest growing human trafficking rings—sex slaves really—in North America."

That got Xander's attention. "All right, now you're talking."

Ever since Xander saved a few young girls from the basement of Miguel Juarez's compound in Chula Vista, California, he'd been hoping that one day he would get a chance to stop that trade run at its origin.

"Thought that would perk your ears." Sam stood and paced the large round table that was cast in the orange rays of the setting sun. "Millions of dollars are changing hands while thousands of young lives are being destroyed. The part that makes this more difficult, however, is twofold. One, they are also moving a massive amount of illegal weapons with these truckloads of young girls. Always several men on board, heavily guarding their shipments."

"And the other problem?" Xander wasn't really concerned with the armed men. What mission didn't have armed men?

"The other problem is more difficult. No one gets close to Javier Romero. His compound is unlike any we've ever encountered. It is nestled in the mountains down in Sinaloa, Mexico. And there is no getting in without being invited."

"Come on, Sam. No getting in?" Xander was skeptical.

"No getting in. But . . ."

"I knew there was a way in." Xander smiled.

"Only because you are who you are."

Xander stood and leaned forward, both palms resting on the table.

"I don't get it. We're going to introduce ourselves before we kill him?"

"Precisely, and you are quite possibly the only man in the world that he would let inside his little circle. And it is the only reason we are taking him on as a target."

"The suspense is killing me."

"Horse racing. The man has a fetish for horse racing. Like you, he thinks the 'Sport of Kings' is the greatest sport in the world."

"All right, I see the connection, but what does that have to do with getting on the inside?"

"Well, Romero has been wanting to break into horse racing in America for years. And for years he has been growing his stables in Sinaloa," Sam continued to explain. "The problem for him is no one will take him seriously in the US because the level of competition that his horses run against is widely considered mediocre at best."

"So you think he will open his home to me, for what, so I'll put in the good word?" Now Xander began to pace.

"Not that simple. After a couple of phone calls as your assistant, I was able to speak with Romero himself."

"Wait, what? So the man who is impossible to get close to now all of a sudden calls you back himself? You're losing me, Sammy."

"No, I know, I was shocked as well. But it seems that the prospect of one of his horses winning a race against the horse of a Kentucky Derby–winning owner was all it took for him to jump all over personally inviting you, and the horse of your choice, down to Sinaloa for an impromptu exhibition race. And he wants to do it this Saturday as part of a show he already had scheduled. A lot of wealthy people are coming into town. He's throwing a party, supposedly to get some hype going for his horses. But I believe it is for something much more sinister."

"What?" Xander was flabbergasted. "This is crazy. Even if I had a horse that was ready to run in a couple of days, there is no way I would interrupt the schedule Gary has mapped out to get them ready for the Derby next May."

Gary Trudough was Xander's trainer for all the Thoroughbreds in his stable. Xander trusted him implicitly when it came to his horses. He always had. And winning the Derby and the Preakness last year with King's Ransom cemented that trust forever.

"All taken care of. I spoke with Gary today and he said he could shuffle some things around if it's what you really wanted. He didn't get it but said you must have your reasons."

"What *I* really wanted? How did you know I would even want to be a part of all this in the first place?"

Sam emphatically placed both hands on her hips. Her face was telling him to "wake up."

"Xander, it is quite literally the mission of a lifetime for you. You get to fly in on your jet, smoke cigars, drink some bourbon, watch one of your precious horses conquer a field of inadequate equines, all while stopping a power-hungry tyrant from shipping innocent young girls off to be degraded and ruined by other power-hungry sexual deviants all across the United States."

Xander stood quietly for a moment. Sam waited patiently.

"Well, when you put it that way . . ."

"Sounds like she nailed this one, son," Jack said.

Kyle agreed. "X, we've got to do this one. It's perfect."

"And it is the perfect cover to have all of us come along with you," Sam said.

"How's that?" Xander asked.

Sam motioned around the table. "All of them can be part of the racing team. Publicist, assistant trainer, and, hell, Jack is an actual cowboy, he won't even have to act."

Xander raised his eyebrows and shrugged, acknowledging that she had a point.

"What about you?" Xander asked Sam.

"Well, I'll be your girlfriend."

"What?" Xander laughed.

"Don't act like it's so out of the question."

Xander couldn't help himself; it had been too long since he'd been around to give Sam a hard time. "No offense, but you really think that they would buy *you* with *me*?"

He of course was just poking fun. Sam was as gorgeous as any woman he'd ever been around. But the beauty of a brother-sister relationship is that you get free license to give each other hell.

"Oh, go to hell. Besides, Romero has a girlfriend around my age. It will be a good opportunity to stay close to you but possibly get some easy intel if I can get her to have a few too many drinks."

"Close to me?" Xander didn't let it die. "Whoa, whoa, I can see right now that we are going to have to set some boundaries for this mission. It's just business, Sam, there won't be any funny business."

"Good God, will you ever grow up?"

Jack laughed. "I sure hope not, this is pretty fun to watch."

"If that is all, I have some more arrangements to make." Sam was through playing games. "Someone actually has to work around here."

"Aw, Sam. You know I love you . . ." Xander paused for effect. "Not in that way, of course. Damn, this is getting weird already."

Sam rolled her eyes and said good night. Jack and Zhanna followed suit, and Xander invited Kyle to have a drink and a cigar before they turned in.

Kyle held up his finger. "Let me just go change my shirt and I'll be right back."

"Change before we smoke?"

"Yeah, it will just take a second. You gonna be right here?"

"I'll pour the drinks."

"Perfect, be right back."

Xander grabbed two glasses from the table as Kyle ran off into the cabin. He walked over to the starboard stern and pulled two cigars from his travel humidor. Kyle didn't seem like anything was terribly wrong, but he knew his friend, and something was certainly off. As he looked back at the marina in the distance, the mountain rising up behind it, the tangerine sky shining on its peak, seagulls floating together on a warm breeze, he couldn't help but be excited. He was right where he wanted to be, with the people he wanted to be with, getting ready to do some terrible things in the name of justice, just as he was meant to.

He reached in his pocket, and after thumbing around for his cigar cutter, he remembered it was sitting on the nightstand in his room. He set the cigars down on the lounge chair and took his glass of King's Ransom bourbon with him inside. He walked around the main salon, and just before he made it through the galley, something caught his eye just outside the entryway. It looked like Kyle from behind. Xander stepped outside the door onto the outer walkway.

"What in the—" Xander dropped his glass, and it shattered on the teakwood below his feet. Kyle whipped around at the crashing sound, startled, and so too was Sam. Kyle didn't realize it, but he still had his arm wrapped around Sam's waist, her deep-red lipstick smeared on his face.

"Good God, X, I thought you were at the back of the boat." Kyle didn't know what to say.

"Nope, but mystery solved, I guess, on why you've been acting so damn weird. How long's this been going on?" Xander wasn't mad. He wasn't even shocked. It just felt odd that they hadn't told him.

Sam pulled away from Kyle. "Nothing's going on, we were, we just . . ."

"Sam, it's fine. I love you guys. I love you even more together. This has been a long time in the making. The only thing I hate is that Kyle won't make fun of you with me anymore. Now *that* hurts."

The tension fell from both Kyle's and Sam's shoulders. Kyle said, "We've been wanting to tell you forever, we just . . . couldn't find the right time."

"It's fine. Really." Xander meant it. He was happy for both of them. "So are we going to have that cigar, or are you gonna finish what you've started there, Kyle?"

"You boys go have your cigar. I'll be in my room, Kyle."

"Vomit," Xander joked. "Is this going to be awkward, me being your boyfriend this weekend?"

Sam sighed. Then on her way inside she said, "No more awkward than you were already going to make it."

Xander smiled at Kyle.

"Touché."

7

Meet the Tarters

With surfboards jutting out the back, a black Jeep Wrangler pulled into the driveway of the beach house that sat on the boardwalk in Pacific Beach, a small beach community in San Diego, California. David Tarter stood staring out the living room window. He was livid. For the last hour he had been pacing the room, waiting on his younger brother and sister to show up with their friend. Waiting on them to show up at the meeting he had given them a full day's notice about. But it wasn't a surprise to David that they were late. His brother and sister did this all the time. Like they had no responsibilities in the world. If it hadn't been his mother's dying wish that he bring them in and take care of them, he would have cut them out a long time ago.

"Is that them?" Jonathan Haag asked David from the kitchen table.

Haag was David's right hand. Had been since they did a couple of tours together a few years ago in the Middle East, and even further than that, all the way back to grade school. They were both well known for their fearlessness. And they were both equally known for their ruthlessness. It's ultimately what handed them their dishonorable discharge papers from the Navy SEALs. The two of them had wanted out for a while. The only reason they'd joined up was because it was the only way the two of them could stay out of trouble. But in the end, all it did was teach them how to find trouble and not get caught.

"Yeah, it's them," David answered.

"This shit has to stop, David. I love your family, but they aren't cut out for this. They just want to play all day and party all night. This stuff is too serious to have them mess it up. And way too expensive if they screw it up for us."

"Look, this is the way it is. You don't like it, find another way to make money."

Haag frowned and shook his head. "I hear you, brother. I know you're doing this for your mom—"

David turned and shouted, "Don't!" His muscles rippled under his black tank top.

Jon held up his hands. David wasn't a man whose anger you wanted directed at you.

"Just get them in line. That's all I'm saying."

"You worry about the job. Let me worry about them."

David heard the doors shut on the Jeep. He couldn't wait until they got inside. This was the reason he'd purchased the two beach houses on either side of this one, so he could keep these sorts of things private, even when it was out in the driveway. He flung open the back door and rushed outside.

"David." A young surfer-looking man with straight blond hair down past the middle of his neck walked toward David with his hands up. "David, calm down, I know we're a little late, but—"

"But nothing," David charged at him, took him by his T-shirt, and slammed him up against the passenger door of the Jeep. "Tommy, you're over an hour late. You think this is a game?"

"No, David, I don't think this is a game. Relax, bro."

"Bro?" David slammed him again.

"David, relax!" a young dark-haired woman shouted from behind him. "It just took longer than we thought to get Greg. What's your problem?"

David turned toward her. "Was I talking to you, Lisa? Huh?" David released his brother and stepped back so he could look at all of them. "Don't give me this 'it just took a little longer' bullshit. You don't think that I can see that your hair is wet and you have surfboards in the back? You don't think I smell the weed and Jack Daniels on your breath? This happens again, you're out. You hear me?" He pointed a finger at all three of them.

"Good!" Tommy shouted back. "You aren't Mom. You can't tell us what to do. We're twenty-five years old, for Christ's sake."

"Yeah? And you act like you're fifteen. So you're out then? You think I need you? Be out. And both of you get your stuff out of the beach house and find somewhere else to mooch."

"Mooch? We've made you enough money to pay for these houses ourselves!" Tommy shouted.

"Yeah, working jobs I trained you for, put together for you, and went along with you on, doing all the work."

Tommy started to pace. "This is ridiculous, bro. We can pull these jobs on our own. We don't need you. We're out."

Lisa stepped forward and used her small but powerful frame to put some muscle into pushing her brother Tommy, trying to bring him to his senses. "No, we are not out." She turned to David. "We are not out. You're right. We were partying, that's why we were late. It won't happen again." She looked back to Tommy. "Right, Tommy?"

Tommy bowed up a little, then after a second, better judgment kicked in. He knew David was his meal ticket.

"Right."

Lisa turned to their friend, Greg, the last one in the group involved in their underground family business. "Right, Greg?"

Greg, a dark-haired version of Tommy, stepped forward. "I got no problem. I'm just happy to be here."

Greg had been a lifelong family friend, the son of one of their mother's best friends. That's the only reason he was ever involved.

Lisa looked back to David. "We good?"

"No, we're not good. All of you get inside, we've got work to do."

8

Make It Reign

The sun was rising from behind the deep blue ocean, casting its first golden rays over the island of Saint Thomas. Kyle, Zhanna, Sam, and Xander decided to go for a morning run along the harbor. They tried to convince Jack to go along with them, but he politely told them that the only running he planned on doing was running the coffee machine. Marv agreed, and the two of them also offered to get everything together for the plane. They all would be flying that evening to Sinaloa, Mexico, meeting Gary there with Xander's latest Kentucky Derby hopeful, Heir to the Throne. Since Throne was actually sired by the father of Xander's Kentucky Derby champion, King's Ransom, Xander thought it fitting that Ransom's little brother be named what he is: the next in line to be the king of horse racing.

"So how good is the new horse?" Kyle asked in between rhythmic jogging breaths. "He's got big *horseshoes* to fill."

"Good one." Xander laughed. "He's even bigger than Ransom if you can believe it. Gary says he's a step faster too."

"Wow. That's really saying something."

"Speaking of fast," Xander changed the subject, "how quickly has this thing between the two of you been moving?" He swiveled his head between Kyle on his left and Sam on his right, the calm harbor full of boats just beyond her shoulders.

"Couple of months," Kyle answered.

"So, how'd it happen?"

Sam said, "Kyle knocked on my door one night, sloshed, probably turned down by half a dozen lasses, looking entirely too pitiful to turn away."

"Broken man." Xander laughed. "Love that angle. Usually only buys you one night. Glad to see you could turn it into something more long-term, Kyle."

"We're just having a good go at it. Nothing serious, Xander," Sam said.

Xander glanced at Kyle and caught a glimpse of disappointment. He decided to give his old friend a break.

"So what's the plan when we get to Mexico?"

The four of them rounded a turn and headed back toward the yacht.

Sam answered, "Romero's people sent over an itinerary. You and I will be staying in the mansion. Everyone else will be in the guesthouse, which I've been assured is five-star worthy. Xander, you and I will join Romero for dinner. Tomorrow will be the exhibition race. This will be our first real shot at gathering some intel. Tonight, while everyone is sleeping, I will try to find a way to get you into the mansion. The CIA does have some surveillance of the property, I will be studying those on the plane. I will find something. I already have blueprints, so I will direct you to Romero's office."

"How do you know we will find anything there?" Xander asked.

"Well, in the last twelve hours, CIA Director Hartsfield has legitimized our little top secret team. They're calling us Reign. I suppose because of your last name, Xander. A king is royalty, guess it has something to do with that. I didn't find it very creative of them, but whatever."

"Ooh, I like it!" Kyle and Zhanna said in unison.

They all looked at Xander. He shrugged.

"I like it. Reign. Sounds strong. They could have done much worse."

Everyone agreed.

Xander got them back on topic.

"Okay, so we are legitimized. How does that help?"

"Now that we are recognized amongst the upper echelon of the CIA, we now have our clearance. Highest level, as promised by Director Hartsfield."

"Wow, that's a big deal, X," Kyle said.

Xander rolled one hand over the other, gesturing for Sam to move on.

Sam wiped away the sweat from her brow and continued.

"Now that we have that clearance, we now know of José Ramirez."

"José Ramirez?" Xander asked.

"He has been undercover in Romero's security for two years now."

"Now we are talking," Zhanna said.

"That's right. Director Hartsfield is going to get him an information drop some time this afternoon. He should be able to provide us with help getting in and, even more so, what to look for when we get there."

"Perfect," Xander said. "This is coming together. You're not so bad at this, Sam."

"Right, because the last four years of us doing this on our own hasn't shown that."

Xander smiled at her.

"What?" she said.

Then he smiled at Zhanna and Kyle.

"What?" they said together.

"Last one to the boat carries the heavy bag of weapons onto the plane," Xander said quickly as he sprinted out in front of them.

He looked back over his shoulder and saw the three of them look at each other, right before they broke out into a sprint after him. As he sprinted toward his boat at the end of the marina, he was excited. For the first time in a long time he was going to be able to get back to doing good in the world, and there was no other motive that came along with it. No search for answers to questions like who killed his parents. No search for a missing loved one to add stress to the already stress-laden situation. And best of all, no burning desire for revenge to cloud his judgment.

He was going to be able to go in and have some fun doing what he did best.

What he did better than any other human on the face of the planet.

Catch the bad guy and make him pay.

9

Romero's Rules

Javier Romero sat alone in the middle of the small grandstand he'd had built for the track he'd bought from the government of Sinaloa a few years back. The track had been in shambles, and the horse racing culture had been as well. As he looked out over his dirt track, the palm trees swaying in the background, it reminded him of Santa Anita, a famous track in Arcadia, California, just as he'd meant for it to when he had it designed.

He tugged on the tip of his white fedora, shading his eyes from the afternoon sun. He sipped on some Kentucky bourbon as he watched his best horse practice just beyond the rail. Even though he was more a fan of scotch whiskey, he had always enjoyed bourbon as well. But this bourbon in particular, King's Ransom bourbon, was new to him. He had his people ship in a few bottles of it because he wanted to have it around when the owner of the company, Xander King, made it into town. He didn't know Xander at all, but he already liked him. He had watched him on Derby day this past May. Romero liked the way the man handled his wealth and success. Liked the way he'd been humble when he answered the media's questions, and he liked the fact that he enjoyed a good cigar, a good drink, and a beautiful woman. Romero knew there would be no shortage of things they had in common. He even liked the fact that Xander had been a military man. Showed that he had great discipline and could handle himself when things didn't always go as planned.

What he liked most about Xander was the fact that he was up for the challenge of bringing his big time Thoroughbred all the way from Kentucky, just for some competition. Romero loved to compete. That's why he stayed in such good shape for a sixty-year-old man. That's why he loved horse racing. And that is why tomorrow was going to be so enjoyable. Xander was going to be flying in on his private plane, and they were going to have a good time wagering on their best ponies and enjoying some of the finer things in life.

"Señor Romero?" a man said from the end of the aisle, getting his attention.

Romero stood up, shaking his head as he tossed back the last of the bourbon.

"What did I tell you? English. I want all of us to be speaking in English until Mr. King leaves."

"I'm sorry, *Mr.* Romero."

"Was that so hard?"

Romero knew that it was over-the-top to have everyone speaking English, but he wanted his guest to feel as comfortable as possible. He always treated guests this way, but a guest who could potentially help him break into the United States horse racing scene was going to get an even more special red carpet rolled out.

Ricardo Sanchez, the tall and thick man who had been Romero's right hand for years, shook his head.

"No boss, not hard at all."

"Good, now what is it?"

"Thoroughbred horse aircraft has arrived."

"Xander?"

"No, he will be here this evening. A Gary Trudough flew in with the horse along with a few other handlers."

"Ah yes. Xander's assistant mentioned that this Gary would be the one flying in with the horse. Make him feel welcome, and let him know that I will be here to greet him when he comes with the horse."

"Of course."

Romero shifted his attention back to the track.

"How are the preparations going for our little dinner party tonight?"

"The chef is prepping, the decorators are bringing in the flowers and all of the other things you requested. They will be ready."

"Perfect. And security?"

"We will be ready as usual."

Romero turned back to Ricardo.

"No, you will not be ready as usual. You will be more ready than ever before. You are the one who said the Sinaloa Cartel got wind of our new back channel into San Diego. They will be coming for us. But it will not affect our guest. Am I clear? If he hears what we do, and that what we do is making it into his country, it could ruin my attempt to bring my racehorses to America. Need I say more?"

"No, boss. We will be prepared for the worst. But we have no reason to believe they will bring the fight to us. There has been no word that will be the case."

"Let's keep it that way."

Romero nodded Ricardo away, reached down for the bottle of King's Ransom bourbon, and poured another glass. The taste was sweet on his lips. He pulled the glass away and studied the brown liquor as it reflected a ray of sunlight. He hated to admit it, but that sweet burn was beginning to grow on him. Just beyond his glass, his racehorse thundered down the straight stretch. He didn't like the timing of having trouble with the Sinaloa Cartel. This time with Xander was a big deal to him. He had been growing weary of the outlaw lifestyle over the past few years. Horse racing seemed a wonderful transition out of it. But he needed the "in" with US racing's golden boy. Therefore, he needed the next two days to go perfectly. A war with the Western Hemisphere's largest cartel was certainly one way to ruin it.

10

The Devil's in the Details

Seagulls cooed as they hovered over the boardwalk just outside the patio of Lahaina Beach House Bar, and at the foot of the sand in Pacific Beach. California was showing off, the sun was shining in its 75 degree way, and the waves were crashing in the distance. The crowd had swelled on the small patio, as it always did at the beachside bar.

"Be honest," Tommy said to his sister, Lisa, and his friend Greg. "Don't you think David is getting us in over our heads with this one?"

Lisa finished a long swig of her Kona Big Wave beer and shook her head.

"It's not that we are in over our heads. David and Jonathan have handled far worse overseas. I just don't know how I feel about selling young girls. Pretty messed up, you know?"

Greg said, "Technically, we aren't the ones selling them. We are just like . . . the delivery service, right? The ones taking the risk. Isn't that why they're paying so much?"

Tommy leaned back and let the sun bake on his face.

"Whatever helps you sleep at night, brother. *Technically*, we are definitely selling them. But I don't really care about all that. They're just a bunch of Mexicans anyway, aren't they?" He took a drink from his beer. "You ask me, we're just transferring them from one bad situation to another."

"You're an asshole, Tommy. And I don't know. I'm pretty sure it makes us terrible people, regardless of their nationality," Lisa said.

David and Jon walked up from behind them.

"What makes you terrible people?" David said.

The three of them jumped. They weren't expecting him to be there for another half hour.

"You three are awfully jumpy, aren't you?" Jon pulled up a chair.

Tommy tried to play it cool.

"Just weren't expecting you so soon, that's all."

David pulled up a chair.

"Well, this is what it's like when someone isn't late for a meeting."

Tommy rolled his eyes.

David continued, "All right. Everything is in place for tomorrow night, except for the cars. We need three of them. They don't have to be anything special, just reliable. The more inconspicuous, the better. Can you all handle that?"

"We can handle that," Lisa said. "But I'm just not sure about this whole thing, David. I mean, what if it were me who was one of those poor girls."

"Then you would just be some poor girl whose family didn't care about her anyway."

Lisa just stared at David. It seemed the inside of him had become as hard as the outside. She figured if you opened him up, the battle scars on his face would pale in comparison to the scars he was sporting on the inside.

"What?" David stroked his dark-brown goatee. "You don't have to do this. I've got several more men coming along for backup as it is. Soldiers. So if you don't want to be cut in…cut out."

"You know she needs the money, David," Tommy interjected.

"Yeah, I know. I told her getting involved with those organized crime scum was a mistake, but she didn't listen, couldn't stop trying to be a card shark, and now she has a mountain of debt and is still back here working with us. But we can make that all go away with one job and a cut of two million dollars."

A wry smile grew across David's face and his partner in crime Jon's face as well. It was the first time David had shared the actual figure they would be paid for the truckload of girls and weapons.

Tommy's face lit up. "Two million d—" He stood up and grabbed the waitress beside the table next to him. "Five shots of tequila please, we're celebrating." He returned to his table. "Two million dollars!"

"Would you sit down, Tommy?" David wasn't happy. He had long thought his little brother was a screwup. He just hoped bringing him in wouldn't be the thing that brought them all down. Tommy sat down and David stood up. His six-foot-four-inch stocky frame towered over the table. "Now, is that a big enough number for you to actually take this seriously?"

Tommy didn't answer; he just looked off down the beach.

"Get the cars tonight. Three spaces in the garages will be open at the house. Just pull right in and shut the door behind you. Lisa, you in or out? There can't be any half-stepping here."

"Don't worry about us. We'll be ready."

"You three are the only worry I have with this entire thing. Everything else will be flawless."

The sun went down, and Tommy, Lisa, and Greg were turning their car into the massive dirt parking lot at the Mattress Firm Amphitheatre just south of San Diego. There was a country music concert going on that night at the open-air venue, so cars would be ripe for the picking. Row after row of cars sprawled out in front of them. The lighting wasn't great, and they would easily be able to get lost somewhere in the middle where no one would be the wiser that their cars were being broken into. By the time the owners heard their car alarms, the three of them would have them started up and be on their way. This wasn't their first rodeo when it came to boosting cars. They had been doing it for fun since they were fifteen.

They parked their car and coordinated with each other once they'd picked out the cars they were going to take. Five minutes later they were on the road, on their way back to David at the beach houses. Lisa checked her rearview mirror and couldn't help but shake her head. The only instructions David gave was to make sure to boost inconspicuous cars. Yet there Tommy was, swerving back and forth in the lanes behind them, in a brand-new Chevy Corvette. Bright cherry-red no less. David was going to flip out. She decided it best to give him a heads-up. She dialed David's number.

"How'd it go?" David answered.

"Fine. Just wanted—"

"Where are you?"

"On the 5 Freeway, almost to San Diego. Listen—"

David cut her off again.

"I'm not far behind you. Haag and I had to pick up a few things. Get back to the house. I'll see you in a few." He hung up.

Lisa set her phone in the seat beside her as she shook her head. David could be a real asshole on a normal day. But when they were about to do a job, he was a nightmare on another level. She couldn't be happier that this was the last time she would be working with him. The last time she was putting herself in these situations. She had done a couple of stints in juvy because of her brother Tommy's influence. She wasn't going to see how prison compared. Just one more job and she could move on to her new career, debt free and worry free. All she had to do was keep them from getting caught.

It was then that she saw Tommy swerving around again like an idiot, and it was then that blue and red lights started flashing from the other side of the road. Her stomach dropped when the cop car turned left into the median, then left again onto the highway behind them. So much for not getting caught. Her moron brother had finally done her in.

She quickly picked up her phone as the police car started to pull Tommy over. To her surprise, Tommy was actually slowing down and pulling over.

"What is it?" David answered.

"Tommy is getting pulled over. We're going to need another car. He's going to jail."

"Shit! I knew he would screw this up!" David shouted through the phone. "No, he is not going to jail. I'll be there in thirty seconds. Head back to the house and put the cars away."

"David! What are you going to do?" Lisa shouted into the phone, but the line was already dead.

She started slamming her hands on the steering wheel of the stolen car. She couldn't believe that Tommy couldn't even do this right. And now David was going to do something even worse and ruin this entire thing. Why did she always have to be the only one with any sense? This was why she had to do this job and then get the hell away from these psychopaths.

Lisa jerked the wheel of the Honda Accord and drove right through the median as she turned around to see if she could at least keep everyone alive. She mashed the gas pedal as her heart pounded. When she approached the flashing patrol car lights, she slowed the car and drove by to see if anything was happening. That was when a black Hummer slammed into the side of the cop car and drove it toward the side of the mountain that sat about thirty feet off the road. She whipped her car back through the median and drove up behind the stolen Corvette. She watched Tommy run toward the cop car, and she bolted out of her car after him.

The only thing she could see was David's back with red and blue flashing behind him, as he rained punches downward.

"David! No!"

The closer she got, she could see the cop taking the beating. His head was bouncing off the hard, packed dirt underneath him.

"You're going to kill him! Someone stop him!"

Jon ran around the back of the patrol car and hoisted David up by his shoulders to break his rage. David turned and shoved his longtime friend backward, then turned toward Tommy. His chest heaving with fury, his hands still balled into fists. His face was full of anger. He looked more like a spun-up silverback gorilla than a man.

"You see what you did?" David shouted at Tommy as he pointed to the bloody police officer on the ground. "You see what happens when you don't take shit seriously?"

"He's alive," Jon said, taking the officer's pulse.

"Hell with you, David! That is your fault, not mine!" Tommy shouted back.

David surged forward and caught Tommy's throat with his right hand, lifted him up into the air, and slammed him down on his back. He got one hard punch in to the forehead before Lisa dove at David and knocked him off Tommy. They rolled and David ended up on top. He raised his fist like he was going to hit her, but Jon stepped in and took hold of his arm.

"That's enough! We've gotta get out of here. We have what we need for tomorrow night. Let's not blow this on some family feud!"

Lisa could see madness in David's eyes. She realized in that moment that he had lost whatever it was that humans have that enable them to empathize with others. The look in his eye was not human at all.

One last job and she was finished.

It was hard to believe, but she was actually scared of her own brother.

Because her brother was a madman.

11

Sinaloa Soirée

Xander's G6 jet touched down in Sinaloa, Mexico. On the way in, the evening sun shed light on a coastal city. On one side, the deep blue waters of the Gulf of California, on the other, the town butted up to the foothills of the Sierra Madre Occidental mountain range. From the air, it seemed a beautiful place to live. From all that Xander had heard about it on the news, and from Sam's intel, it could be at times quite the opposite for those who resided there. Unless of course you were one of the many drug lords who called Sinaloa home.

Xander's trusted pilot, Bob, lowered the stairs on the G6 with the push of a button. Jack wore his cowboy hat and his deep-purple King Stables polo shirt. Zhanna and Kyle did the same, sans the cowboy hat. They all needed to blend in with the team, and they definitely looked the part. After showing everyone all the new weapons and gadgets, Marv decided to stay behind on the yacht and set up his electronic office there. No one could blame him for that. Xander dressed the part as well. He needed to look like the rich man Romero expected to meet. He chose a lightweight navy sport coat, a white button-down shirt, matching navy-blue dress slacks, and a pair of tan leather oxfords. His suit was perfectly tailored to his six-foot-three-inch, 215-pound frame. "Athletic fit," his tailor called it. And finally, Sam dazzled as the bourbon mogul's girlfriend in her long white summer dress. Her long, dark hair fell down her back from underneath her matching white sun hat.

"Damn, you are stunning," Kyle said just before wrapping his arms around her and giving her a kiss.

Xander moved in and shoved him into the seat to his right. Kyle looked up to find a smile on Xander's face.

"Keep your paws off my woman, asshole." He laughed.

They all shared in the laugh until Sam, being Sam, made sure everyone understood the stakes. She looked at Kyle. "There can be no more of that. We blow our cover and we'll have to shoot our way out of here." She immediately looked over at Xander and held out her hand. "And don't you say it. I don't care if you think that would be fun, we aren't going to do it."

Kyle stood, a confused look on his face. "I thought that was exactly what we were coming down here to do."

Sam shook her head. "This is nothing more than to gather information. After we find proof that Romero is indeed trafficking these girls as we suspect, then we will return to make sure he no longer can."

"Borrring." Xander gave Sam a wink.

"Oh, shut it. You get to drink your bourbon and watch your horse race. And you get to have me on your arm. Others would kill to be in your shoes."

Xander looked down at his shoes. "They are nice shoes."

Sam made sure she didn't smile, then motioned for everyone to exit the plane. The five of them descended the stairs into the warm evening air. A stretch limousine and a large Mexican man awaited them at the bottom.

"I feel like we're going to prom," Xander whispered to Sam.

"Prom? Is that yet another of your silly traditions? Sounds dreadful."

"It's an excuse for teenagers to drink and talk their dates into handing over their virginity."

"Okay," Sam said, smirking, "not so bad then."

The limo drove through a massive iron gate, then wound its way up another portion of the mountain that Romero's mansion was tucked into. As they stepped out of the limo, a sprawling Spanish-style residence loomed before them, complete with the orange-red terra-cotta tile roof and the typical eggshell-colored stucco exterior walls. There were several soldiers dressed in all-black tactical gear surrounding the front entrance of the house. This was definitely a first in all of the dinner parties Xander had ever attended. The oversized oak front door opened, and out walked a stunning dark-haired beauty in a red dress, on the arm of a silver-haired older gentleman, who would most likely be classified as a stud. Though he was in a suit, it was clear that for a man near sixty that he was in damn good shape.

"Mr. King. So good of you to come to Sinaloa." The man walked down the steps with his woman. "This is my wife, Lola, and I apologize for what looks like an army here to greet you. But this is the life of a wealthy man here in Mexico."

"Apologies not necessary. Better safe than dead." Xander smiled.

"I like that." Romero laughed.

Xander took his hand and gave it a firm shake, kissed Lola's hand and said hello, then introduced Sam as his girlfriend, Samantha. It was an odd thing for him to hear coming out of his own mouth.

"You are very beautiful young lady. Mr. King is lucky to have you on his arm."

"That he is." Sam offered her hand.

Xander knew this whole charade was hard for Sam to swallow. She was about as far from a country club "how do you do?" wife as anyone could get.

"Please, call me Xander. And this is my team, Zhanna, Kyle, and Jack." He pointed to the three of them.

"Nice to meet you all," Romero said. "I look forward to seeing what your horse can do tomorrow afternoon, Xander. For now, would the three of you be so kind as to follow Juan to your quarters in the guesthouse? Dinner will be waiting for you there."

The team did as he asked and followed after Juan.

Romero continued, "And, Lola, would you please show Samantha around the mansion. Hopefully she has a thing for artwork and the two of you can discuss. I'd like to have a drink and maybe a cigar with Xander in my study before dinner if that is all right with everyone?"

Everyone agreed, and Xander and Sam followed their hosts into the mansion. The interior was as one would imagine, full of opulence and marble. Lots of marble. Sam and Lola split off to the opposite side of the mansion, and Xander followed Romero into his study. In reality, it was more of a library with a desk. Full of dark wood shelving, lined with stories that seemed to span a couple of thousand square feet. Romero went over to a decanter and poured a few fingers of bourbon into two crystal whiskey tumblers.

"Neat?" Romero asked, making sure Xander was okay with his bourbon straight up.

"Is there any other way?"

"I was afraid I would have to ask you to leave prematurely if you said no." Romero smiled.

Xander didn't want to, but he instantly liked Romero. He was charming, which was expected, but the way it seemed sincere was throwing Xander off a bit. The man was also a salesman by nature. Xander could tell this because the scent emanating from his glass was his own bourbon that Romero had poured for them.

Touché.

"You have good taste."

Romero reached his glass forward and clinked Xander's. Then he raised the glass toward him, referencing the bourbon with his eyes. "As do you, my friend."

Romero then pulled two Davidoff Nicaragua Toro cigars from a small leather travel case that was tucked in the breast pocket of his khaki-colored sport coat.

Now Xander had a full-on man crush.

"So tell me, Xander, what is your favorite thing about life?"

An odd question, but one Xander liked. He liked everything about this drug lord. What he didn't like was the fact that even though it was early, he just couldn't see Romero as the type to be involved in something like human trafficking. Sam would be kicking Xander in the ass for being wooed by the kingpin, but Xander would never let something like bourbon and a cigar interfere with something as serious as selling young women into slavery. Something wasn't adding up.

Romero took a puff of his cigar and looked at Xander expectantly.

"Winning," Xander finally answered.

"Winning? I like this. Anything in particular?"

Xander smiled. "Everything . . . in particular."

"Cheers to that. How did you get into horse racing?"

"It's in my blood, as is this bourbon. Kentucky is the most beautiful place in the world. Its culture seeps into your veins and becomes a part of you forever. No matter how far you try to run."

Romero smiled. "You are very passionate man. I see a lot of myself in you."

A beep from Romero's mahogany desk interrupted their conversation. Romero's face scrunched in frustration. He walked over to the desk and picked up the receiver.

"I told you, no interruptions."

A good thirty seconds went by. All that came out of Romero's mouth as he listened were a few one-word questions. Xander could see that his demeanor had changed once he hung up the phone.

"Everything all right?" Xander asked.

Romero finished his bourbon in one drink, set down his glass, and placed his cigar on the ashtray. He followed that with a deep sigh.

"I am not quite sure how to say this."

Uh oh.

Xander finished his bourbon and set down his glass.

"That doesn't sound good."

"I am afraid it is not."

Romero removed his sport coat, picked up a remote, and hit a button. On the wall, a painting turned into a television monitor.

"What exactly am I looking at, Romero?"

"That is at the foot of my property. Those men are the Sinaloa Cartel. Ever heard of them?"

Xander gave a wry smile, then spread his arms wide.

"You mean you didn't come by all of these nice things honestly? Shame on you, Javier."

Romero smiled.

"You are not frightened? This is in real time. In my line of work, sometimes, I'm afraid, you piss off some very vengeful people."

In front of them on the television screen, the night-vision camera showed a horde of men approaching the gate. All of them clearly armed.

"Tell me about it."

Xander knew all too well what it was like to have some bad men with a lot of resources after you.

"I ask you again, you are not frightened by this?"

"Not unless you leave me standing here unarmed."

"You know how to handle a weapon?"

"Come on, Romero," Xander said. "Let's cut the shit, shall we? I know you are a drug kingpin, and you know I used to be a Navy SEAL. We aren't the type of men who don't check into people's backgrounds before we open ourselves up to them."

Romero nodded his head and began to roll up his sleeves.

"I am very sorry that I have brought you into this. I have extra men at the mansion because there was a very slight chance there might be a threat. Please believe me when I tell you that if I thought this could actually happen, I would never have brought you here."

Xander did believe the man standing in front of him. But Xander had to know for sure about how deep it went before he could move on.

"I need one question answered before shit gets real." Xander nodded toward the security footage that now showed a gunfight at the gates.

Romero nodded for him to continue.

"I don't care how you've made this money or how you live your life. I really don't. With one exception."

"Go on."

"Do you traffic young women into America and sell them to the highest bidder?" Xander was blunt.

Romero paused for a moment, then walked over to Xander.

"This is why you are here? Not for horse race?"

Xander looked back up at the screen where guns continued to flare on the black-and-white live feed.

"Make no mistake, Romero, Heir to the Throne was going to smoke your horse tomorrow in that race. But in the interest of saving time, I had to see for myself if you were the one doing the trafficking as some intel might suggest."

Romero was stoic. He looked Xander straight in the eye. "I

have heard these rumblings myself. I give you my word, as a man: it isn't me."

Xander searched the man's brown eyes. Nothing inside them told Xander he was lying.

"They say your men are involved. If not you, then who?"

Romero finally broke the stare and looked down at his feet as he shook his head.

"I have tried to deny this and keep this embarrassment from coming to my doorstep. But it is the reason the Sinaloa Cartel is here tonight. And it is part of the reason for many sleepless nights."

"Who?" Xander was not concerned with Romero's lack of sleep.

"My son."

12

Mexican Standoff

Xander could see by Romero's demeanor that it was a sore subject. And frankly, they currently had bigger fish to fry. The two men glanced up at the television on the wall, and it showed the cartel breaching the gate. This wasn't how Xander saw his Friday night going, but things rarely work out the way you think they will. Especially when you are keeping company with criminals. Though even for Xander a full-on turf war was a bit much.

Well, not really.

He didn't exactly *want* to fight an army of half-trained thugs, but he also didn't have a choice. They were coming whether he wanted to be involved or not. Whether his team wanted to be involved or not. This wasn't about fighting for Romero and his cause; it was about fighting for survival.

"Follow me," Romero told Xander, and he walked straight toward the bookshelf on the far wall.

"We don't really have time for *Pride and Prejudice*."

Romero grinned as he pulled on a book on the third shelf. Something clicked behind the shelving, and the entire section began to move inward like a door.

A secret room.

"Did I mention I like your style?" Xander told him.

A light flickered on inside the hidden room, and three walls of weapons awaited them. It was a glorious sight for a soldier like Xander. The room was a lot like the one in his basement in Lexington. With a quick glance, there were a lot of the same weapons as well.

Xander said, "This is great for you and me, Romero, but what about my team?"

"Ricardo is bringing them in from the guesthouse. He is also gathering the ladies from the gallery. They will be safe until we arm ourselves and make our way to them, so don't worry about Samantha."

"That is one woman I have *never* had to worry about. Trust me when I tell you, she'll be just fine."

"You are full of surprises, Mr. King."

"You ain't seen nothing yet."

As the two of them picked out their weapons of choice and filled a bag with enough for the rest of the team, Xander could feel the adrenaline start to leak into his veins. As he removed his sport coat and rolled up his sleeves, excitement filled his system.

I must be one sick son of a bitch.

At the back of the mansion, Lola was showing Sam the gallery. Though Xander likely had far more money than Javier Romero, Sam could instantly see that their spending habits could not have been more different. Xander would never have a room dedicated to expensive artwork. It wasn't that Xander wasn't sophisticated enough to appreciate great artwork; he would just consider it a waste of money to spend millions of dollars on what looked like something a fourth grader could paint.

"And this, this is a Jackson Pollock," Lola said as she pointed to a canvas with what looked like random splashes of paint.

Sam wanted to act impressed, but she couldn't. The "artwork" looked as if the artist accidentally tripped and fell, spilling the paint on the canvas and then was too lazy to clean it up. A million dollars later and he was a genius.

Lola could sense that Sam was unimpressed.

"Oh good, I see you are like me."

Sam snapped out of her trance.

"Excuse me?"

Lola placed her hand on Sam's arm.

"I don't like any of this . . . *crap* either. But Javier loves it."

"Oh good, so you see this as drivel as well?"

"If by drivel you mean a waste of money, then yes."

It was then that the two of them heard something just outside the room. Lola didn't have the experience that Sam did; that's why she wasn't alarmed at the sound.

"Are you expecting company?" Sam asked as she walked over to the window.

"I'm sorry?"

"That was a gunshot, and unless those are your husband's men coming toward the back of the house, I'd say we've got a problem."

The look on Lola's face was sheer terror. She rushed over to the window and peered out into the night. Then she looked back at Sam.

"We need to get back to Javier."

Sam was about to agree, but the French doors behind her exploded inward and before Lola had the chance to scream, Sam shoved her to the ground. She then spun toward the men in black and reached up under her dress. Strapped to her right thigh was a Glock 19 pistol. Before the men could register that the beautiful woman in the sexy white dress had pulled a gun on them, Sam ended their evening abruptly as she put two bullets in each of their chests.

She then rushed over to the window to check the outside perimeter. They only had seconds before more men would be on top of them.

"We have to move, now," Sam told Lola as she helped her up from the floor.

"Who the hell are you?" Lola said in awe.

"Apparently I'm a trouble magnet."

Sam jerked Lola out in front of her and told her to lead them to the front entrance. Just outside the door, more gunmen were fast approaching.

Xander and Romero walked into the foyer at the same time Lola and Sam were walking in from the other side of the house.

"What the bloody hell is going on?" Sam said to the two of them.

Romero took in the sight of Sam. Xander could only imagine what he was thinking. Sam looked about as sexy as a woman could as she stood there, rocking that beautiful dress, pistol at the ready.

"Told you there was no need to worry about her," Xander said to Romero. Then to Sam, "Apparently we flew right into the middle of a turf war."

"Bollocks."

Just then the front door opened, and Romero, Xander, and Sam shifted their guns toward it, anticipating the worst. Instead, Kyle walked through the door. He immediately threw up his hands in surrender.

"It's me! What the hell is going on around here? They said we were under attack? Do you plan shit like this for fun, Xander?"

The three of them lowered their guns as Romero's man, Ricardo, ushered in Zhanna and Jack behind Kyle.

"They are halfway up the road, señor."

"How many?" Romero replied.

"Ten. Maybe fifteen."

Sam interrupted. "Well, there are more at the back. Have you no security there?"

"They cannot come in from there. It is a ravine," Romero said.

"The two dead men in your art gallery beg to differ."

Six of Romero's armed men came through the front door, and he directed them to the gallery.

"I am so sorry, Samantha."

"I'm fine, but Lola might be a little out of her element."

Romero motioned for Ricardo to take her away, then asked Xander, "Are all of your crew soldiers?"

"Fortunately for you, yes," Xander answered as he reached into the bag of weapons. "Jack, I grabbed this one just for you." Xander pulled out a sniper rifle and tossed it to Jack.

Jack tipped his cowboy hat back and marveled at the weapon. "Shewee! This is a Desert Tech SRS-A1. 'Bout as accurate as these new rifles come!"

"Figured you'd like that. Romero, where is a good place for Jack to perch? He's one of the best shots I've seen, so pick a spot and let him work."

Gunshots rang out at the back of the house in the direction of the gallery. Sam gave Romero an "I told you so" shrug.

Sam said, "Have we got a plan?"

Xander locked two magazines into the two Berettas he'd grabbed from the secret room. They weren't his weapon of choice —Glock 19—but they would do.

"Yeah, survive," Xander answered. "Kyle, you go spot for Jack. Make sure he has some backup ammo." Sam tossed Kyle two extra six-round mags for Jack's Desert Tech rifle. "Romero, put two men at the top of the stairs to watch Kyle's back."

Romero raised his eyebrow. "You're barking orders in my home?"

Xander squared up to him and looked him dead in the eye.

"You're damn right. You dragged me into this mess, I'm not going to let you get me or my friends killed too."

As Kyle and Jack marched up the stairs, Romero squared up to Xander and puffed out his chest. For the first time, Xander saw the qualities that made Romero a successful drug lord. Beneath the charismatic exterior was a hard man.

"We don't have time for an alpha-male pissing contest," Sam said. She stepped forward, getting Romero's attention. "I know you don't know us, Mr. Romero, but I beg you, let Xander put us all in the position to survive whatever you have got us into here."

"She speaks of you as if you are some sort of warrior. I like you, but it looks to me that the years away from the military may have made you soft."

Xander let out a sigh. Then he turned toward three of the armed guards who were with them in the foyer, then looked back at Romero. Just before he was about to challenge Romero's statement with a show of action, the window in the sitting room adjacent to where they were standing crashed inward with the momentum of a man diving through and rolling to a knee. As the intruder raised his gun toward Romero, Xander push-kicked Romero to the ground, and as the bullet from the intruder's gun hit the banister behind where Romero had been standing, Xander pulled his Beretta and shot the gunman dead. Two more men followed through the window, and a combination of Sam's and Xander's bullets put them down in a flash.

Romero looked up at the two strangers who had just saved his life. Sam adjusted the shoulder strap on her dress that had fallen down her arm as she turned to make sure Romero could see her.

"You see your men standing behind me?"

Romero glanced over her shoulder at the three men dressed in all-black tactical gear. Not one of them had so much as gotten their guns off their shoulders before Xander and Sam dispatched the enemies. Romero nodded and reached his hand toward Xander. Xander took his hand and helped him to his feet.

"I apologize for questioning you, Xander." Then he looked past him to his men. "You two, to the top of the stairs, and you, go see if they need help out back. Whatever Xander and Sam need us to do, we do." Then he said to Xander, "I am a business man, not a soldier. But I can hold my own against these thugs."

The men moved into their instructed positions. Gunfire erupted out front. The rest of the cartel army had made it to the mansion.

Xander said to Romero, "We survive this, you tell me where the next drop is in your son's little trafficking ring."

Romero hesitated.

"I haven't spoken with my son in more than a year."

13

Primal

"What was that back there?" Sam asked Xander as they moved over to the shattered window.

Xander peered through the broken glass from a crouched position and watched the tips of Romero's soldiers' guns flash as they fired defensively into the night.

"Romero says it is his son who's in the sex slave business."

"And you believe him?"

Xander looked over at Sam. "I know what you're thinking. And I know the man makes his living as a criminal, but yes, I believe him."

"Bloody hell, Xander. I'm shocked that your heart hasn't gotten you killed before now. As many terrible things as you've seen, from so many horrible people, and you still want to believe in humanity."

"Sorry we all can't be as cynical as you, Sammy."

As the gunfire continued just outside the window, Sam

replaced her half-empty magazine with the full one in her thigh strap. She decided it best to drop the conversation for now and focus on surviving the night.

"So what do you want to do here?"

Xander's expression softened, and his mind focused on the task at hand.

"We don't know how many are coming. That is a problem. If they have anything more explosive than guns, we are sitting ducks in here."

"Agreed."

Xander pulled out his phone and typed a group text that included Zhanna and Kyle:

Z, keep Romero and men at back of mansion. Do everything you can to keep the gunmen from breaching doors. If you can't, message K and have J move his sniper rifle to back to help cover u. K, J should have visible targets in seconds out front if not already. Make sure he knows his targets before he fires.

Zhanna messaged back first: *Will do, right now not much movement back here.*

Then Kyle's message came in: *Wait, why would Jack need to be sure who he is firing at? Aren't they all bad guys? What the hell are you planning, X?*

Xander messaged back: *Just tell him not to shoot the sexy couple coming up from behind.*

Kyle: *Christ.*

"Made your plan, have you?" Sam asked.

"Remember the service entrance on the aerial topography map of the compound you showed us earlier?"

"The one with the dirt road leading up to the left side of the mansion? Of course."

"You think the cartel knows about it?"

"No way to know that."

"You think you can navigate the rocky terrain in between the service road and the main drive in that dress?"

76

Sam began to slip off her high heels.

"To sneak up behind a bunch of gun-toting thugs? I can bloody manage."

The night had cooled since Xander and Sam had arrived at the mansion an hour earlier. As Xander shut the service door behind him, a chorus of various insects called out into the night. The heat of the night combined with the feeling of going off into battle reminded him of all the nights he'd spent with the Navy SEALs, sneaking up on an otherwise unsuspecting enemy. Without fail, every time he had found himself in a situation like this, the feeling of becoming something other than himself always came over him. As silly as it sounded, it really felt as if he were something like a lion in the jungle, stalking his prey.

It was an odd feeling when he first experienced it years ago. One that almost threw him off his game entirely when it crept up the back of his spine. He remembered it like it was yesterday. He and a small team were in the desert just outside of Jalalabad in Afghanistan. They had chased one of Bin Laden's senior generals to the foot of the Hindu Kush mountain range that bordered Pakistan. As he and his team stalked across the creek, he remembered the strangest feeling coming over him. One so strong that it stopped him dead in his tracks, the water of the creek rushing around his legs. It was something primal. Something that he was sure had been buried deep in his DNA from cavemen days, a time when they hunted for survival. That was what it felt like, because Xander and his team were doing just that. Though they weren't hunting for food, they were hunting a man, and it was kill or be killed. At the time, his commanding officer had to snap him out of it. Xander remembered the large man grabbing him by his com pack and shaking him until the feeling crawled back out from under his skin. Now, every time he was in a similar situation,

Xander could feel those same primal feelings gnawing at his subconscious. The difference for him now was that he had felt it enough to know how to control it. Instead of fearing it, he welcomed it. It was his source of focus.

"Are you all right?"

Sam sensed that Xander was in another head space. As Xander walked forward on the dirt path toward the darkness, she must have been able to feel his electricity.

"I can't believe I ever thought I could stop doing this," Xander said to her as he tucked one of his pistols into his belt line. He replaced it with his Marfione knife, preparing for a possible silent attack. "This is what I was meant to do."

Though Xander couldn't see it through the darkness that enveloped them, Sam wore a wide smile. "That makes two of us."

Xander and Sam, with the kinship only two warriors could share, walked off the dirt path, once again running alongside each other toward the danger.

14

Watch Your Back

As Xander and Sam walked off the beaten path and stalked their prey, Kyle was looking out the master bedroom window through the laser range finder that Jack had one of Romero's men find for him.

"What's that crazy sum bitch up to now?" Jack asked.

"He and Sam are trying to flank the gunmen. I guess he didn't like the idea of waiting for death to come to him."

"Probably a good strategy. How long you boys known each other? Hang on, hold your ears."

Jack squeezed the trigger on the sniper rifle, and Kyle watched one of the approaching cartel gunmen disappear from sight.

"Been blood brothers since we were eleven. Been finding trouble ever since."

"Awfully unusual for a civilian like yourself to follow trained soldiers into situations like this. You might be even crazier than Xander is."

"There's one," Kyle said, breaking the conversation to point out another target. "A hundred and forty yards—"

"I see him." Jack squeezed the trigger and another gunman disappeared.

"Nice. And as far as me and Xander go, after he finished with the SEALs, I was always around anyway, so when I figured out what he was doing, we just decided I might as well know how to handle myself. One thing led to everything else after that."

"You're brave, Kyle. But I reckon you've had just about as good a trainer as you could get. That sure helps."

The gunfire was beginning to escalate below them. Spotting the men coming out of the brush wasn't easy, and Jack knew they had to be careful.

Jack said, "I figure Xander and Sam are closing in about now. We best be real careful before we shoot again. We lose either one of them and we're all in trouble."

Another blast from a sniper rifle echoed across the mountain.

"Jack?" Sam whispered.

"Jack," Xander confirmed.

Sam and Xander had made a loop around the back of the approaching army of men. They didn't see anyone below them, and that gave them hope that they were coming up the back side of the last of the cartel. They were crouched together behind a row of shrubs. Both of them were covered in sweat as they listened for any clues. Over the calls from the insects, they heard some rustling up ahead in the direction of the mansion.

"Stay with me," Xander told Sam. Then he made a move out from behind the bushes.

He hadn't taken the time to notice whether the moon was out in force. But judging by the darkness, he didn't see how it could have been. Every step was a misstep; he had no idea how Sam was managing to do it barefoot. He danced around a couple of cactuses, and with the light of the front of the mansion a couple hundred yards to the north, the clatter of automatic gunfire serenaded their steps. That was when Jack's sniper rifle began firing at a much faster rate. Then Xander felt a vibration in his pocket.

A text from Kyle: *Get back to the mansion. The first few through were just scouts, at least a dozen of them just came out of the dark and took out all the front guards. Jack is about out of ammo. We've gotta move!*

Xander stopped and texted back: *Get to a secure room upstairs and hole up. Let Z know which room. Sam and I are on our way.*

A final sniper round blasted into the night.

"We gotta go, they're taking the front of the mansion," Xander shouted back to Sam.

He began to run up the mountain toward the mansion. As they approached, the floodlights from the roof shone down on a few men rushing toward the front door.

"There! On your right." Sam whisper-shouted to Xander, drawing his attention to the trees.

Xander saw the three men watching each other's back from the tree line. He tucked his pistol into the back of his belt and hit the release button on his knife, shooting the blade from its hiding place inside the handle. He could faintly see Sam behind him now. He motioned for her to stay to the left, and he showed her his knife, letting her in on how he planned to deal with the three unsuspecting men. Sam veered off to the left, heading directly for the front door. Xander narrowed his eyes and focused on the men crouched at the edge of the brush. That primal feeling needled at the back of his brain once again, and adrenaline heightened his senses as he moved in. He readied the knife in his right hand and steadied the rush that was pumping through his veins. An excited sweat threatened to impair his handle on the knife, so he wiped his palm down his pant leg to keep it dry. His heart pounded faster in his chest with each step he took toward them. The terrain around him was loud. Each move he made on one plant or another caused a noise. If he maintained this speed, they would hear him before he could strike.

Xander stopped for a moment. He was only twenty feet from the men now. One of them radioed something in Spanish to a member of his team. Xander took a deep breath and saw that Sam was now in position, ready to rush the front door when Xander was finished with his quiet kill. The man in front of him put the radio away and readied his gun. They were about to move. Xander's hand tightened around the knife's handle as he leapt forward toward the man in the middle. A second later, his knife sank into the back of the man's neck. Before the other two men had time to react, Xander had retracted his knife from their comrade's neck, stabbed right hitting the next man in the left side of his neck, and immediately spun 180 degrees in the opposite direction and plunged the blade into the right eye of the third man.

When Xander looked up, the last few of the dozen or so men Kyle had mentioned were running into the front door. He took back his knife from inside the man's face and sprinted toward them. Sam darted out of the tree line to meet up with him on his way there. Even though they had gone undetected, and taken out three men, Xander wasn't satisfied with what had happened. He had hoped to get there sooner and take more of them out before they entered the mansion. However, at least the men who were now inside weren't expecting anyone but their allies to be coming in behind them.

15

Dance with the Dead

Xander and Sam both stopped just outside the mansion's front door. Xander pocketed his knife and pulled both of his pistols. As they caught their breath, gunfire erupted inside the mansion. These strangers were firing on his friends.

And they were going to pay for it.

Just before they went to move, Sam reached up and wiped a smattering of blood from the side of Xander's face.

"Red might just be your color," she told him.

"I'm telling Kyle you were hitting on me."

Sam just smiled.

"All right then, up or down?"

"You go up and check on your boyfriend, I'll go see how Zhanna and Romero are doing."

Sam nodded.

"Don't risk your life for this Romero bloke. I assure you he isn't worth it."

"Maybe not, but Zhanna is."

The two of them readied their pistols, and Sam whirled around and kicked in the door. The next fifteen seconds was like a choreographed dance. A violent yet methodical groove that only Xander and Sam could perform. A high-speed death tango that felt, in the moment, more like a slow and smooth waltz. Although they hadn't practiced this synchronized cadence specifically, it was an art they had mastered together through years of battle. As they breached the door, Sam did a front roll and shot the first two men she saw on her left. Xander shot four times up the stairway with his left pistol as he simultaneously took out two men on his right who turned to see who had kicked in the door. As the men dropped dead to the ground, Xander turned and shot the gunman on the left side of the room who had raised his gun to shoot Sam, who had just elbowed an attacker who grabbed her from behind, spun into him landing a knee to his stomach, and put a bullet at close range through his forehead.

With soft yellow lights glowing overhead, Sam watched the man whom Xander had shot drop dead, and as her victim also fell, she gave Xander a nod of appreciation for the assist. That was when the two of them heard men yelling at the back of the mansion in the direction Zhanna and Romero had gone earlier. Xander, knowing Sam was low on ammo, tossed her one of his pistols, and the two of them split up, Sam going upstairs, Xander to investigate the shouting.

As Xander rounded the hallway that took him to the west wing of the mansion, the voices grew louder. They were shouting in Spanish, and though Xander didn't understand their words, there was no mistaking their tone. As he walked past the dining room, there was a large open archway that led into what looked like a massive room. It was clear the shouting was coming from there, so Xander moved swiftly to the end of the hall and sidled up to the opening. The men continued to shout; then he heard the distinct sound of the slides of pistols being pulled back and released. Someone was ready to shoot. In a slow motion, Xander moved his head around the wall and saw two important things. First, three men were standing over a silver-haired man lying on the ground, with what looked like blood pooling around him. Second, through the window on the far wall, he noticed a woman steadying a pistol in the direction of the three men.

Zhanna.

Because the men had their backs turned to Xander, he quickly waved his hand once, and immediately Zhanna turned her pistol on him. He ducked back behind the wall in case she pulled the trigger on reflex, but when all he heard was the men continuing to shout at Romero, he spun himself around the wall, nodded to Zhanna out the window, and shot the two men on the right in the back as she took out the gunman on the left.

"Behind you!" Romero shouted, pointing his finger at the second entrance to the room on the far wall over Xander's shoulder.

Xander spun while simultaneously dropping to a knee, flicked his right arm up and squeezed the trigger twice, dropping the man walking in the doorway. Romero and Xander heard two more shots on the other side of that wall, followed by a fiery redhead walking through the doorway, changing out her pistol's magazine as she confidently strutted their way.

"Thanks for assist, Xander," Zhanna said.

"Thank *you*."

Xander rose to his feet and walked over to Romero. Romero was much paler than the tan version of himself from earlier in the night. A leaking hole in the side of your stomach tends to have that effect. No one knew that better than Xander. There were still nights he would wake from a nightmare, reliving the night on his yacht a few months back when he was blasted in the stomach himself. It was a strange thing to see your own blood flowing freely from your body. That stuff wasn't supposed to make it to the outside. Xander still had pain once in a while from his nasty wound.

"Where are the rest of your men?" Xander asked Romero.

"Dead." He looked up at Zhanna. "If it wasn't for her, I would be as well."

"What am I? Chopped liver?" Xander made a motion to the dead men lying at his feet. The men he'd just killed to save Romero.

"No . . . I—"

"Joking." Xander stopped him. "Don't waste your energy. Do you think you can walk?" Xander extended a hand to help the wounded man to his feet, but before he could get to it, he heard gunshots from upstairs. His arm recoiled like he had reached for a hissing snake; then he reached instead for his gun and bolted for the doorway.

"See if you can stop the bleeding!" Xander shouted to Zhanna on his way out.

As he jogged down the long hallway, he heard more gunshots above him. The gun sounded like Sam's Glock, but through multiple walls and a flight of stairs, he couldn't be sure. As he approached the banister, he eyed the top of the stairs. He didn't see any movement. It was then that he remembered telling Kyle to message Zhanna what part of the house he and Jack were in. Xander pulled his phone from his pocket and pulled up Kyle's reply.

Z, if you make it upstairs, we're in the master bedroom closet. On the right side of the house.

Perfect.

Xander tiptoed up the stairs. He hadn't heard another gunshot. He hoped that meant Sam had taken the rest of the cartel gunmen out, but he couldn't know that for sure. He turned right at the top of the stairs, per Kyle's text to Zhanna, and moved down the dark hallway. No one had managed to hit the lights up there, and he was happy that was the case. Life and death happens in fractions of a second when you are playing these deadly games. Darkness could aid in providing a millisecond hesitation from the enemy, and that would be long enough for Xander to take advantage. The house was quiet now. Too quiet. Xander opened three doors in the hallway for a quick check inside as he made his way to its end. One door left. According to Kyle, this was where Xander would find them.

He reached for the door handle, and just as he was getting ready to give it a twist, he heard something beyond the door. A squeal? A sob? He couldn't be sure, but it sounded like a woman. His mind computed several things at once. Zhanna was downstairs, Sam could easily take these thugs out, and he hadn't seen another woman other than Romero's wife—

Romero's wife.

Xander kicked in the door, and as soon as he did, a gunshot rang out. The room was dark, but when the muzzle flashed, out of the corner of his eye he saw a woman tied to the bed with two men hovering over her. As soon as he heard the blast, he dropped to the ground. If the man had been a good shot, Xander would be dead. As it turned out, Xander didn't feel the burning sting of a bullet, so this time he was lucky.

But that wasn't going to last.

He rolled to his right, and just as he did, he heard two more gunshots, followed by the splintering of hardwood as the bullets burrowed into the floor where he had just been. From his stomach, Xander whipped his gun around and squeezed the trigger. The man let out a shout and began to hop around. Xander had hit him in the leg. He moved his gun up the silhouette in front of the window and pulled the trigger again.

The shouts of pain stopped.

As Xander scrambled toward the light coming from a half-shut door on the wall beside him to flee from the gunfire the other two men would surely be raining down on him, a worry flashed in his mind. According to Kyle's text, this was the room he and Jack were in. But clearly they weren't. Xander dove through the door and kicked it shut, then dove once more for the claw-foot tub against the wall to his right. Just as he pulled his leg down into the porcelain tub, gunshots blasted, and after blowing holes through the bathroom door, the bullets ricocheted off the marble floor and walls around him. He should have been worried about himself, but all he could think about were the gunshots he'd heard when he was downstairs. He had assumed they were from Sam's gun. But since she, Kyle, and Jack weren't where he expected, he worried that maybe Sam had been ambushed by the men who were torturing Romero's wife on the bed.

His mind snapped back to what he could control, and that was getting rid of these two gunmen so he could then get answers about where his friends were. He pulled up his pistol and shot out the lamp shining on the sink counter. More bullets came blasting through the door in response to the noise he made.

"Ah! Oh God, it hurts!" Xander shouted. Not his best performance. "Please! You got me! Por favor!"

The first gunman kicked in the door. They had believed him. Maybe there was a future for Xander at the Academy Awards after all.

Xander sat up and spent his last two bullets on the large shadow that moved into the bathroom. When that shadow fell to the ground, Xander was staring at two arms extended toward him. He threw himself backward and lay down flat in the tub as fast as he could, and it was just as two more shots were fired in his direction. Then he heard two more shots, but they sounded like they had come from farther away. Maybe the hallway. He eased his head up to see above the lip of the tub, and saw no one. Then the light came on, and Sam in all her ferocious beauty walked around the corner.

"There's no time for a spa treatment, Xander," Sam said with a wry smile on her face.

Xander pulled himself out of the tub as Kyle walked into the room. Xander gave him a sideways look.

"What?" Kyle said, shrugging his shoulders.

"What? Don't you know your right from your left?"

"What are you talking about?" Kyle was genuinely confused.

"You told Zhanna that you and Jack were on the *right* side of the house." Xander swapped out his last magazine in his Beretta.

"Yeah, the right side."

Sam turned and gave him a look.

"What?" Kyle asked.

They gave him a moment. Then he turned as if he would be facing the house, trying to figure out what they were talking about. His shoulders slumped and he turned back to them.

"Oops?"

"Oops?" Xander said. "Pretty big oops there, brother."

"Oh, I'm sorry." Kyle held up his arms. "I must have been sick that day you trained me on how you must always be facing the house to call out a side."

Sam scoffed. "Some things fall under the category of common sense, sweetheart. Good thing you're cute."

"Uh, I hate to interrupt, but does someone want to help me untie this young lady?" Jack said from beside the bed.

16

The Tendency to End Up Dead

The group finished squabbling over which side of the house was which, helped Jack untie Romero's wife, then made their way downstairs. The mansion looked like a war zone. It had been a while since anyone had heard a gunshot, but everyone was still on edge as they reached the war-torn foyer. Bullet holes and bodies were the new decor, and as Zhanna helped Romero in from the hallway, he looked like if he wasn't careful, he would fit right in soon.

"You don't look so hot, you going to make it?" Xander asked.

Romero removed his arm from around Zhanna's back and stood on his own. He was wobbly at best.

"I'll be just fine. My men just radioed that the perimeter is clear. I can't thank you enough for your help. Is everyone in your group all right?"

"They're fine. So much for the horse race tomorrow, I guess."

Romero looked as if he might protest.

"Save it, we're leaving. We've had better welcomes."

"I'm sorry about this, Xander. Is there anything I can do to make it right?"

Xander didn't hesitate. "Tell me where I can find your son."

"My son?" Romero played dumb.

Xander was over it.

"Look, Romero, we both know I didn't come down here for a horse race. I came down here because there is a human trafficking operation tied to your name in the intelligence circle. We can play friendly all you like, but there isn't a damn thing funny about selling little girls into slavery. Now, either it's you or it's like you said and it is your son. I'll find out either way, so let's make this easy."

"It's not that simple."

Xander racked the slide on his Beretta. "Oh, it's exactly that simple."

Everyone was quiet for a moment. Romero winced and placed his hand over the bandaged wound on the side of his stomach. Two of Romero's men walked through the front door, their assault rifles down by their sides. Romero took a deep breath, straightened his posture, and gave Xander a long look.

"I thought we would make good friends, was I wrong?"

"I've got plenty of friends. Which is it, Romero, you or your son?"

Romero glanced at his men, then took a sweeping look at Sam, Zhanna, Kyle, and Jack. It was clear he was trying to decide if there was a way out of this conversation. Xander cleared his throat, letting Romero know that there wasn't.

"What I told you in my office was true. I haven't seen or spoken with my son in a year."

"And you also said he was the reason the cartel was here tonight. That you'd been trying to keep him from trashing your name."

"I am businessman, Mr. King. I would never have my hands in

such things that you are speaking of. That being said, I don't know where my son is. And if I did, I couldn't tell you. Regardless of what he has done, he is still my blood. You have to understand that."

"I do understand," Xander told him as he tucked his gun in the waistline of his pants. "But you have to understand that I will find him, and stop him."

Romero took a step toward Xander. Sam raised her gun, and so too did Romero's men. Now the room was on edge. The two men were standing face-to-face, neither of them willing to back down.

"Don't be fooled by the friendly demeanor I have shown you on this night. I assure you, I am not the sort of man you want to find yourself on my bad side. If you go after my son, you will have an enemy in me." He took another step forward. "You must know that you don't want an enemy like me."

This time it was Xander who took a step forward.

"And you need to know that my enemies have the tendency to end up dead. All of them."

Just as the tension was about to boil over, José, the undercover CIA agent who had been in Romero's fold for more than two years, walked in from the hallway.

"Sam, Xander, I have new information regarding the latest trafficking shipment that will be moving across the border."

Romero turned in José's direction, a look of disbelief on his face.

"Traitor! I trusted you!"

Romero went to move toward José, but Zhanna kicked his legs out from under him. His wound had drained his strength, and he dropped to the ground with ease. But he still had a fire inside him, and it was clear that he didn't like to look weak.

"What are you waiting for? Shoot them!" he shouted to his men at the front door. But they were too slow to react: Sam had already pulled on them.

"No, no," she said to the gunmen. "There's been enough killing for one night. Drop the guns and you won't be next."

"Shoot them!" Romero shouted again, sounding desperate. But his men recognized there was no way to win this one, so they laid their weapons on the floor. "Cowards." Romero was disgusted.

"Listen," Xander said to the now-unarmed men, "get him some medical attention." Ignoring Romero, he then said to the rest of his team, "Let's get out of here. José, you can fill us in on the way to the airport."

"All right, what do we know?" Xander skipped the small talk and got down to business with José. They helped themselves to Romero's only SUV that didn't have blown-out tires from the shoot-out earlier, and Kyle was driving them back to the airport.

"You really know how to make an entrance," José said. "You always leave this kind of carnage behind?"

"It tends to follow us around," Xander said. "So what do you know?"

"Right. An undercover FBI agent has sent word that a ship-ment is being finalized tonight for the San Diego border, and should be there around nine tomorrow evening."

Sam spoke up from the front passenger seat. "Wait, there is an undercover agent working with the ones responsible, and they sent us here, what, on a wild-goose chase? They've known the entire time?"

"I'm not sure about the specifics, ma'am," José said. "Last I heard the agent had gone dark. Been weeks since the agent had checked in. I'm assuming the FBI considered her dead."

"And now, tonight, this agent all of a sudden reappears?" Xander was trying to understand. "Seems like an awfully big coin-cidence, don't you think?"

"I don't know, sir. This is all third party to me. As you know,

I've been in the dark myself. The only reason I knew this information at all was because I was given a burner phone at my intel drop this morning. I guess because they knew you were going to be here, that I might need access to information. An encrypted email just came in during all of the commotion. That's all I know."

"I understand," Xander said, then shifted focus to Sam. "We need a conversation with Marv, stat. He'll be able to clear this up for us, give us our real target, and stop wasting our time having us fight other people's battles. If this is the way it is going to be working with US government agencies again, you can consider me retired."

Sam just nodded and turned to get to work on the situation. They needed information, and they needed it fast. Xander didn't like the way things were shaping up. He had put his team's lives on the line, and maybe for nothing. That didn't sit well with him at all. He knew Sam was thinking the same thing, and he knew she would soon get to the bottom of it.

17

Taken

As Xander's newly formed clandestine unit, Reign, was seemingly chasing their tails in Sinaloa, things in another part of Mexico had become downright scary. Sixteen-year-old Carrie Taylor's life was about to change drastically, and what was worse was her eleven-year-old sister, Bethany, was there too.

The two girls were on a cruise with their parents, and out and about for the day at their first port of call, Puerto Vallarta. Carrie's mother and father had been discussing whether or not to let Carrie make a little money babysitting her sister for a while, and since her parents wanted some alone time by the beach, Carrie was allowed to take her sister shopping a few blocks away. It was the worst decision her parents ever made.

"Can we go see if they have any postcards?" Bethany asked her big sister. Her eyes wide as half-dollars, her smile as broad as the ocean just down the road.

"Why? Are you going to send one to your boyfriend?" Carrie teased.

This had been an ongoing hot button between the girls. Carrie knew her little sister had a boyfriend; she had seen the notes Beth kept "secret" in her top drawer. She couldn't help that her mom made her do laundry and she had to put Beth's clothes in that drawer. It was cute, her sister's first crush. She wished she could tell her that all boys will do is break your heart, but she didn't want to ruin her sister's fun with her own already cynical view.

"I don't have a boyfriend, Carrie!"

"All right. Whatever. But we better hurry, the stores are probably about to close and Mom and Dad don't want us out after dark."

Beth threw her arms around her sister, then led the way down the street full of tourist-trap shops and cheap Mexican food. Carrie just laughed as her sister's blonde pigtails bounced along the way. The sun had begun to set. Carrie looked up at its beautiful color and for a moment almost called her sister back. Her parents had been adamant about being back to the cruise ship by sundown. And while it wasn't quite that time yet, darkness was certainly closing in.

Instead, she chased after her sister. She needed some lotion with some aloe in it anyway. She had fallen asleep on the beach earlier, and her lobster-red skin was making her pay for it now.

"Wait up, Beth"

"There." The man pointed out the girl with the sunburn to his partner. "She's perfect."

"You don't think she's too old? Boss said find a young girl, don't you think he meant younger than her?"

"Well, you saw the girl she was talking to, didn't you? She's much younger, we'll take them both, make even more money."

The two Mexican men exited their vehicle and began to walk up the street to the store the girls had disappeared into. They didn't look like criminals, didn't look like bad men at all, but they were about to do a very horrible thing.

They tried to act normal as they approached the novelty store. The two of them walked inside and made their way to the back where a refrigeration unit housed various soft drinks and waters. The girls were there as well, laughing and looking at all the different postcards.

"Ooh, I think he'll like this one, Betty Boop," the dark-haired girl with the sunburn said to the little one. She would be just what their boss was looking for. Young, just now blossoming into a woman. She would bring top dollar.

"Shut up, Carrie! I just want one for my teacher!"

"Okay, squirt. Just pick one and let's get out of here. We have to get back to the boat."

After a few more minutes, the girls had finished paying and walked back out into the street. The two men followed closely behind. Their car was just a block away now, and the girls were walking directly for it. With each step the girls took, the men took two. They were closing in on them now. One man motioned to the other to go ahead and move across the street, conveying that he could come in from the other side in case one of them tried to run. This wasn't their first time doing this, and it showed.

"Bethany, come back this way," Carrie called to her sister.

Bethany did as she was told and slowed her pace. Carrie knew she was excited to get back and show their mom which postcard she picked out. It was then that she saw her reflection in the store window to her right, and then she noticed a second figure walking not too far behind her. Carrie whipped her head around to see who was following on the sidewalk at her back. The man smiled and gave a friendly wave, but something didn't feel right.

"Come here, Bethany," she said, trying to think of a reason to make her sister come all the way to her. "One of your pigtails is falling out." She knew that would work; her sister couldn't stand one hair on her head being out of place.

This time, instead of just slowing down, Bethany turned around and began walking back in Carrie's direction. She was only ten feet away, but it might as well have been a mile. Before Carrie knew what was happening, before she could even react, her sister had been scooped up in some strange man's arms. The cry for help was on the edge of her lips, but before she could get it out, there was something keeping her lips from moving.

A hand.

The same hand from the friendly hand wave a moment ago. She could see the man that had a hold of her reflecting in the store window. At the same time, she was watching a different man try to stuff her little sister in the back of a strange car. Panic clawed at the frames of her consciousness. She didn't know what to do; she just knew from all the episodes of *Dateline NBC* that her family had watched that she could not let them get her and Bethany in that car.

So she began to fight.

First she kicked back behind her, and the man grunted in pain at the unexpected blow. When he lifted her up off her feet, she rammed the heel of her sneaker straight backward, and she must have hit the sweet spot because in a blink she was free of the man's grip.

"Help! Help us!" Carrie screamed as she ran toward the strange car. Her sister was kicking against the man who had a hold of her. "Let her go!"

There were a few others on the street around them, but they all seemed frozen in shock. She was going to have to do this on her own if they were going to get away. She sprinted forward, and all she could think to do when she made it to the man was club him in the back of his head with her purse. She took the purse in her hand, stepped forward, and swung at him as hard as she could. The man was so caught off guard that he dropped Bethany.

It worked!

She took another swing at the man and hit him on the shoulder. Her heart was pounding, and adrenaline rushed through her veins.

"Run, Bethany! Run!"

She turned to take a swing at the man she had kicked in the groin, because she knew he would be coming up behind her. And sure enough, he was. But this time, she missed. He was able to dodge her purse and grab Bethany by the shirt as she tried to run past. Just as Carrie was going to lunge at the man to help, she felt a hand wrap around her leg, pulling her backward.

"No!" Carrie screamed. "Let go of her! Someone, PLEASE!" She barely found the breath to scream. Her lungs burned as panic drained her stamina.

She lunged forward once more and kicked her leg up, breaking free of the grip from the man on the ground. "Let her go!" Carrie jumped on the man's back. Bethany was sobbing in fear, struggling to run forward and get her shirt loose of the man's hand. Carrie began beating down on the man's head with both fists, and finally he was forced to let go of Bethany's shirt.

"Run, Bethany! Go get Daddy!"

Carrie felt two hands wrap around her waist, and before she knew it, she had been thrown to the ground. Her elbow plowed into the concrete, and she screamed as pain bolted through her nerve endings. Her scream forced her sister to turn around. Through the man's legs in front of her, she could make out her sister's face in the glowing streetlight.

Fear.

"Run! Go!"

"No, Carrie! I won't leave you!" Bethany cried. "Let go of her!" Her voice echoed through the street.

The two men picked Carrie up off the ground and began attempting to shove her in the backseat of the car.

"Go now, Beth! Go get help!"

Finally, right before Carrie was forced inside the car, she saw her sister turn, and once again watched as her pigtails bobbed away from her. The door slammed behind her. She was terrified. What did they want? Where were they taking her? She didn't know any of the answers, but she knew she was in serious trouble.

At least they didn't get her little sister too.

She screamed, felt a thump on her forehead, then everything went black.

18

Son of a Drug Lord

"Coffee?" Xander said, offering Sam a cup from the freshly brewed pot.

The jet hit a pocket of turbulence, Xander wobbled, and hot coffee lipped out of the rim of the mug that he had extended toward Sam. She managed to dodge it like a cat on a hot tin roof. She gave Xander a warning look from her seat, but then smiled when she noticed that Xander's expression looked impressed.

"Just keeping your skills sharp, Sammy."

"My skills are just fine, thank you," she told him as she took the warm mug from his hands.

Kyle plopped down in the chair beside them.

"So what's next for Reign?"

The sound of a name for the team still felt a little odd to Xander, but he was warming to it. He was proud of the way they all performed back at Romero's mansion. Not that it surprised him, because he had seen them all in action before, but it was nice to know he was going to be able to count on them when the shit inevitably hit the fan. They left Romero's and Sinaloa on as good of terms as one can when a man has pledged to go after another man's son. Xander could see in Romero's eyes that he wanted to stop him, but he was witness to Reign's performance, and though he was a proud man, Romero knew they were also the only reason he still drew breath.

Before they went wheels up, while Xander and Kyle had gone to make sure Gary and Heir to the Throne made it safely out of Sinaloa, Sam and the rest of the crew began to formulate a plan for what was next. Based on what José had said, it was clear they had to start with the info that had come in from the undercover FBI agent. And that is where Sam's work had been focused the last couple of early morning hours. Deciphering who, what, and how credible this new information was from this recently "dark" agent.

"Can I just have a second?" José said before Sam could answer Kyle's question of what was next. "I just want to thank you for getting me out of there alive. For a minute there, I wasn't sure how that was going to happen. Two years in deep cover, seeing the things that I have seen, I thought being free of Sinaloa and Romero was a pipe dream. Thank you all for that."

Xander clinked his Red Bull can against José's coffee mug. José looked to be in his midthirties. Long dark hair pulled into a ponytail, olive skin, brown eyes, and what looked like a physique ready for any physical challenge.

"Thank *you*, my friend," Xander said. "The longest I've been undercover was a month, and it was hell. Constantly trying to be someone else is exhausting. And thank you for your invaluable information." Xander took a sip of his energy drink. "So do you think we can trust what Romero is saying about his involvement in the human traffic ring?"

"I think you can," José said. "I saw no signs of his involvement in that sort of thing. Don't get me wrong, Romero is a ruthless man, but only when it comes to his drug business and people remaining loyal to him. That is why I thought I would have to die to get out."

"Okay, so you believe him when he said it was his son?"

"Honestly, he must have thought a lot of you, Xander. Even though he and his son don't get along, as loyal as he is, I am shocked he told you that."

"I was too."

"But yes, I believe him."

Sam set down her coffee mug that read "Talk to me when this is empty" and powered on her iPad as she looked at José.

"So what do you know about Romero's son?"

"Nothing really," José answered Sam. "I haven't seen him in over a year. And even when he was around, it was always a short visit. He and his father would argue, then he would leave. That's it. Rumors were that he was a real spoiled asshole who kept getting in over his head, and Romero was constantly bailing him out."

"Like now?" Xander asked rhetorically.

Zhanna brought over some eggs and bacon from the galley and passed the plates around to the team.

"Here is breakfast. Where are we going now?" she asked.

"Why don't you bring us up to speed, Sam," Xander suggested.

"Okay, according to Eliza Sanchez, the undercover agent, we are dealing with a real wild card in Romero's son."

"Can we give him a name already?" Jack interjected.

"Francisco Romero." Sam gave Jack a wink. The old cowboy tipped his hat. "The last couple of years he apparently has been trying to break out of his father's shadow and create a name for himself."

Kyle laughed. "Ah, the dream of every young son of a drug lord."

Sam continued, "As José eluded, it was a rocky start at first. He tried to set up several different operations, to no avail, needing

Daddy to get him out of trouble. That being said, over the last year, and probably the reason you haven't seen him, José, Francisco has been able to set up a trafficking ring consisting of all the major ports up the Mexican Riviera. Mainly, of course, Mazatlán, Cabo, and Puerto Vallarta." Sam glanced up at Zhanna. "And Mazatlán is where we are heading now. An American family just reported their sixteen-year-old daughter being taken last night in Puerto Vallarta. Witnesses confirmed it."

"So why we are not going to Puerto Vallarta?" Zhanna asked.

"The drive to get to California runs right through Mazatlán. It's a shot in the dark, but I'm hoping we can make it there in time to cut them off. The sooner we can fight them, the less time they'll have to deal the girls. It's very likely they will try to sell a few of their kidnap victims in Mazatlán. They won't sell what they consider their 'high-dollar' girls there, but American men on vacation will pay good money for a young Mexican girl."

"This is a sick-ass world we live in," Jack said. "We have got to get these sons of bitches before they can do this to these poor girls anymore." He then turned toward Sam, a look of disbelief on the old man's face. "So I reckon what I'm hearin' you say is that the white girls go for a premium? And those premiums are paid by men in our own country?"

"That's right, Jack." Sam nodded. "Wealthy businessmen in the US. I guess they've done everything else in their lives, so they get bored and dabble in the black market."

Kyle was taken aback. "This is sick. We have to stop this. So you're telling me that these assholes go from port to port stealing young American tourists right from their vacations? What sick bastards would do things like that?"

"Sons of drug lords trying to make names for themselves," Xander answered.

Sam added, "Not just American girls. I know this sounds awful, but the men in the US doing the buying like a variety. So they are picking up girls from a lot of different places. These ports in the Mexican Riviera are just the easiest pickings, so they are the most frequented. If we shut this operation down, cutting off the head, the rest of the body will die."

"Francisco Romero." Kyle said his name with great disdain.

"That's right," Sam said. "We take out Francisco, we take the entire operation down."

"What makes you think Francisco will be here in Mazatlán? Why wouldn't he just let his men do the dirty work?"

"Sanchez's intel is that he is very controlling because it is all still so new. He stays with the shipment until the handoff in Tijuana to ensure nothing goes wrong. Then he has his money, so it no longer involves him. He never has to cross the border, which is where the biggest risk lies."

"So then we only know half of the information?" Xander said.

"Half?" Kyle sat up. "What do you mean?"

"Right, Xander, only half," Sam said. "We aren't yet sure who receives the shipment and then takes it across the border to finish the sales. But they are believed to be Americans."

Kyle stood up. "I mean, we are talking about this like these girls are a commodity. Like they are something as insignificant as drugs or something."

"To these people, that is exactly what they are," Xander said. "And that is exactly why this entire operation dies tonight."

"What do you mean tonight?" Sam asked.

"You know exactly what I mean, Sam. We only take down half the operation if we just stop them here in Mazatlán. The Americans responsible for the other side of this thing have to be stopped as well. Otherwise it's a failure."

"I disagree." Sam was stern.

Xander shook his head. "So you're telling me that if someone took Kyle but we got him back, you wouldn't be going after the men who took him? To make them pay? To stop them from doing it again?"

Sam glanced at Kyle, then back to Xander. Her face was solemn.

"Of course I would make them pay. But that's different, Xander."

"Not to me it isn't. Any one of those girls could be my niece, Kaley. Each of those girls *is* somebody's niece . . . somebody's daughter. Everyone involved in this operation is going to pay. If not because it is what they deserve, then because it will send a message to anyone else considering giving an operation like this a shot in the future." Xander paced the walkway in between the couches for a moment, thinking. "Do we even know what type of vehicle we are looking for? Where is this Agent Sanchez under-cover? With Francisco?"

Sam sighed. "This is the frustrating part of this, and honestly, it smells fishy to me. The intel from Sanchez is very vague. The day she was supposed to give a report on what she had been investi-gating stateside was the day she went dark. They were expecting to receive information from her about both ends of the trade, but it never came. She is from California and she requested this assign-ment, which is why they put her on it, but no one is sure where she is or why the intel is so incomplete."

Xander shook his head. "What great help the government is. Good thing we have all their resources," he said sarcastically. "Something is definitely off. Do you think she's compromised?"

"Her superior said she's been nothing but exemplary so far. But as you know, Xander—"

"That doesn't mean a damn thing."

"Right."

"So we don't even know what vehicle we're looking for?" Kyle asked.

"No," Sam answered. "But Francisco has his own plane. Just because he is known to be controlling the shipments doesn't mean that he rides with them the entire way."

"You think he could be at the airport?"

Sam looked annoyed by their lack of information.

"Until we know what vehicle they are transporting the girls in, where the exact drop point is, and who is taking the girls into San Diego, we don't really have another option other than the airport."

"She's right," Xander agreed, looking at Sam with a smirk. "So are we playing 'Mr. and Mrs.' again when we land?"

19

Captive

It was hot and dark, and the suffocating air stank of body odor. Other than the rumbling below her, the sound of tires rolling down pavement, oh, and the screaming and crying of other young girls around her, that was all that Carrie knew of where she was. Their cries were heartbreaking. Even though it was in a way comforting to know she wasn't alone, it nearly wrecked her soul to know that there were other girls that these monsters had taken.

She had switched vehicles more than once, but other than that, the sounds of men speaking to each other in Spanish, which she didn't understand, along with the blackout blindfold yielded nothing in regard to where she was or where she was going. Or just how many innocent young women were going along on this terrifying ride with her.

She could feel her hair glued to her forehead with her own sweat. Her hands were still tied behind her back, just as they had been for hours on end. The cries continued around her. The floor below her was hard like metal, like what the bed of her uncle's pickup truck was made of. But they weren't outside, it was definitely some sort of van—a van that was now beginning to slow, and Carrie felt her body shift to the left as the vehicle turned off the road. She worked at the gag in her mouth with her tongue. She was close to pushing the cloth out past her lips. She didn't know what good it would do, if any, but maybe if she could convince someone else into spitting theirs out, she could at least have someone to brainstorm with.

She continued to work at the gag. It had completely soaked up any saliva in her mouth, like a splash of water on a cotton ball. Ironically, the rest of her was wringing with sweat. She knew from what Mrs. Beasily said in health class that she was becoming dehydrated. The first sign is usually a headache, and her forehead was pounding. The dry of her mouth made it all the more difficult to work her tongue against the cloth. But she was close. As the van continued to slow, her heart began to pound. As bad as the back of that van was, she would stay in there forever if they would just leave her alone.

The van came to a stop, and she heard doors open and shut. An electric shock of fear burned cold over the top of her skin. Her breathing began to quicken as she anticipated what could possibly be next. Then doors closer to her opened, and she felt the back of the van dip down and warm air whoosh in. They were coming inside to get her. She began to cry. She began to whimper. And as she felt a hand wrap tightly around her arm, she screamed into the gag.

"Stop crying now," a man with a Spanish accent told her. He wasn't angry or hostile; it was a soft command. "Everything will be all right now. No need to cry."

She felt a tug at the back of her head, and before she knew it, bright light pierced her eyes as the blindfold was removed.

"You see, we are not monsters. Whoever took you, they were the monsters. I am here to take you home."

For the moment, all Carrie could see was a black figure with a bright light silhouetting around him. There were other shadows at the back of the van. She gave a few blinks, trying to move the tears that perpetuated the blur. As her eyes began to adjust, a short man slowly began to be revealed in front of her. As she blinked some more and calmed herself, she could see that though he was Mexican, he looked nothing like the men who took her. He looked more . . . refined. Could what he said possibly be true?

"You are scared, I understand," the man said. "Those men who took you, they are gone now. I am here to take you back to your family."

Carrie felt a flutter in her stomach. Could it be true? Could he be taking her back to her parents? To her little sister? Hope swelled inside her. She remembered watching a show once where undercover cops posed as drug addicts and bought from the dealer to catch them in the act. Could this be something like that? Could the switching of vehicles earlier have been this undercover officer taking possession of her?

As she processed this information, the man turned to whoever was outside the back of the van and nodded. She noticed a pistol tucked in the back of his white pants. Then she looked at his belt buckle: a gold H. A very expensive brand, Hermes. She had seen the same belt on some of the fashion bloggers she followed on social media. Then she glanced down at his shoes. They too looked very expensive. And when she caught a glimpse of his watch, it was the unmistakable shape of the watchmaker Hublot. She knew from her obsession with all things fashion that there was no way an undercover officer would be wearing that belt or those shoes, and not in a million years could he afford that watch. They weren't here to take her home; this was just another step in whatever bad things they had planned for her.

She wanted to scream.

She wanted to run.

She glanced around her and saw three more girls, all around

her age, all bound and gagged. Carrie took a deep breath in through her nose and back out. She felt the panic creeping up her spine, but what good would panicking do? This most likely wasn't the first time these men had done something like this, so she knew they had a plan in place if she started to freak out. And it would probably be them knocking her out. She swallowed a hard, dry swallow and decided that she would play along for now. She would wait for an opportunity better than this one; then she would make her escape.

"I'm going to untie you now and remove this terrible thing from your mouth, okay? You don't have to scream or be scared, I am here to help you. You understand that?"

Carrie nodded.

The other girls were beginning to squeal, and two more men entered the back of the van. The cheesy but well-dressed man walked her out the back of the van. Two men were there to help her down, and while they were untying her, she was looking directly at one of the most beautiful women she had ever seen. And noticing behind her, she realized she was at an airport. For a brief moment, that feeling of maybe, just maybe, they were actually saving her rushed through her. The pretty woman was definitely out of place, and by the look on her face, she wasn't happy. Or maybe what she was seeing, saddened her? Like she couldn't believe someone had done this to Carrie and these other girls. Could that mean they were actually rescuing Carrie?

"I can't watch this," the pretty woman finally said. Then she turned and walked away. There was anger in her stride.

Carrie couldn't have been more confused. The man untying her shouted for the woman to stop, but she just kept walking. The man said something to another man beside him in Spanish, then went walking after the lady. Carrie was trying to piece together the dynamic of their relationship, but what did she know about relationships? She was only sixteen. She looked back over her shoulder toward the van, and that was when thoughts of being saved left her forever. Because there was another van, with more girls like her in it. And she turned around just in time to see a man hit a girl, who was making a lot of noise, on the back of the head with the end of his gun.

Carrie folded up inside herself, doing her best to shut everything down. If there was a way to go numb all on her own, she needed to dig deep and find it.

Her sanity—and her survival—could very well depend on it.

20

The Girl Who Knew Too Little

Bob had to circle Xander's jet in a holding pattern while a smaller private plane ascended into the air from the runway below. After landing safely, they taxied over to the small private airport terminal, and a hot breeze blew inside the jet as Bob lowered the door.

"Stay put while the missus. and I go and poke around." Xander smirked and gave a wink to Kyle, then grabbed Sam by the hand.

Sam quickly removed her hand from his. As usual, unamused by what he found humorous. She turned her attention to Kyle.

"Kyle, while we probe the staff at the airport for information, can you check in with Marv and see if he's been able to gain clearance with the Mexican government to tap into surveillance cameras in this area?"

"Of course."

"We also need any footage he can find from the kidnapping in Puerto Vallarta. At least to see who we are dealing with, and get a read on what type of vehicle they are using. We also need pictures of the latest kidnapping victim, and any relevant information about her."

"Done." Kyle began to dial Marv on his phone. "But what if he hasn't obtained clearance from Mexico?"

Jack swiveled around in his chair. "Tell 'em to get that info anyway."

Kyle looked from Jack back to Xander.

Xander smiled. "What he said."

Xander shaded his eyes from the sun, and he and Sam made their way toward the airport entrance. In just a few strides from the plane his skin was on fire, and it felt as if his shoes were melting into the pavement beneath his feet. In the distance, a van pulled out of the airport parking lot, but his mind didn't register anything beyond that.

"What makes you think anyone in here is going to cooperate with a couple of inquisitive white people?" Xander asked Sam as he looked at her through squinted eyes.

Sam tugged at the zipper on her purse.

"Still weird seeing you with a purse."

"I *am* a woman you know, Xander."

"Whatever you say." He laughed.

Then Sam produced a thin black leather case that looked like a folded wallet.

"You're going to pay them off?"

Sam opened the wallet and inside was a picture of her next to the acronym CIA.

"There are *some* perks to being backed by your government."

Xander smiled.

"I've seen better pictures of you."

Sam slapped him none too gently across the face with the leather case. Xander acted as if he were really hurt, and then smiled. "Why, Mrs. King, is this our first fight?"

Sam rolled her eyes and walked into the air-conditioned lobby of the private airport. Xander followed, but instead of enjoying the cool air that swirled around him, a familiar feeling tickled at the back of his subconscious. He stopped just inside the door to indulge the feeling. A flash of the van he watched exit the airport a few moments ago floated in front of his eyes—the source of the tickle that set off alarm bells in his head.

Sam turned around. "Are you all right?"

He wasn't sure if he was or not. The feeling that something was off about the van wasn't leaving him. He nodded to Sam and told her to go ahead. He watched as she walked toward the front desk. Out of the corner of his eye he noticed a woman staring out the window in the direction of the airport exit. Her back was turned, but there was something very familiar about her. Xander took a step to the left and pulled out his phone. He sent a text to Kyle, asking him to have José remind him of the name of the undercover FBI agent.

Eliza Sanchez, Kyle replied.

Xander knew he had never met Eliza Sanchez, but in some corner of his mind this woman in front of him was familiar, and he didn't know if the two could be connected or not.

The woman by the window was wringing her hands. There was clearly something bothering her. When she brushed her long dark hair back behind her ear, it reminded Xander of why she seemed familiar. In a flashback to the pool in Cabo when he watched Gabriela walk out of the water in all her gorgeous splendor, she had tucked her hair in exactly the same way.

Xander's blood ran cold.

What was she doing here?

Could it be a coincidence?

Was he going to run into Antonio and his thugs?

He didn't have time for all that nonsense, but he couldn't avoid her either. As Sam tried her hand at questioning the woman at the front desk, Xander made his way to Gabriela. There wasn't a whole lot of noise in the lobby, so the squeak of the bottom of his shoes against the polished tile announced his arrival before he could call out to her. When she turned toward him, her face wore a look that was nothing short of shock.

"Xander? What are you doing here?"

"Hello, Gabriela, I was just going to ask you the same thing."

She stumbled over her words, trying to find the right thing to say.

"I-I . . . I am on my way back to Los Angeles."

Xander took a few steps closer. He could see that she was shaking. He closed the distance and put his hand on her shoulder.

"Are you okay?"

She told him yes, but he could see a resounding no in her water-filled brown eyes. She threw her arms around his neck and hugged him. She was trembling, and she began to sob into his shoulder. He wrapped his arms around her and gave her a reassuring squeeze before he pulled her back and looked into her eyes.

"Gabriela, I need you to tell me what's going on. I can help you. Why are you here? Mazatlán isn't exactly a stopover from Cabo to LA."

"I can't, Xander. There is nothing you can do. I made a terrible mistake getting involved with Antonio, or whoever the hell he really is. I just need to get back to the States, I need to find out who to call. The police, the FBI, I don't know!"

She once again began to cry. Xander was confused.

"Wait, Antonio is here? Now?"

She shook her head no and gave a hard swallow, trying to stop the tears. Xander could see the fear in her eyes.

"Gabriela, you need to tell me what's going on. I can help."

"Is everything all right?" Sam said as she walked up to the two of them. "Do you know this woman?"

"Yes," Xander said. "It's a long story."

"It always is," Sam said.

"Who is she, Xander?" Gabriela asked as she finally calmed herself. "What is going on? Why are *you* here?"

Sam said, "We don't have time for this, Xander. The lady at the front desk had no flight plan for the plane that took off just before we landed. She described the man that chartered the plane, and it sounds like Francisco."

"Francisco?" Gabriella looked surprised. "Are you talking about the white plane with the red stripe?"

Sam shifted her weight and put a hand to her hip. "Yes."

Gabriela looked back at Xander. "That was Antonio leaving in that plane."

Xander's head swam. They were there to find Francisco Romero. What kind of coincidence could it be that Antonio was here? And Gabriela? It wasn't a coincidence. That realization hit him with the force of a moving train. And when he thought back to the moment in Cabo when he picked Antonio up and threw him in the pool, then pictured Javier Romero back at his mansion in Sinaloa, he suddenly realized that there was a resemblance.

"What is Antonio's last name?" Xander asked her.

He had a feeling he wasn't going to like the answer.

"Romero."

Xander looked at Sam and found that she had already caught on. She immediately pulled out her phone.

"Kyle. Could you please ask José what Francisco Romero's middle name might be?"

Xander looked at Gabriella, who was clearly lost. Then back to Sam.

"He's sure?" Sam said into the phone. "We need you and Zhanna inside please." Sam ended the call. "Francisco Antonio Romero."

Xander was quiet for a moment. He couldn't believe it.

Sam must have seen the confirmed realization in Xander's eyes. She held her arms out at her sides, giving him the eye. "You want to fill me in on what the bloody hell is going on?"

21

Sam Doesn't Speak Country

Kyle and Zhanna walked into the airport just as Xander finished explaining to Sam that the run-in he had in Cabo was actually with Francisco. She was trying to digest the coincidence.

"I obviously didn't know at the time who he was, but it makes sense now, knowing what we know," Xander explained.

Sam looked at Gabriela, then back to Xander. "Must you always complicate things by involving women?"

"Complicate things? She should be able to make this easier." Xander took Gabriela by the hand. "We need to know everything there is to know about Francisco. Not the least of which, where his plane is headed."

"Who are you guys?" she asked. "I'm not implicating myself in what he is into. I had no idea, I thought he was into real estate and maybe some small drug thing on the side. He told me he would help me get an acting job. Said he knew some producers in Hollywood. Maybe I should call a lawyer."

Sam flashed Gabriela her CIA credentials.

"Really?" Xander said.

"CIA?" Gabriela's demeanor shifted from concerned to downright terrified. "I don't have anything to do with this, Xander, you have to believe me. As soon as I saw the girls in the back of the van, I told Antonio—Francisco to leave and never speak to me again. I swear! That's why I'm here, and not on that plane, and not in that van!"

Xander's stomach dropped. He knew exactly which van she was talking about. If they had landed just ten minutes earlier, those girls would be safe and Francisco Romero would be dead or in custody.

Xander shifted focus.

"Kyle, get us a car, preferably an SUV. Sam, see if they have the tail number to Francisco's plane, and get Marv to find a way to track it." Xander turned to Gabriela, took her shoulders in his hands, and looked sternly into her teary eyes. "Tell us everything you know about where the plane and the van are going, and who exactly is inside both."

"He'll kill me if I tell you. He said he would find me and kill me if I told anyone what I saw."

"I'll kill you right here, right now if you don't," Sam said. Not an ounce of remorse in her tone.

"Sam," Xander said, "you're not helping. Call Marv."

Sam held his glare for a moment, then diverted it to her phone. Kyle and Zhanna headed over to the Hertz rental counter, leaving Xander alone with the frightened Gabriela. Xander moved the hair from the right side of her face, back behind her ear, trying to convey to her with his eyes that he would take care of her.

"What did you see, Gabriela? Where are they going?"

"It was horrible." She began to sob. "They were just stuffed in the back of that van, tied up, bags over their heads. Blindfolds over their eyes. It was awful!"

"How many girls were in the back of the van?"

"There were two vans, but they consolidated to one. Six in that van . . . I think."

"You think?" Xander raised his voice.

"No, I know. There were six!"

Xander turned back to Sam.

"Get Marv to see if he can tap into a traffic camera somewhere along the road to see where the van is headed. There are six girls in the back of it."

"Five," Gabriela spoke up.

Xander was getting frustrated.

"You just told me there were six, which is it?"

"There were six, but he took one of the girls with him on the plane. I saw them putting her inside while Antonio—or Francisco, whatever the hell his name is—was berating me."

Xander turned back to Sam. "One in the plane, five in the van." Then he said to Gabriela, "Where is the plane going?"

"I-I don't know."

"Think, Gabriela. Something he said, some clue?"

"He didn't say anything about it, I swear!"

Xander believed her. There are certain things in life that you would have to be a complete sociopath to fake. And he didn't get sociopath when he looked at her. He could see genuine fear for the girls in Gabriela's eyes. Until they knew where the plane was going, he knew they had to focus on the van. It wasn't going to be easy getting it stopped without harming any of the girls. They were headed for a delicate situation. Xander was more known for crash and burn when it came to taking out the bad guy. He was going to have to finesse this one. And he knew that meant putting himself and his team in even more of a dangerous spot.

A flashback to Moscow ran through his mind. He and Sam were on a motorcycle heading for the airport when three SUVs intervened, trying to block their path. They should have never made it out of that one alive. He hoped for everyone's sake that this would be nothing like that.

"Got the SUV," Kyle said, snapping Xander out of his trance. "Jack is bringing in a bag of weapons. I'll pull up out front. José is staying with Bob to make sure the plane is safe."

Xander nodded to him, then looked back at Gabriela. "Stay here. You can fly back to San Diego with us."

Gabriela didn't say a word; she just threw her arms around Xander's neck again. She needed comfort, something Xander was normally very good at when it came to beautiful women, but his mind was on the task at hand. He gently removed her arms from around his neck.

"I'll have my pilot, Bob, come and take you back to the plane. You can wait there. Hopefully we won't be long."

He instructed Sam to give Gabriela her cell phone number in case they got separated. Sam didn't seem too happy about it, but she obliged. Jack came in from the tarmac with a big black bag over his shoulder. He met up with Xander and Sam, and the three of them walked out front and jumped inside the black Chevy Suburban with Kyle and Zhanna.

"Head north. I saw the van turn that way when we were walking into the airport," Xander told Kyle.

Kyle hurried the SUV down the road to the airport's exit, but when he came to the main road, he slowed to a stop.

"Uh, which way?"

"North," Xander answered.

Kyle looked back at him in the rearview mirror, confusion on his face. The four others all chimed in together, "LEFT!" Kyle mashed the gas pedal to the floor and headed north. Xander couldn't help but laugh, because even though he wasn't looking at her, he knew Sam was rolling her eyes.

The Suburban full of Reign, the CIA's newest clandestine unit, sped into the shining sun on Highway 15—the driver not even understanding which way was north. Xander thought to himself that either the CIA had severely lowered its standards or they had put far too much faith in him and Sam. He knew they would get the job done, but he was also glad they were allowed to call all the shots and didn't have someone with them who would let the higher-ups know just how little one of their teammates knew about this business. That said, Xander also knew that it didn't matter. Kyle had learned over the years where he could be of help and where he would just get himself killed. All that mattered to Xander was that he knew his friend would die for any one of his team members. That was enough for him.

"Any word on the plane?" Xander asked Sam.

"Marv said three planes with all the same sort of makeup left Mazatlán one right after another. They all have checked in so far with their corresponding air traffic towers. So far they are all complying. Marv is reaching out personally to each plane to find out where they are going and to ask for a passenger manifest. That doesn't mean they will comply, but for now, we at least will be able to watch them all until we find out what is what."

"Okay, good, I guess," Xander contemplated. "If we can get through this fairly quickly, our jet will all but catch up with any of those three smaller planes."

"What's the plan once we get close to van?" Zhanna asked.

Xander smirked when he turned and looked to Jack, his resident sniper extraordinaire. "You ever shot from a moving vehicle before?"

Jack returned the smirk with one of his own that grew out from under his white mustache. "Does a fish shit in the ocean?"

Xander smiled as he glanced over at Sam.

"Does a what?" Sam asked, disgusted confusion on her face.

Kyle and Xander laughed. Zhanna, being Russian, didn't get the expression either. Xander put his hand on Sam's knee.

"It means he has, Sam."

"You country boys have your own language entirely."

Jack smiled as he pulled his sniper rifle from the bag.

"Daggum right we do."

Sam, unimpressed, could do nothing more than shake her head.

22

Smoke and Mirrors

"This is a mistake, David," Lisa told her brother as the two of them stood outside the garage of one of David's beach houses in Pacific Beach. Though it was a touristy area, it was quiet that afternoon. Most of the commotion came from the beach side of the house on the boardwalk. Vacationers were heading out to brunch along with the young locals just waking up after a night of partying. Lisa longed for her surfboard and some waves, but at the moment that was the furthest thing from her reality.

"It's not a mistake. It's two million dollars. For two days' work, tops. And now for only one girl this time."

"This time?"

"Yeah, they aren't going to pay us two million dollars for one job. When we do this right, they give us the money, then we are on the hook for a couple more. That's it."

"Oh, is that it? Just a couple more times of selling girls into slavery. No biggie. How the hell are you okay with selling a girl into God knows what?"

David stared at her for a long moment. His brow furrowed, his eyes angry. "Are you saying you're out? You knew what we were doing on this one, and it wasn't a problem two days ago."

"Yeah, that was before you beat the hell out of a cop and left him for dead. Before you turned on your own brother—"

"Turned on my brother?" David shouted. "Tommy almost ruined this thing last night because he is a moron. If you want out, fine. I don't have time for this shit anymore. It's your debt that I am trying to erase here. Did you forget about that?" A pause. "Did you?"

She hadn't forgotten, but him reminding her brought her back to the middle of her dilemma. She absolutely wanted out. She couldn't imagine the guilt that would come after indenturing a sixteen-year-old girl to a creepy old rich man. But she was afraid she didn't have a choice. If she didn't repay her debt, everyone would know what she did. Including her fancy job she started not long ago. The one that David would kill her for if he knew about it. The one good thing about a brother who never really cared about you, is that you can easily keep things from him. Even a whole other life.

"Well?"

"Well what, David? This is just hard for me. Have you forgotten what your father used to do to me? Huh? The same thing that these strange men are going to do to this poor girl. And once again, you are just going to let it happen!" Lisa wasn't planning on bringing up the abuse she had suffered at the hands of Jim Tarter. But this operation was beginning to hit too close to home. She needed to keep her cool, though, for just a little while longer; then she could be finished with it all.

She could see that her words had cut through David's rough exterior. He turned his back to her for a moment. He didn't even acknowledge what she said. When he finally did speak, it was yet another slap in her face.

"I'm hearing a lot about the past, Lisa, and it tells me that your head isn't here in the present, on the task at hand. So one last time. This is your debt we are clearing here. Are you in, or are you out? I'm not asking again."

Lisa wanted to scream. She wanted to claw his eyes out. She wanted him to feel what it felt like to be raped, to be beaten. But most of all, she just wanted never to see him again. And getting through this last job was the only way to do it. And now he was already talking about other jobs.

"You know I can't be out, David. You know I have to have that money."

"Okay then, not another word about it. Let's get down to business. Tommy found another car, I assume?"

"Yes, he got rid of the Corvette. But Greg is out. After what you did to that cop, he couldn't be involved."

David nodded. "Good. More money for you. Now, the rest of the men will be ready to meet us at the Burbank Airport. They'll have a van, and they have an identical one for us."

"Then what do we need all these stolen cars for?" Lisa asked.

"Smoke and mirrors."

"That's it? We're risking our lives for your plan and all the detail you're going to give us is smoke and mirrors?"

"All of you are on a need-to-know basis," said David. "When you need to know, I'll tell you. Just be ready."

David's cell phone rang. He looked at Lisa and confirmed the details one last time before answering. "We leave here at one o'clock. That will put us in LA around four or so with traffic. Make sure Tommy is still good to go without his butt-buddy, Greg, tagging along. No mistakes."

Lisa gave him a nod.

"Hello," David answered his phone. "Hey, Jon, is everything

all set with the rest of the men?" A pause. "Good . . . Yes. The plane left Mazatlán a few minutes ago. Everything is a go. See you at one."

23

Mr. Unflappable Is Actually Human

Highway 15 stretched out in front of Reign's SUV about as far as their eyes could see. The afternoon sun had risen to its peak, and the asphalt hummed beneath their tires as they sped north toward the kidnapper's van.

"Is that . . . ," Kyle started, but he trailed off as he squinted his eyes in an attempt to make something out in the distance. He even leaned forward in the driver's seat to try to bring it into view.

Zhanna squinted and leaned forward as well from the front passenger seat. "I see it too. Is like black dot?"

"Yeah, is like black dot. I think that might be them, X. Was it a black van you saw?"

"Yes," Xander answered as he performed a press check on his Glock. When he looked up, Sam was looking him over. "What?"

"So, is it everything you've been missing?" she asked.

"Missing? What do you mean?"

"You got your first taste of it at Romero's mansion. Now, here we are again, getting ready to run down the bad guys. Is this what you were hoping for when you called to tell me you wanted back in?"

Xander was quiet for a moment. He glanced toward the front seat and noticed Kyle glancing back at him in the rearview mirror. Zhanna had turned to face him, and he could feel Jack breathing down his neck from the third row behind him. It was a good question. One he hadn't really contemplated. Getting back into the action felt natural to him. It felt like home, like things were back to normal. A completely screwed-up normal, but normal. Judging by how interested everyone seemed in hearing his answer, he could sense this was a topic the four of them had previously discussed without him.

"Not really sure what you're driving at here, but yeah, this is exactly what I expected getting back into bed with the four of you, if that's what you mean."

Sam gave him another long look.

"What? If you've got something to say, Sam, just say it. You all are acting like this is some sort of intervention or something. I gotta say, your timing is a little off."

"You joke, Xander, but you went through some serious things five months ago. And you haven't really talked to any of us about it. Not even Kyle."

"Oh, is this what I can expect now that the two of you are together, Kyle? She's going to start speaking for you?"

Xander was trying to remain calm, but this subject was quickly making him uncomfortable. Though he didn't let on, he knew exactly what Sam was getting at. His father. And she was right: he hadn't spoken to any of them about it, because he had purposefully done his best to forget about it completely.

"Don't be like that, X. You know it isn't like that. Sam, this is hardly the time to—"

"No, you know what?" Xander felt his blood pressure rise. He didn't really understand why, but this was making him angry. He turned and scowled at Sam. "You want to talk about this now? Let's talk about it."

"Xander—"

"No, Sam, you brought it up, so here we go. I was forced to slit my father's throat because he had my mother killed and was coming after me, his own son."

They were rapidly gaining on the van in front of them, only about a mile separating them now. But to Xander, it may as well have been a hundred.

"And before his blood was dry, someone killed my Derby-winning horse and kidnapped the woman I love."

The hum of the tires rolling over the blacktop was the only sound made for several seconds. Everyone in the van was stunned into silence. They had never seen Xander lose his cool, not like this. Sam had hit a nerve that Xander himself didn't know was so sensitive. Now they all understood that Mr. Unflappable was actually human.

"That what you wanted to talk about? I'm fine now, it's all in the past."

"Clearly," Sam said without thinking. She regretted it immediately, because the fury in Xander's eyes vanished, and pain forced its way in. "I'm sorry, Xander. I shouldn't have brought it up."

Xander was quiet. He was doing his best to bring his breathing back to normal, but his chest was heaving. Sweat ran down the small of his back and his skin was crawling due to the feeling of weakness that was overwhelming him. He didn't like feeling vulnerable; it wasn't something he was used to.

"Really, it was terribly insensitive of me. Can you forgive me?"

Xander took another deep breath.

"It's fine, Sam. It's obviously more of an issue than I thought it was."

Kyle spoke up from the front. "You don't owe us anything, X. Just know you can talk to us whenever you need to."

Zhanna and Sam nodded in agreement.

Xander wanted nothing more than to open the door and jump right out of that SUV. So he decided right then and there that that was exactly what he was going to do.

"Get me close to the van."

The subject change caught everyone off guard. They weren't sure how to respond. Kyle just looked at Xander in the rearview, a question in his eyes.

Xander explained, "It's too risky for Jack to try to shoot out a tire."

"I can hit the tire, Xander. I won't let a bullet go stray and hit one of them girls through the back."

"I know you won't, Jack. What I mean is, the van is going too fast. If you pop the tire, it may send the van out of control. If it crashes, we may hurt more than one of the girls."

"Damn, you're right," Jack agreed.

"What is getting you close to van going to do?" Zhanna asked.

Xander leaned forward and hit the button that opened the sunroof. A whoosh of warm air swept through the van, and his plan became clear to everyone.

"You dead isn't going to save anyone," Sam said, raising her voice over the wind blowing above them.

"Yeah? You have a better plan?"

She didn't. He could see it in her eyes. They all knew the van wouldn't stop unless they stopped it. Those men would be willing to die for it, because if they didn't make it where they were going, they'd be dead anyway. Their SUV closed in on the van, only a few car lengths ahead of them now. Xander tucked his Glock into the back of his waistline and squinted ahead at the van.

He shouted over the wind once again. "There's a cargo rack. That will make it easy to grab onto. Kyle, just keep her steady and when you see him jerk the van into you, steer into them. That will give me the smoothest transition. Just don't swerve too hard into them. The last thing we want is to drive them off the road."

From the driver's seat, Kyle's face showed all kinds of concern. "How in the hell am I supposed to know how hard to . . ."

He stopped talking when he noticed Xander had already poked his head through the sunroof.

The wind whipped past Xander's head, instantly drying out his eyes. It felt like going down a ski slope at full speed with no goggles on. He removed his sport coat, took the sunglasses from the inside pocket, then tossed the sport coat to the ground. The sunglasses instantly helped his eyes see that they were now upon the van. Kyle steered the SUV into the oncoming lane as it pulled up beside the van. Whoever was driving the van didn't waste any time, immediately swerving into their SUV. Kyle wasn't ready for it. When the two vehicles clashed, Xander's rib cage knocked against the opening of the sunroof and the Suburban swerved left. Kyle corrected the swerve, and Xander knew he couldn't hesitate. He pulled himself up through the opening and squatted down, hand on the side rail of the luggage rack. The wind was blowing him back, but he managed to hold on. The van was getting closer now, and as he adjusted his stance to ready himself, he slipped and went down on his side.

His dress shoes from the night before had zero traction, adding greatly to the difficulty of making the jump. He pulled himself back up to a squatting position, and out of the corner of his eye, he noticed the driver of the van jerk his hand to the left. Simultaneously, he felt Kyle pull to the right; he too must have seen the man's hand. Just before the two vehicles came together again, the thrum of adrenaline palpated through Xander's entire body.

Definitely his drug of choice.

He felt so alive in that moment that everything slowed down for him. His vision tunneled as it focused on the luggage rack atop the black van. Every sense heightened, every muscle taut and ready. Millimeters before the vehicles collided, Xander launched himself toward the roof of the van.

At least he tried to.

As he applied pressure downward against the roof of the SUV with his right foot, instead of the boost up and forward he was expecting, his shoe slipped right out from under him, sending him almost straight down to the pavement. But through excellent timing on his part, and sheer luck, the gap between the vehicles had closed, and it was only the direction he had given Kyle to swerve into the van that saved his life. As the two vehicles collided, Xander's torso bounced off both of them as he reached his hand toward the vertical rack along the top left of the van's roof. He felt the two vehicles begin to separate beneath him, and just as his body plummeted into the gap, his left hand squeezed around the metal rack.

His body dropped and slammed against the side of the van, his shoulder wrenched as he held on. The double yellow lines streaked just below him as he pulled his knees up to his chest. He knew he didn't have a moment to spare. The minute the driver of the van saw him dangling there, he would swerve right back into their SUV and crush Xander between them. Sure enough, as soon as Xander began to pull himself up, the van swerved left. The only thing Xander could do was close his eyes and brace for impact. He squeezed his already cramping hand with all his might as he felt the burn of fatigue settling into his forearm.

Instead of feeling impact, he heard tires squeal against the pavement. He glanced over and watched their SUV spin out of control off the side of the road. Kyle had done the only thing he could to keep from making a Xander sandwich, and it saved Xander's life. He glanced back up at his hand. The thought of letting go to stop the pain flashed across his mind.

Instead, he dug deep and squeezed harder as he wiped that thought from his brain.

No way he was leaving these girls to these bastards.

Besides, he always had been a glutton for punishment.

24

Along for the Ride

The black van carrying innocent young girls on the inside and one determined ex–Navy SEAL on the outside surged forward down the Mexican highway. Xander held his knees to his chest, keeping his shoes from catching the churning pavement below as he swung his right arm up and grabbed the rail beside his left hand. It was none too soon either, as that hand was burnt. His right foot found the back bumper, and he pushed off as he pulled himself up. The hot wind blasted through his sweat-soaked shirt. As soon as he steadied himself, the van began to swerve back and forth. They were trying to get rid of the pest on their roof.

Xander wasn't about to wait for their next move.

He slid himself forward, grabbing the next horizontal rack up as he went to his stomach. This greatly diminished the pushback of the wind, and gave him a moment to reach his right hand behind him and grab hold of his pistol. He then leaned out over the front passenger side door and saw a man staring back at him in the side mirror. As the van swerved to the left, the man in the passenger seat reached out his arm and pointed an AK-47 skyward.

Xander was ready.

Before the man had the chance to squeeze the trigger, Xander shot a hole in his hand, and the gun dropped out of sight to the pavement below. Xander followed that by shooting downward through the window, and the scream that reached his ears a second later told him he had hit something.

The van swerved once again, but Xander had a good grip with his tired left hand, and he had wrapped the toe of his shoe around the rack behind him. He knew the driver was about to get desperate. An understandable reaction when a madman on the roof just shot your partner. Twice. So he knew he had to act fast. Not only for his safety, but if the driver was frightened enough, he might do something rash and put the girls in the back in danger as well.

Xander leaned out over the side of the van and reached down past the window, his fingertips grazing the door handle. But he couldn't quite grab it.

He unraveled his foot from the rack behind him, giving him the extra inches he needed. But as soon as he pulled the passenger door open, the driver hit the brakes, sending Xander forward on the roof. The only chance he had to keep from flying off was to relinquish his gun and grab hold of the rack with his right hand as well. His pistol skittered over the pavement, the tires of the van squalled against the blacktop, and his legs whipped around to the front side of the van as he held on for dear life.

The van mercifully came to a stop.

Xander had managed to hang on.

And he just managed to get himself back fully onto the roof when a succession of bullets blasted from a semiautomatic weapon from inside the cabin of the van. The glass of the front windshield shattered, spraying out over the hood of the van and the highway in front of it.

It was then, for the first time, that he was able to hear the girls screaming.

The sound filtered in through his ears, straight to his heart, and his stomach clenched as the feeling of desperation flooded him. He was their only hope.

From atop the van, Xander reached into his pocket and unclipped his Marfione knife, hit the blade eject button, and slid over the passenger side of the van. As soon as his feet hit the pavement, he sank the four-inch blade into the side of the neck of the man who had just stepped out the passenger door. As quickly as the razor-sharp blade slid in, Xander pulled it out; there would be no need for another strike. The man was already dying.

A spray of bullets flashed through the open door. Then he heard the driver's side door open. The man was heaving for air. The gun popped off again, and another string of bullets passed through the van out the door just in front of Xander. He wasn't afraid for his life. But he was afraid that this man was panicking, and those bullets could easily find their way through the back of the van to the girls. He had to do something before—

Another bullet fired; then he heard a click. The gunman's magazine was empty. However, this wasn't this guy's first time with a gun. Xander could tell by how quickly he had managed to eject the magazine and was already inserting a fresh one. There was only one play here.

Xander stepped in front of the open passenger door, and as the man pulled back the bolt on his AK-47, loading it, Xander took the blade of his knife between his thumb and forefinger, pulled it back by his ear, and as if he were throwing a dart, released the blade after a forward flick of the wrist and watched it soar end over end through the cabin of the van before it sank into the man's hand that held the handle of his gun. The AK-47 dropped to the pavement as the man grabbed for his hand.

Xander immediately stalked around the front of the van. Glass from the windshield crunched beneath his shoes. The short, dark-haired, olive-skinned man staggered back from the open door and pulled the blade from his hand. Sweat ran down his pain-ridden face. He looked down at the gun he had dropped, then back up to Xander. Realizing he wouldn't be able to get to it in time, he readied the knife and took a fighter's stance. Xander didn't so much as slow his pace. He walked right toward him as the man swung his arm forward. Before the man's swing could land, Xander punched the man at the elbow, forcing him to drop the knife. The driver of the van staggered back from the blow, putting his hands up in a boxing stance. Blood leaked from the knife wound in his right hand as he shouted at Xander in Spanish.

The concern was gone for Xander now as he stood and glared at the unarmed man. The screams and sobs from the back of the van decidedly took away any consideration of showing him mercy. The man threw a right hand at Xander's head. He was quick, but the punch missed when Xander moved his head to the left. It had almost zero power behind it. The man threw a left hook next, but instead of dodging it, Xander stepped forward and drove the crown of his head into the bridge of the man's nose. The man screamed as blood flooded from his nostrils. Xander wrapped his right hand around the man's throat and pinned him against the van.

"Where is the plane going to land?"

Blood ran from the man's face down onto Xander's hand and arm. He wiggled, grunted, but gave Xander no response.

Xander drove his knee into the man's groin.

"Where?"

The girls had stopped screaming. The only sound was the Mexican man groaning in pain from the force of Xander's blows.

"It's okay, girls, you're safe now," Xander shouted to them. Then he tightened his grip around the man's throat and spoke in a lowered voice. "You're going to die right here if you don't tell me where Francisco's plane is going to land."

The back door of the van busted open so fast that it put Xander in an automatic reflex position. And if he hadn't turned toward it, putting the man in his grasp between him and the back of the van, he would have been killed. Because before he could make another move, bullets from a pistol were hitting the man he was holding so hard in the back that it was shaking his now-dead body in Xander's hands.

He did the only thing he knew to do and continued to use the man as a shield as he walked toward the gunfire.

POP-POP-POP-POP-POP

The girls resumed screaming and the gunman kept firing. Spent shells were ringing as they fell to the pavement. Xander just kept walking forward, pulling into himself as he did his best to stay behind the much smaller man he was now holding up with two hands.

POP-POP-POP-POP-POP-CLICK

Xander threw the dead man to the ground and drove his right hand into the chin of the man holding the empty gun. This man was much larger, but he was slow. He took Xander's punch well, but his counter might as well have been in slow motion. Xander parried it with his left hand, grabbed the back of the man's neck with his right, and yanked his head down as he drove his knee up to meet the man's forehead. The man fell straight onto his back, unconscious. But Xander didn't have time to put him away before he saw something streak past him out of the corner of his eye. He flinched, fearing the worst, but then saw long blonde hair floating in the wind.

"Wait, it's okay!" he shouted.

One of the girls hadn't waited to see whether or not the good guy had won. Xander couldn't blame her for that. She was running in the direction of Sam and company, so he knew she would be okay. But before he could console whoever was left in the van, a young girl had leapt out of the back and was kicking her unconscious captor as hard as she could as she sobbed.

Xander's heart broke. Though he knew they were safe now, God only knew what damage had been done to these poor girls' psyche long-term.

"It's okay, you're safe now." He tried to use a calm voice. But his words never found her ears. She screamed at the man on the ground as she kicked him. She was going to hurt herself if Xander didn't step in.

"It's okay," he said a little louder as he took hold of the outsides of her arms.

The girl was in a fit of rage. She turned into him and continued her assault; though her wrists were bound by rope, she pounded her fists against Xander's chest. The look on her face would be one he would never forget.

Sheer terror.

"It's okay, you're safe. I promise, I'm not going to hurt you." He maintained a calm voice.

The girl sobbed as she continued to fight.

"I'm an American, I'm going to get you back to your family."

She pounded on him one more time, then her eyes shot open. She stopped swinging at him. The word "family" had gotten through to her. Her blue eyes were swallowed by red streaks of terror. Tears flowed like an open spigot down her rose-colored cheeks.

"You're okay. You're all right."

He didn't know what else to say.

He watched it set in that what he was saying was true. When she realized she was no longer being held captive, the sobs came even harder. Three more girls managed their way out of the back of that van. All of them wearing the same terrified look on their faces.

Their lives would never be the same.

Their innocence had been stolen.

And they were the lucky ones.

Francisco and whoever had been involved in this, no matter how small their role, were all going to pay.

Every . . . last . . . one of them.

25

Sliver of Hope

"Would you please shut her up?" the Mexican man—the one they were calling boss, and the one the pretty lady had walked away from—shouted to one of his men at the back of the plane.

Carrie had tried a moment ago to calm the girl beside her. She knew nothing good would come from making these people angry. At the last minute, they had decided to bring the younger girl along with them. While Carrie was glad that she wasn't alone, she was heartbroken that this girl, who looked as if she wasn't a day over thirteen, had been brought into this. Whatever *this* was. The girl reminded Carrie of her sister, Bethany. That made things even harder, because all she wanted to do was be back safely on their cruise ship, trying her best to keep Bethany from annoying her. She longed for that, something she never thought she would say. But right now, this girl beside her really needed to calm down. She was really agitating the man in charge.

"Hey," Carrie whispered to her.

Like her, the girl's hands were bound by rope behind her back. They had put them on the floor of the plane in the very back, where the luggage was supposed to be.

A big bald man, whose face looked as if someone had just beat him up, turned from the seat in front of them, shouted something in Spanish, and made the little blonde girl cry even harder. Carrie knew she had to get through to her.

"Hey," she said a little louder, raising her voice above the hum of the plane's engine. "It's okay. We'll be okay if you just look at me . . . okay?"

The girl sniffled once, then stifled the oncoming cry as she raised her head to meet Carrie's eyes.

"We're going to be okay, I promise. We just need to do what they say until we land. Then I'll find a way to get us away from them. All right?"

The girl swallowed hard, tried to speak, but when words failed her, she just gave Carrie a hopeful nod. Carrie scooted closer to the girl, kissed her on the forehead, and gave her a smile. Comforting the girl somehow brought her own anxiety level down a notch.

After quieting the girl, the terribly dressed man with the shifty eyes at the front of the plane left the two of them alone. The small victory somehow gave Carrie a sliver of hope. Though she had no idea who these men were, where they were taking her, and what they planned to do with the two of them once they got there, at least they were okay for now. She would dip into her knowledge of mystery shows that she had watched on television so much over the years to find her next move. She knew that every opportunity would be a small one, and if she hoped to get away, she would have to be ready.

26

Airport Not-So-Security

Their rented SUV came to a screeching halt in the middle of the road, right in front of Xander and the four girls he was trying to console. Sam jumped out first, and Kyle was right behind her.

"Did you get the girl?" Xander asked.

Sam walked up, concern on her face. "She's in the back, Zhanna is tending to her. Are you all right?"

"You missed a hell of a show."

Sam glanced at the four girls, then back to Xander. "I'm sure you'll fill me in later."

Xander caught her drift. The girls didn't need him patting himself on the back in front of them.

"I've called the US Embassy," Sam said. "They're sending a couple of officers to meet us at the airport. They'll handle getting these girls back to their families."

A young dark-haired girl spoke up. "Are they really going to get us back to our families?"

Xander went to place a hand on her shoulder, but the girl recoiled. She had been through a lot, for her, trust was going to have to be earned from now on. Xander pulled his hand back, giving the girl some space.

"They are. This time tomorrow you'll be with them."

She made a move toward Xander, then paused, then decided she couldn't hold back. She lunged at him, threw her arms around his waist, and gave a hard squeeze. Then she looked up at him.

"Thank you, Mister. Whoever you are."

Xander didn't know what to say, so he just gave her a pat on the back of the head and told her she was welcome.

"Come with me, girls," Sam said. "It's going to be a tight squeeze, but we don't have far to go."

"You're our hero," the girl said, letting go of Xander and following behind Sam. "You saved all of us."

Xander smiled and gave her a nod, then swallowed the lump in his throat.

Kyle put his hand on his friend's shoulder. "Looks like you've once again come out unscathed. I'd say you were like a cat, but they only have nine lives. You spent those years ago."

Xander looked back at the van, and at the carnage he left behind. All in all, by his standards, it wasn't so bad. He and Kyle put the two dead man in the back of the van first; then, after restraining the man Xander had knocked out, they threw him in as well. They got back in the Suburban and headed back to the airport.

"Any word from Marv, Sam?" Xander asked.

"Yes. He has checked with all three pilots, and all three swear they have never heard of a Francisco or an Antonio Romero. Two of the planes are charters, and one is a businessman's plane. Two of them say they are headed for the Burbank Airport, and one is flying to LAX. They are all compliant in every way, but obviously we know one of them is lying. Unfortunately, we won't know which one until the planes land. There are a lot of small airports in

LA, so there is a chance that at the last minute they could make a switch. But they would have to know someone to be able to fly in under the radar."

"Kyle," Xander laughed. "Did Sam just make a pun?"

Kyle looked back and smiled.

"She did, but I'm not sure it was intentional."

"Right," Sam said, "Because the two of you are the only ones with a sense of humor."

Xander shrugged, implying a yes.

Suddenly everyone in the van was thrown forward into the seat in front of them. Kyle had slammed on the brakes in the middle of the highway, just in front of the airport.

Xander recovered from the startling stop and squinted toward the terminal entrance.

"What is it? What do you see?"

"I just saw someone with a rifle over their shoulder walk into the airport."

Jack spoke up. "Could it be the embassy officers?"

Sam handed Jack the sniper rifle. "You tell us."

Sam rolled down the window, and Jack took the rifle in his hands. He peered down the scope, searching the front parking area of the private end of the Mazatlán airport.

"See anything?" Xander asked.

"Unless the US Embassy sent a Mexican vigilante military outfit to pick up these girls, we got ourselves a problemo."

Xander scanned the area surrounding the building that the men were circling. There was no way they could drive safely through the entrance and out to the plane. They were going to have to improvise to keep the girls safe. He knew those men were there to take the girls, dead or alive.

Xander pointed away from the building, toward the tarmac. "Kyle, see that spot in the fence back there? Where the gap is in the parked planes on the other side?"

The runway was just beyond where he was pointing.

Kyle put the SUV in reverse, swinging the front end toward the point Xander had motioned to in the fence. He gunned the engine, and the SUV sped forward.

Kyle looked at Sam. "I knew I shouldn't have listened to you and declined the rental insurance."

They all braced for impact with the tall chain-link fence.

"Keep your heads down, girls!" Zhanna shouted.

Just as Xander picked up his phone to dial his pilot, Bob was already calling him.

Xander answered, "You see what we see, Bob?"

"Already fired up the engines. I'll be ready to head for the runway as soon as you shut the door."

"Good man. We'll be coming in hot."

Bob chuckled. "Is there any other way you come in?"

Xander ended the call and dug inside the bag of weapons as the SUV crashed through the fence. The girls screamed when the fence made a loud crashing sound as it gave way to the truck's force.

"There, on the left!" Sam shouted, pointing out Xander's jet.

Jack had been keeping an eye on the armed men through his rifle's scope. "That got their attention, Kyle. We'd better be ready for a fight."

Kyle swerved toward the G6 as Zhanna helped Xander pass around some hardware. A pistol for each of the boys and a couple of M16s for her and Sam.

"What's the plan?" Kyle said.

Xander press-checked his Glock 19 as he scanned the area in front of his jet.

"Pull in sideways. Make the truck a barrier in front of the jet's door. Zhanna, get the girls to the back of the plane and then get our back from the door opening. The rest of you, just help me hold them off from behind the truck. Any idea how many there are, Jack?"

From behind the scope, "Two trucks just came flying through the entrance. I'd bet on eight, just to be safe."

"Eight?" Kyle said. "That won't be nearly enough."

He sped for the entrance of their large private plane, then slammed on the brakes as he jerked the wheel to the left. The SUV skidded to a stop, exactly where Xander had requested. Zhanna flung the door open and rushed the girls up into the plane. José was waiting at the open door. There would be no waiting for any embassy officers. The girls would be flying private back to the States.

Xander looked over his shoulder and saw the two SUVs Jack had mentioned, now speeding toward them. As he shuffled out the passenger door on the plane's side, he readied his pistol.

"Jack, take out the passengers. Leave the drivers, we can't have the trucks smashing into the plane."

"Roger," Jack said as he hoisted the sniper rifle to his shoulder and leaned around the corner of their SUV.

"Sam," Xander said. "How'd they know we were here?"

To give Jack a bit of cover Sam stepped up onto the running board of the truck and fired a couple of times over the roof in the direction of the oncoming SUVs. She then furrowed her brow and flashed Xander a stern look.

"Where do you bloody think, Xander? Where just about every problem we've had comes from with you. The girl."

Xander stepped up on the running board beside her, firing a couple of shots of his own.

"Bullshit, Sam. That's just your go-to excuse these days."

Sam fired a couple more times, and both she and Xander watched as the windshields of the oncoming trucks exploded in fairly quick succession. Jack had shot both passengers, just as Xander requested. The two trucks swerved a little, then skidded to a stop about twenty-five yards in front of them. From behind the team, Zhanna was joined by José, and from their elevated position the two of them continued firing their weapons, keeping the men from getting any good shots at the four of them.

"You sure about that, Xander? How the hell else would they have known?"

They both fired a couple more times, joining the sniper blasts from Jack and the pistol shots from Kyle.

"I don't know, Sam. But I'm telling you, it wasn't Gabriela. There must be a mole."

"Oh, there's a mole all right." *POP-POP-POP.* "And she looks like J.Lo."

27

Sherlock Holmes Has Nothing on Xander King

A couple dozen more rounds from Reign's weapons and the Mexican crew that was sent to stop Xander and company decided they weren't getting paid enough for the job. The two passengers Jack had so graciously managed to put holes in with his sniper rifle probably helped influence that decision. Xander instructed his team just to leave the rented SUV where it sat. Sam said the CIA had people to clean up messes like that for them. Xander was beginning not to hate having a US agency there to deal with the things he never would.

After their ascent took them over ten thousand feet, Xander made sure everyone was okay, then finished passing out waters and snacks to the four girls spread out on the couches at the back of his plane. Weary from the chaos, he walked back to his seat next to Sam. The jet engines hummed, and sunlight poured in from the great blue beyond just outside the windows.

"Shall we finish our conversation?" Sam asked.

"You mean your Spanish inquisition?" Xander wiped the sweat from his brow and let out a frustrated sigh. "Can I at least get a bourbon first?"

Kyle walked up, three glasses full of ice in one hand, a bottle of King's Ransom bourbon in the other. Sam and Xander each took a glass, and Kyle poured a couple of fingers into each one. Kyle clanked their glasses and sat down opposite of them. Zhanna, José, and Jack sipped from their own glasses a row back. They all were weary, but Xander could tell by the way Kyle looked at him that he felt Xander was the most out of sorts.

"What?" Xander said to Kyle.

"Why don't you go take a hot shower, relax for a minute?"

"Look that bad, do I?"

Kyle shrugged. "You've looked better."

Xander took a sip of his bourbon, swirled the glass, and for a moment just wanted to change the subject.

"How are sales?"

He was asking Kyle about sales of King's Ransom bourbon. Xander started the company almost immediately when he left the Navy SEALs. He never imagined it would take off like it had the past year. His horse with the same name as the brand, King's Ransom, winning the Kentucky Derby had a lot to do with that. It was all kinds of good publicity. The last five months, he had received only a few updates from Kyle about how the company was doing. Kyle would spout off a bunch of dollar figures, but that didn't matter to Xander. He was going to be giving the profits to charity as it was. He didn't need the money. He just loved having his own piece of Kentucky—home—everywhere he went. The thing he cared most about when it came to the bourbon company was that it was available all over the United States. That was where Xander drew his source of pride.

"They are great," Kyle said. "We are in over thirty states now. I know you like that."

Kyle knew Xander well. Twenty years of friendship will do that.

"Now seriously, will you go clean up? We'll try to get some more info while you do. That way we at least have some direction on where we should land."

"Los Angeles," Sam said.

"You have an update?" Xander asked, hope in his voice.

"No, but we know they are headed to one of the airports there. Additionally, three of the four girls are from there. I figure that is a good place to start."

Xander glanced toward the back of the plane. The girls were huddled together, eating their food. All of them looked relieved to be safe, but there was a heaviness to their eyes. He looked back to Sam.

"You think they're going to be okay, Sam?"

Sam took a drink, then paused to ponder the question.

"I think they will be."

Xander couldn't tell if she was placating him or if she really thought they would be okay. Either way, the notion of a shower began to sound better and better. But a nagging question hung in his mind.

"I'm gonna go wash off, but do you really think that Gabriela tipped Francisco that we were there?"

Sam rolled the ice in her glass with the tip of her finger.

"I don't know anything about this woman. And neither do you. But I told you that Bob said she wasn't in the airport when he checked before we took off. Now, I didn't see her get in the truck with those men, but she definitely didn't stick around for a ride home."

Xander thought about it for a moment. Sam had a point. If Gabriela was who she said she was, and lived in California, why wouldn't she stick around and fly back with them? Her story about why she was with Francisco didn't make a lot of sense. And besides her, there weren't many other options of who could be the mole. Then it hit him.

"Have we found anything else out about this 'dark' FBI agent?" Xander said.

"Only that she hasn't been with the FBI long. Why? What else is there to know?" Sam said.

"It just seems so strange that the FBI doesn't know more about where she is right now."

"It does," Sam agreed. "But when undercover, there are many times when an agent can't come up for air."

"True, but okay . . . so she goes dark for a while, then turns up out of nowhere and only gives one little slice of information? And that's it? There is a very high likelihood she is the mole. Can we get a picture of her?"

Xander's wheels were spinning.

"Of course. What are you thinking, Xander?"

He didn't want to tell Sam what he was thinking. Because it would mean that Sam was right about Gabriela. And there were few things Xander hated more than admitting when Sam was right.

"Go on then. Out with it?" Sam nagged.

"Okay, so this FBI agent, she's a she . . ."

"Sherlock Holmes has nothing on Alexander King," Sam interrupted.

Xander rolled his eyes.

"Can I finish?"

"Please."

"So, she's a she, and if she hasn't been with the FBI long, she is probably also fairly young."

"Okay . . ."

Sam was trying her best to give him a moment.

Xander finished his thought. "So we have a young, female FBI agent from California, who is undercover, and she has a Latino name. Sound familiar?"

"I don't get it," Kyle said.

Sam picked up her phone.

"You believe that Gabriela's real name might be Eliza Sanchez."

Kyle had a *lightbulb moment* look on his face. "That's why you want the picture of the FBI agent! You think Eliza Sanchez is Gabriela!"

Sam put the phone to her ear and gave Kyle a condescending pat on the head. "Just don't ever lose your looks, all right?"

Zhanna leaned in from beside them. "But this would mean that FBI agent is compromised. Working for Francisco instead of US government."

Xander stood up.

"It's the only thing that makes sense. Who else could have tipped Francisco off that we were in Mazatlán? And that quickly?"

"Does make a lot of sense," Jack agreed.

José nodded as well.

The five of them listened to Sam leave a message for Marv. Xander began to feel like things were closing in on them. They didn't have the answers they needed, but they needed them fast. They had managed to save four girls from a horrific future, but there was one more on her way to that peril at that very moment. And while Xander knew they would find Francisco and shut him down, he also knew that was the easy part. Keeping the young woman out of some monster's hands while doing it would prove much more difficult. Their timing and precision would have to be far more delicate because of it.

"I'm going to get cleaned up. By the time we drop these girls off in LA, we have got to know our next move. If not, we're probably going to be too late."

"We'll find her, Xander." Sam tried to assure him. "Half the CIA is working on it."

Xander turned toward the back of the plane as he began to unbutton his sweat-drenched shirt.

"Not sure that's really a vote of confidence at this point."

28

Born to Fight

Hot water washed over Xander. He closed his eyes and let it massage his back. He rolled his head in circles a few times, trying to get his neck muscles to relax. He hoped it would lead to the same feeling in his mind. It did not. As much as he tried to clear it, his brain kept dialing up the conversation that Sam had started back in the SUV. Instead of fighting it, he let the images overload his senses, as they had many times since the day he slammed the blade of his knife into the side of his father's neck.

He thought after avenging the betrayal his father perpetrated against his family that he would stop having the dreams, but they still came, clear as the day it happened. It started as it always did. Replaying the day when he was a teenager, the day that changed everything. The vision was always the same. The black van would screech to a halt in front of his parents' home, and two men wearing black ski masks, carrying assault rifles, would jump out and open fire. He watched as the bullets smacked into his mother's body, until she lay on the ground, leaking blood, dead. Then Xander would look left and see what he thought were bullets entering his father. But they weren't. Now in his memory he can clearly see what he couldn't have known as a child. That the other gunman firing at his dad wasn't using actual bullets at all. They were blanks.

This was where the memory turned into a new movie in his mind. The scene no longer ended as it had that day; now it ended instead with his teenage self jamming a knife into his father's throat.

Xander rubbed the hot water over his face, and with both palms against the wall of the shower, he leaned full weight against it, and sobbed. His heart was still broken for his mother. His heart was still broken for his friend Sean, who died trying to help Xander in Syria. And his heart still hadn't recovered from the loss of King's Ransom, and it still longed for Natalie.

They say that time heals all wounds. Xander supposed, as his tears mixed with the water from the shower, that in some ways that was true. But in his case, all those terrible things, mixed with what happened to Sam in the basement of Sanharib Khatib's compound, were still there in the form of gaping wounds. Over the last five months, all those wounds had been doing was festering. And though he only showed his friends the face of the Xander he wanted them to see, inside he was on fire. And seeing what these men were doing to these young girls only poured gasoline on those flames.

As he stood there, drying his eyes and calming his sadness, he realized that the revitalizing feelings that had crept back in from being back in action had nothing to do with feeling that adrenaline flowing again. Somehow being able once again to make some bad people pay for the terrible things they were doing was throwing water on the fire that burned inside him, if only for a brief moment. And it was right there in that plane, on the way to try to right some more wrongs, that he understood that this life of risking his own to hold people accountable for their actions was the very thing that would keep him sane. Whether he liked it or not, this was his purpose.

He understood himself in that moment more than he had at any time since that life-altering day when his mother was murdered. Xander understood that everything in his life had led to this revelation. All the events in his life that led him first into the Navy, then to becoming a SEAL, and all the missions he carried out with Special Ops had rendered him the perfect man for the job. He realized that running into Sam all those years ago was no coincidence at all. She was the perfect person to help him on this journey. She was just as broken and yet just as perfectly trained as he was for this. And having Kyle around to keep him grounded were all perfect pieces to the puzzle that made his team exactly what they were supposed to be.

Xander shut off the water and wrapped a towel around his waist. He opened the door of the shower and walked out with the steam. He stepped over to the sink, wiped away the fog from the mirror, and for the first time he truly recognized the man staring back at him. His eyes wandered over his machine of a body. A machine that he had been forging for years. He ran a finger over a scar along the outside of his shoulder. A flash of being shot in his bedroom as he protected Natalie played in his mind. He then ran his fingers over the scar on his stomach, and a flash of that shotgun blast on the back of his yacht sent the illusion of pain to that very spot.

He put both hands on the vanity and leaned in close. His eyes were bloodshot from the emotional moment in the shower, but Xander did not see weakness. He saw a man staring back at him who had found his purpose. Though anyone else on his team could easily have told him that purpose long ago, knowing who you are is something you can only figure out for yourself. He knew now why that fire had been permanently planted inside his soul. It wasn't as he had always thought. It wasn't planted there to ruin his life or to make him miserable. It was planted there for no other reason than fuel. Fuel for the machine that he had become. That fire was something that he had always used to do extraordinary things. And now he was finally at peace knowing that it would always be there, waiting for him to tap into when he needed it. It was the thing that had always made him special, and it would be the thing that would carry him through those moments when all hope seemed lost.

As he looked deep inside himself, he could feel that fire burning at that very moment.

White hot.

There would never be another question about what he was to do with his life. The bourbon company, the horse racing, the jet setting, all those things were great. But Xander, at heart, was a soldier. And the only thing that would ever get his full attention for the rest of the time he remained on this earth would be just that.

Fighting for those who couldn't fight for themselves.

For the first time it had become crystal clear.

It was what he was born to do.

As he realized this, Xander watched a smile grow across his face. It was as if he had just been made whole.

He also realized that whoever was responsible for hurting these young girls was about to pay the ultimate price.

29

Ghost of Battles Past

As Xander King was experiencing a moment of clarity, David Tarter sat behind the wheel of his black Hummer, having the complete opposite kind of moment. Instead of things becoming clear, they had just become incredibly muddied. He slammed his hands against the steering wheel, hard, several times. He was frothing at the mouth. He was so close to getting the job done of delivering a girl for two million dollars, and an unnecessary complication was the last thing he needed. He had just ended a call with his contact on the job, and it appeared that a ghost from his past was somehow hot on his trail.

David and Xander King went way back. And the memories weren't what you would call fond ones. In fact, Xander had been the reason David and Jon were court-martialed from the Navy. That fact had been burning a hole in David's gut ever since. As he sat there wondering how it was possible that Xander was involved, he couldn't wrap his mind around it. He heard stories of Xander leaving Special Ops to go vigilante, and he heard about what happened in Paris a few months back, but why he would be involved in this baffled David.

This changed everything. Though he wasn't scared of Xander, he couldn't help but remember the caliber of soldier he was.

"You finished with your little hissy fit?" David's partner, Jon, finally said. "Who cares if Xander is involved?"

David turned toward him. The Los Angeles sunshine blasted through the front windshield and aided in hardening David's scowl.

"We all better care."

"Come on, David. That little rich boy ain't gonna do shit," Jon said.

"Do I have to remind you how exactly it is that we came to be sitting here?"

David rolled down his window, picked up a pack of cigarettes from the console, lit one, and took a moment. He wanted Jon to take a moment as well. As he sucked on the cigarette, he transported himself back to Afghanistan. Back into that small little hut of a house. And back to the sights, smells, and sounds that brought an end to his and Jon's military careers. Their SEAL team had just cleared a small village, and he and Jon thought they may as well be rewarded for their trouble. Most of the other SEALs knew this sort of thing went on, but they didn't partake. They also didn't interfere. The women there weren't human to David. They were trash. So he had always felt he could do whatever he wanted with them. It didn't matter if they were good-looking or not. War was lonely, and they were still women, even though it was hard to tell that by the clothes they wore.

All the other team members had moved on that night. David and Jon thought they had the woman to themselves. But one young, cocky, self-righteous son of a bitch had doubled back to make sure the two of them were okay. And when he found them on top of that woman, he couldn't just close the door and leave well enough alone.

"No, asshole. I don't need reminded," Jon said. "I remember exactly how Xander chose that Muslim bitch over his own brothers. At first, when he walked in, I thought he was just jealous 'cause we had found her first."

David smirked.

"Didn't you offer for him to join?"

"Yeah, that's what set him off."

"That, or it could have been her squealing," David said. His smirk grew into a proud smile.

Jon returned the smile.

"I've never seen a guy fight like that, though. Damn he was strong. My nose is still crooked from that night."

David tossed his cigarette butt out the window, his face scrunched in disgust.

"Fuck that son of a bitch. Only reason he got the best of us that night was because we were literally caught with our pants down."

"I agree, that's why I don't understand why you care. You ask me, this is a good thing."

"Good thing," David furthered his scowl. "How the hell is a complication a good thing?"

"Because now, not only do we get to make two million for a relatively easy job, but we also might get revenge."

David was quiet for a moment. He felt the scowl on his face slowly move to intrigue. The thought of taking down Xander King was almost as good as the two million dollars.

Jon said, "See. It's a good thing."

David picked up his phone and scrolled to his brother's name in his contacts and tapped to call him.

"This changes everything," David said to Jon while the phone rang.

"How do you mean?"

"If we do get a shot at King, which hopefully we are long gone before he ever knows what happened, we can't be having any amateur bullshit mucking this up. Get ahold of the crew and tell them to get to the airport early. We need to have a meeting."

Jon nodded and went to his phone.

David told his brother over the phone. "Tommy, you and Lisa get here ASAP. We need to talk."

"But we are in the middle of—"

"I don't give a damn what you're doing. Things have changed. Get here, now."

David ended the call. Francisco's plane was set to arrive in the next hour. He knew they needed to regroup. He didn't have any idea how much Xander knew about where they were, or where they would be taking the girl, but they all had to assume he would find out, and they needed to be ready.

Jon said, "The men are on their way over. You're going to cut your brother and sister out of this, aren't you?"

"I'll still pay them for their trouble, but there is no way in hell they are ready for what's coming tonight. *If* we should happen to run into King."

"Agreed," Jon said. "Are *we* ready?"

David lit another cigarette, opened the truck's door, and nodded for Jon to follow him. The lift gate opened, and the two of them walked around to the back of the Hummer. David lifted a black tarp, revealing a large cache of high-powered weaponry. Everything from a Barrett .50-caliber sniper rifle to an AirTronic GS-777 rocket launcher.

David smiled through his cigarette as he puffed a cloud of smoke into the air.

"You're damn right we're ready."

30

Better Than Nothing

"Told you so," Xander told Sam.

Sam looked up at him from her phone. Her expression was not what you would call amused. "Are you going to follow that up with a nanna-nanna-boo-boo? How old are you again?"

Xander made an "oooh" face at Kyle.

"Well," she said, "this certainly isn't Gabriela."

The picture on the screen of her phone was sent to her by Marv. It was of the undercover FBI agent, Eliza Sanchez, and she looked nothing like Gabriela. The woman in the photo was more J.No than J.Lo.

"So this is no help to us?" Kyle said.

Sam closed out the picture and turned toward Xander and Kyle. "Not really, no. And they do not know Eliza's current location, so we can't be sure if she is working with Francisco, the criminals taking possession of the child, or neither. But we have to assume that she is at least in bed with one of them.

There isn't another explanation for how they found us in Mazatlán."

"Any other useful information?" Xander asked.

"Nothing useful. Nothing at all really. Only where she went to school, the date they made her an agent, and so on."

Jack leaned in. "They check ya pretty good when ya go into the FBI. Anything about her family?"

"None to speak of. Her parents died when she was young. She bounced around the system for a while until she landed in a foster home as a teenager. Nothing noteworthy there about the foster parents."

Xander didn't like the sound of any of this. Knowledge is power. So far, they had almost zero power. Other than knowing that Francisco Romero is involved, they really knew nothing. They didn't even know if the FBI agent, Eliza Sanchez, was compromised or not. And if she was, they didn't know her location. They didn't know where Francisco was going with the girl he captured. They had no clue who was going to be taking possession of her when he did get where he was going.

They had nothing.

Until Sam's phone rang.

"It's Marv," she told the group. She put the call on speakerphone. "Hello?"

"Sam, I have good news."

"Let us have it, Marv," Xander said.

"Hey, Xander. Sorry this has been so confusing. We will be doing a full investigation into how the FBI handles their agents after this."

"What's the news?" Xander cut to the chase.

"Right. All three of the planes out of Mazatlán are definitely going up the coast of California. We are certain, due to the timing of it all, that one of them is Francisco."

"Great, where are they?"

"You aren't too far behind them actually. About an hour, I'd say. And you are quickly gaining on them. Both your jet and these planes are following the same path. I'd bet my job he's going to land somewhere in Los Angeles."

Xander and Sam looked at each other and smiled.

"That *is* good news, Marv," Xander said.

"Doing all we can from here. I'll keep tabs and let you know where they land. But for now, I would just stay the course where you are going. You have to get those girls off the plane and out of harm's way before you go after him anyway."

"Sounds good, Marv."

"I'll be doing my best to track down this Agent Sanchez. My bet is that if we find her, we'll find whoever is running the trafficking ring from the US end of the trade."

"I agree. Talk soon, my man." Xander nodded that he was finished.

Sam ended the call. "All right, at least we have something."

"Better than nothing," Xander agreed. "All I have to do is get my hands on Francisco. He'll be begging me to find the others involved in this thing after that."

"So we'll stay the course then," Sam said. "Hopefully by the time we hand over the girls to the FBI waiting for us at LAX, we'll have more to go on. I just hope the hour we're behind won't be long enough for Francisco to make the handoff."

"All the more reason we need more information about Eliza Sanchez. She is the key to this thing. We find her, we find the second party involved in this trafficking ring."

31

The Ultimate Betrayal

David Tarter was holding court in the corner of the parking lot at the private terminal at the Burbank Airport. This end of the airport was mostly unknown, and due to its proximity to downtown Los Angeles and the movie studios, it was mostly frequented by celebrities who craved a little discretion. For Tarter, as well as Francisco Romero, discretion was the word of the day. Employees at this terminal were trained to keep their mouths shut, making this the perfect place to transfer their package.

David was going over the plan with his team of ten ex-military men. He had worked with all of them previously, and that was the way he liked it. No surprises. The eleventh man on the team was up in the tower. David had done a tour with him back in Afghanistan, and for twenty-five thousand dollars he would be helping to get Francisco's plane in without anyone noticing. He was explaining all of this to the team behind his black Hummer and their three black vans that were parked side by side. He had

Jon add signage to the sides of the van advertising: Whistle Dry Cleaning. "If it's not clean as a whistle, it's not Whistle Dry Cleaning." Jon had taken the liberty of adding the punchy slogan. David wasn't amused.

As he finished explaining how they would get the girl, and how they would split off, each van ending at a separate destination with only one arriving at the real drop, Tommy and Lisa pulled into the parking spots adjacent to the vans.

Tommy got out of the car with haste, and David could see very clearly that he wasn't happy.

"You started the meeting without us?" Tommy said.

David turned, stalked over to Tommy, and grabbed him by the shirt, quickly putting an end to the questioning.

Lisa remained in her car. She was going to let Tommy get it out of his system before she approached. She knew David was a ticking time bomb, and she knew that Tommy coming at him in front of his men wasn't going to end well. She tried to tell him, but Tommy never listens. Besides that, she had no idea what she was going to do. She hadn't slept at all the night before. The thought of selling a young girl to some rich monster, to rape her and do whatever else he pleased to her, made her sick. This had felt wrong from the first time David mentioned this was the next job. It went against every fiber of her being. But she was lodged directly in between a rock and a hard place.

She owed money to the wrong people. They would kill her if she didn't pay them back. But how could she ever live with herself if she not only let David do this but was a part of it herself? Her palms were sweating. Her heart was thudding. And her stomach was tied up in knots. She glanced out the window and watched David grab Tommy by the shirt and toss him against the back side of the van. How did she get herself into this mess? People, *inno-*

cent people were going to die if she didn't put a stop to it. As she watched David assault Tommy, she flashed back to David beating that cop half to death the night before. He was crazy. He didn't care who got hurt, and ultimately she knew that included her.

She had to stop him.

Lisa sent up a silent prayer as she pulled out her phone and dialed the number that was sure to be her downfall. She had backed herself into this corner, trying to remain loyal.

She realized in that moment that loyalty to the wrong people was the quickest way to bring yourself down.

David smashed his forearm into Tommy's throat as he pinned him against the van. How dare he come at him in front of his own men. Brother or not, that disrespect could not be tolerated. Rage flooded his body. He needed to make an example of Tommy.

David drew back his right hand and threw it forward, smashing Tommy in the gut. Tommy let out a grunt, then dropped to his knees.

"You're out!" David shouted, towering over his much smaller brother.

Tommy looked up, but he couldn't speak. There was no air left in his lungs. Instead, he held his stomach and coughed for a breath.

"Both of you! I should never have brought either one of you in on this one. It is way above your pay grade. Get off your knees and get the hell out of my sight."

Tommy gasped a few more times but still couldn't find words. David heard Lisa's car door open, so he turned his rage toward her.

"Come get your good-for-nothing brother, and both of you get the hell back to San Diego!"

Lisa was barely out of her car, and David had already started in on her. Screaming at her to get her brother. He was psycho. This only confirmed that she had just made the right decision. And for whatever reason, he was yelling at her, telling her she was out. Out? Could he really mean it? This was perfect. She could just go and grab Tommy, and get the hell out of there just in time.

"Are you deaf, Lisa? Come get your brother and get the hell out of here."

She *had* heard him correctly. It was a miracle. Lisa rounded her car and walked straight toward Tommy, who was on his knees gasping for air.

"Jesus, David. What did you do to him?"

Why was she talking to him? Just pick up Tommy and get the hell out of there. Don't make things worse, it would all be over soon.

"Just get him the hell out of my sight. Go back to San Diego and boost some cars or something useful. This big boy shit ain't for the two of you."

David had given her an out, and she wasn't going to wait around for him to blow another gasket. She walked over to Tommy and helped him to his feet. He was still gasping for air. While she was on the phone in the car, David must have hit him. Unbelievable. His own flesh and blood. She was so glad she wouldn't have to deal with David anymore. She was finally going to be able to do some good. Make a difference in the world. She could finally be on the right side of things and make sure people like her foster brother, David, never hurt anyone else again.

Lisa put Tommy's arm over her shoulder and turned toward her car. She was going to get out of there just in time.

David was pissed at his brother, and Lisa. But he was happy they weren't going to be around to screw things up. He watched as Lisa put Tommy's arm over her shoulder and turned toward her car. Just as he was about to finish making sure his team was on the same page, his cell phone began to ring. He pulled it from his pocket, and the number on his screen instantly made him nervous. He knew this was not going to be good news. He had seen Lisa on her phone in the car; he should never have trusted her.

"Hang on, Lisa. Wait right there for a second."

Lisa turned toward him. The look on her face told him exactly what the private investigator who was calling was about to tell him.

"I'm just going to get Tommy out of here. He's hurt, David."

David held up his finger. "No, I'm going to need you to wait right there for a minute."

David nodded to Jon, and Jon pulled a pistol from his hip holster, training it on Lisa and Tommy.

"What the hell is this, David?"

Fear wrapped around Lisa's question.

"Just wait one minute," David said.

Then he turned his back to them and answered the phone.

Lisa couldn't feel her fingers. Somewhere between making the call in the car and Jonathan pulling a pistol on her, her nerves finally fried. Why would he be telling her to wait? What could he possibly want that was so important she couldn't just do what he said and get the hell out of there? Her spine was on fire. A distant voice in the back of her mind was telling her just to run. Drop Tommy, and run. She couldn't believe she ever tried to cover for David in this whole thing. She had put her entire career at risk. If it wasn't for the money she owed, she would never have tried to throw the FBI off track in Mazatlán. From the looks of things now, she may have only made it harder on David.

As she watched his body language, the back of her mind was now screaming at her to get out of there.

But she didn't run.

"Hello?" David answered his phone. "Yeah." A pause. "Yeah." Another pause. "You're sure?" One last pause. "That's what I hired you for. How long do I have?"

Those were the last words that Lisa heard David say. The last words she ever heard anyone say. Except for her own voice as she pleaded for her life. In front of her, David put away his phone, pulled out his pistol, pulled a silencer from his pocket, and fastened it to his gun.

"David? I'm going to go now, okay?" Her voice quivered.

David didn't answer; instead he began to walk toward her. A knowing look on his face. Not sad, not angry, just . . . sure.

"David, what's wrong?"

He raised the gun as he closed the distance between them.

"David! David what the—"

The last thing she saw was a spark at the end of the silencer.

––––––

Tommy dove away from Lisa as blood spattered everywhere from her forehead. David didn't want to shoot her, but he didn't have a choice.

She was a traitor.

"David! David what did you do?!" Tommy screamed as Lisa's body collapsed to the ground.

Dead.

"What did you do?!"

David turned the gun on his brother.

"Did you know, Tommy? Did you?!"

Tommy began to sob.

"David, what did you do? Why would you do that to Lisa?"

"Answer me!" David shouted.

"Know what?" Tommy began to backpedal away from David on the sidewalk.

David could see the fear in his eyes, but he couldn't tell if his brother knew or not. Fortunately for Tommy, and thanks to Lisa, he didn't have time to stand around and find out.

"David, what's going on?" Tommy shouted through gasping breaths. "Why did you do that to our sister?"

David couldn't hold it in.

"She isn't our sister, Tommy. Not even half. She's not our blood, and her betrayal showed that blood matters."

"What are you saying, David? What are you talking about?"

"I'm talking about Lisa, aka FBI Agent Eliza Sanchez! The stray that our hippie mother took in, and now it's come back to bite us!"

Tommy looked dumbfounded. His eyes were wide, and his chin may as well have been scraping the concrete.

"FBI? Eliza? She hasn't gone by that name in more than ten years. What are you saying? She's dead, man! You killed our sister! FBI? She doesn't even have a job. She was fired weeks ago. There's no way!"

"She wasn't fired, Tommy. She was undercover. Giving up her own people who took her in."

"You killed her, David. You killed our sister!"

"NOT our sister!" David screamed. "She just ratted us out. I've had her phone tapped for the last few days. Since she started acting weird about this job. You know what, I don't have time for this shit. There is no way you didn't know. But I don't have time to deal with you right now. I have to pick up the pieces your FBI agent just scattered. If you say one more word, I'll shoot you right between the eyes."

Tommy didn't say another word.

"How bad is it?" Jon said.

David turned to him. "The FBI are on their way."

"What? Here? So we're through?"

"Hell no, we aren't through. Get ahold of Francisco. Tell him to go ahead and land, but wait at the plane for our instructions."

Jon was baffled.

"What? You just said the FBI is coming. He can't land here."

"The PI said she only told her handler that we were here armed. Said she would explain the rest later."

"David, they will be checking every plane that comes in," Jon explained.

The look of frustration was heavy on David's face. The last thing he wanted was to complicate things, but he knew Jon was right. It would make everything more dangerous if they stayed and tried to make it work there.

"You're right. Call Francisco, tell him to go to plan B. Tell him to divert at the last minute and to stop communicating with the towers. His pilots will have to be careful coming in to miss traffic, and quick getting back out, but it's the only option we have. I don't like it being so close to the drop, but our shell game of vans should still provide us with a shadow. We just have to get them out of here now, before the FBI knows what we're driving."

Jon turned to their men.

"Split up in each van and get to Atlantic Aviation at the Santa Monica Airport. We don't have a man in the tower there, so I'll be instructing Francisco to land, let the girl out, then take off. We'll need to be ready to scoop her up and get the hell out of there." Jon turned to David and pointed at Lisa, dead on the ground. "What do you want to do with her?"

David looked down at her in disgust.

"Leave her. Let her friends at the FBI deal with her now."

Jon nodded, and the band of mercenaries split off, some of them going to the Santa Monica Airport, some of them going to set up around the house where they would be bringing the girl. David wasn't happy about anything that just happened, but at least they were still in the game. He had a backup plan for all of this. Time in the SEALs taught him that nothing ever went according to plan, and you had to be ready for anything. His decision to tap Lisa's phone had saved their ass. He learned long ago to trust no one. It hadn't let him down yet. And not letting her and Tommy know the details of the drop location just helped him avoid a two-million-dollar loss.

David was feeling damn good about himself as they pulled away from the airport on their way to the biggest payday they had seen yet. But he knew it would be short-lived.

"Better call our man in the Middle East," David said to Jon.

"I was thinking the same thing. No way out of this one now that Lisa gave us up."

"No. I was ready to get the hell out of here anyway. But now we need that money more than ever. And we have to do *whatever* it takes to get it."

Jon pulled out of the parking lot in the Hummer.

"Burn this city down if we have to?"

David looked at his partner in crime.

"And we may have to."

32

Good Thing We're All Crazy

Xander and the rest of Reign watched impatiently as Sam finished a call at the front of the airplane. She seemed animated, and that made Xander nervous.

She finally ended the call and walked over, shaking her head all the way over to them.

"You're not going to believe this."

Not good.

"You were right about Eliza Sanchez, Xander. That if we found her, we would find the party responsible for the trafficking."

"Okay, so they found her. That's great!"

"Sort of."

"Sort of?" Xander was confused. "So they didn't find her? Spit it out, Sam."

"They found her all right. Dead. Just outside the Burbank Airport."

"The FBI agent is dead?" Kyle said.

"Shot in the head out in the parking lot."

"Damn . . . so what happened?" Xander asked.

"Apparently, that was where they were going to do the exchange."

"Who was going to do the exchange?"

"This is the crazy part," Sam said. "They aren't clear on all the details, because she only gave her handler at the FBI a quick sentence before hanging up. But she was there to do the exchange along with her brother."

Xander stood from his seat.

"Her brother? I don't get it. The FBI said she was undercover. How could she be undercover with her own brother?"

"I know, it is all very convoluted. They are still working it out themselves. Marv thinks that she was undercover to keep them in the clear. The FBI didn't know it was her brother. Remember, the report on her was that she was placed in a foster home. To a Melissa Tarter. The filed report was that she was going undercover to stop a small organized crime ring. The name she gave was Jonathan Haag. They gave her the detail because it was close to her home, and because it was a small-time ring. They thought it would be a good way for her to cut her teeth with the Bureau." Sam noticed that Xander had zoned out. "Xander, what is it?"

"That name, Jonathan Haag. I did a few tours with a Jonathan Haag." Xander's mind was jumping all over the place. Alarm bells were going off like crazy. "What did you say the woman's name was again that took Eliza in?"

The plane began to change its pitch and moved into its descent. They were getting close to the airport.

"Melissa," Sam answered.

"Melissa what?"

"Um, Tarter, I believe he said."

Xander's expression went from confusion to revelation.

"Ho-ly shit."

"What?" Kyle said.

"I know who's behind this."

"Right, I just told you, Xander, Jonathan Haag," Sam reminded him.

"No, he's involved, but he isn't the one in charge."

"So you know something the FBI doesn't?"

"The FBI agent said it was her brother, right?"

"Right."

"His name is David."

Jack chimed in. "How the hell do you know that?"

Xander turned to him. "Because I had David Tarter and Jonathan Haag kicked out of the military for raping a woman in Afghanistan. She must have named Jon so she wouldn't be implicating her brother if something went wrong. She must have changed her mind at the last minute. It wouldn't surprise me if David was the one to pull the trigger himself."

"This is crazy," Kyle said.

"And if it's Jon and David, David is definitely in charge. Jon used to follow him around like a little puppy. So the FBI missed the exchange?" Xander asked Sam.

"No, none of the planes we were tracking have landed yet. All they found at the Burbank airport was Eliza, dead. None of the chartered planes landed there."

"So they moved exchange point?" Zhanna said.

"Yeah," Xander said. "But the question is, where? And they should already know this by now. In a high traffic area like Los Angeles, if a plane diverts course, alarm bells would be going off right and left."

Sam's phone began to ring.

"It's Marv."

Sam put the call on speaker.

"You're on speaker, Marv. What have you got?"

"Hello, Reign. A controller at the Burbank Airport just reported a plane diverting last minute, no longer communicating with them. This has to be Francisco Romero and our girl. They are either going to LAX or to Santa Monica Airport. I'll let you know ASAP. We are scrambling SWAT to both airports and freezing air traffic. If we want to keep this girl safe, we'll have to be delicate. We'll do our best to clear a path for you to land, but there is a lot of traffic over Los Angeles."

Xander said to Kyle, "Go ask Bob how far out we are." Then he announced confidently to Marv on the phone, "He's going to Santa Monica Airport. No way he tries flying blind into LAX, one of the busiest airports in the world. Have the team go there, but keep them away from the plane. We can't have anything happen to the girl."

"It might be too late to get a team there in time. He's probably landing now if he's going there."

"Bob says five minutes if it's Santa Monica," Kyle shouted from the cockpit.

"We're five minutes out, Marv. Tell tower to clear a path." Xander said.

"Will do."

Sam ended the call.

"What's the plan once we land?" Jack said.

"Do our best to not let Francisco's plane leave," Xander said.

"You mean, like block the runway?" Kyle said.

"I'll leave that up to Bob. He'll know better than me. But as for us, we have to be ready for a gunfight. David and Jon are real assholes, but they are highly trained soldiers. The men they have with them that we'll run into on the ground will be too. Let's get the girls into the bathroom. They'll be safe there."

"Son," Jack said to Xander, "I don't know what you done in a previous life, but you got a crazy-shit magnet installed in you somewhere. 'Cause every situation we get into, you attract the craziest of shit."

Xander nodded with a raised eyebrow, agreeing that Jack was probably right.

"Then it's a good thing we're all crazy too then, cowboy. Fight fire with fire."

Jack's response was to pull out his Colt Python and check its status, then he grabbed his sniper rifle from its bag to get it ready for action. Everyone else followed suit readying their own weapons. They didn't know exactly what they would be flying into, but they sure as hell weren't going to be caught off guard.

33

Playing Chicken . . . with an Airplane

Xander's jet descended into Santa Monica Airport. The sun had yet to set, so it was easier for Bob to navigate the circling crowd of planes waiting to be cleared for landing. Inside the plane, Reign was hoping for the best but preparing for the worst. Best-case scenario: law enforcement foiled the handoff of the young girl from Francisco Romero to David Tarter. Worst-case scenario: the plane landed before anyone was ready, and they were able to unload the girl.

Now that it was out in the open who was responsible on both ends, thanks to the recently deceased FBI agent, Xander knew that Francisco, David, and everyone else involved would eventually get what they had coming to them. The concern was obviously for the girl. If Tarter did manage to get her from Francisco and made it out of the airport, that was a real problem. In this situation, some might have thought since David and his crew now had a lot of heat on them, that he would forget the exchange and run for cover. But

Xander thought the opposite. He figured it was now more important than ever for Tarter to finish the transaction. He would need the money, which figured to be substantial, to make his getaway clean.

It didn't surprise Xander that Tarter and Haag were caught up in this sort of racket, given how he found them raping that woman in the Middle East. He just couldn't believe the coincidence in them being involved in this case, which he happened to be pursuing. Xander knew a lot of people, good and bad, so he supposed it was bound to happen. But this was just crazy.

If David knew that Xander was after him, it would change things. He would think differently. Because he would want revenge. He never forgot the look in David's eyes when he stopped him from hurting that woman. And that look only became angrier when he and Haag were court-martialed because of it. Either way, it didn't matter to Xander. The kind of scum that would sell a child into slavery wasn't any more of a motivating factor. Because it was David didn't further motivate him either. What it did do was make him understand that the danger in this mission had just been taken up a few notches. Both Tarter and Haag were good SEALs as far as skill. And a couple of Navy SEALs on the other side of the fight would always be a tougher go. He made sure that the rest of the team understood that, and that each risk they took would be greater because of it.

They couldn't see any major commotion from their position just beyond the runway. Then Bob's voice came in over the loudspeakers. Just as they were about to touch down.

"Traffic controller said the plane in question touched down four minutes ago. Hang on, they're radioing back in."

Sam looked at Xander. "You think they've had enough time to hand off the girl?"

Xander got up to go to the cockpit. "Four minutes? I'd say so. If Tarter was ready, they probably already have her."

Bob chimed back in. "Xander, the controller is asking us to

abort the landing. They say Francisco's plane is heading for our runway, going to take back off."

Xander made it to the cockpit.

"It's up to you, Bob. I don't want that plane to leave, but I don't want to put us all in danger. Especially those innocent girls in the back."

"I understand. All I can say is that we are a lot bigger than they are. If we touch down before they get off the ground, at the very least they'll be forced to swerve off the pavement. And if they're going very fast, it could stop them."

"Your call, Bob."

"I say we run their ass off the runway."

"I'll tell everyone to strap in for a bumpy landing!"

Xander rushed back to the cabin, leaned over the chairs, and told everyone to buckle up.

Sam said, "I take it we aren't aborting?"

Xander smiled.

"Aborting isn't really our style."

Everyone strapped in, and Xander ran back up to take a seat beside Bob. Looking through the front windshield, they were already just in front of the runway.

Bob clicked a few buttons on the instrument panel. "Controller said they are coming our way, hold on."

Bob went three green and full flaps, and a few seconds later, the plane bounced as the tires screeched against the pavement. Sure enough, in the distance there was a plane heading straight for them. It was a very surreal moment. Xander had been through a lot of wild things since joining the navy, but playing chicken with another airplane was definitely a first.

But they didn't play chicken for long.

The much smaller CJ2 veered off the runway in front of them, sliding sideways in the grass that separated the runways. Xander immediately unfastened, told Bob to stay with the girls until everything was secure, and bolted for the back of the plane.

"We've got them," Xander announced.

Everyone else unstrapped, stood, held on to the tops of their seats as Bob slowed the plane. Before coming to a stop, he stomped on the rudder, turning the plane around to the left, then throttled forward until they were right beside Francisco's jet. Xander lowered the stairs and bounded down them, sprinting for the back end of the plane, pistol extended in front of him. The stairs had already been lowered on the CJ2, but no one was coming out. In the distance Xander heard multiple sirens. He hoped they were after Tarter so they could tie all of this up in a nice neat bow before nightfall.

Xander approached the jet's entrance with caution.

"There's nowhere to go, Antonio, or Francisco, whatever name you're going by. Lay your weapons on the floor of the plane, and all of you come out with your hands up!"

The rest of Reign joined at Xander's back.

"Kyle, you and Jack go get us a car," Xander said, not taking his eyes off the jet's open door. "We need to be ready to move on Tarter after we nail Francisco down."

"On it."

Xander shouted toward the entrance of the plane again. "The longer you sit in there, the longer I'm going to beat you before I turn you in!"

Nothing was coming from the plane's entrance. Just a dim yellow light, no sound.

"Okay, I'm coming in!"

Xander took two steps toward the stairs, when finally he saw a pair of hands flash from the direction of the cockpit.

"Keep your hands where I can see them!"

"Okay! No problem!" a man with a Spanish accent shouted. "He made me do it. I am so sorry!"

"Now the rest of you, get your ass out here!"

The same voice spoke as his head poked around the corner. "It is just me, señor! He made me do it. They all left, told me to fly back to Mexico! I swear!"

"All right then, nothing for you to worry about. Come on down here and we'll sort this out."

Reluctantly, the man finally came out from around the corner, his hands as high as they would go. He walked down the stairs, and Xander grabbed him and shoved him into the arms of José.

"So there's no one else in there?" Xander glanced back at the man, then trained his eyes, along with his gun, back on the opening.

"No one, I swear!"

Xander made his way up the three steps, took a breath, then swung to his left inside the cabin. His finger ready to pull the trigger. But the pilot was telling the truth. The plane was empty.

"Damn it!" Xander lowered his gun and looked back out at Sam and Zhanna. "They're gone."

He looked out beyond Sam, and driving straight toward them were a gang of cop cars. Out in front were two Chevy Tahoes with blue lights flashing in the front windshield.

"Sam, get Marv on the phone. We need to know what he knows. Francisco must have gone with Tarter."

José held on to the pilot as Zhanna looked up at Xander.

"This is bad for girl."

"Really bad," Sam added.

Xander could have done without the two of them stating the obvious.

34

An Enemy of My Enemy Is My Friend

For five minutes, the girl had been holding on to Carrie so tight that it had become hard for Carrie to breathe. She didn't know what was going on, but it was clear something had gone wrong. The way they had rushed her off the plane and hurried the two girls into the back of the Hummer. The way the man was driving wildly. The way the big man in the front passenger seat had been in a screaming match with the man who kidnapped her. Someone clearly did something wrong.

When she had gotten carried off the plane and heard police sirens in the distance, she thought for a moment they had a chance to get away. But almost immediately, the Hummer came speeding up to them, skidded to a halt, and there she was, captive again. She couldn't tell if the men yelling at each other was a good thing or a bad thing, but it was seriously getting heated. She raised her head above the backseat for a moment, but immediately lay back down. She gave the younger girl a squeeze and whispered that everything was going to be all right. She wished someone could tell her the same thing.

"I told you, there was a mole! But I have it handled!" David shouted at Francisco.

David never liked being questioned, but he especially hated it coming from this 1980s-looking Mexican douche-lord.

"You call this handled?" Francisco Romero shouted back. "I should be on my way back to Mexico, but here I am instead, packed into this truck, running from the police!"

"Why are there two girls, Romero? Huh? You said one girl."

"The man wanted two girls, he gets two girls. You were going to be paid two million dollars. Two million!"

The truck swerved, tossing everyone around inside. David recovered and turned all the way around in his seat, pulled his Beretta from his hip holster, and trained it on Francisco's forehead.

"*Were* going to be paid? *Were*?"

Francisco's men pulled their guns and pointed them at David. Jon shouted at them from the driver's seat.

"Put the damn guns down! All of you! Are you insane? We've got to work together now. And by the way, Francisco, we have a plan for this, so everyone just relax!"

David didn't lower his weapon, and neither did Francisco's men.

"The police are looking for this Hummer," Jon continued. "We've got it covered."

He turned left, then pulled into an open garage space in a car repair shop. As soon as the Hummer entered, the garage door shut behind them, and inside were all three black vans and some of David's men.

"What is this?" Francisco asked.

"Plan C," David said, lowering his weapon and getting out of the Hummer.

David had called his men away from the Santa Monica Airport at the last minute. He knew it was a risk, but he knew if the vans were burnt, the job was finished. He gambled, and it paid off. Now they just had to transport the girl—girls—to the drop and make the exchange for the money. This was the part that David was worried about the most. This was the first time he would be doing something like this, and it was the main reason he had wanted Lisa to be involved. He was going to have her take the girl and exchange her, with the promise that her parents were there waiting. Let Lisa handle the delicate work while he and his men watched from various positions around the block. He didn't know what sorts of problems could come from doing an exchange like this, so he had men in place to be ready for a variety of problems. Police interference, the man buying the girl not being where he was supposed to be, and he even had men in place at the pier across the street, in case the girl tried to make a break for it.

David wasn't going to lose this payday. Not to a snitch of a "sister," not to the police, and not to Xander King if he should so happen to interfere.

Francisco and his men followed David out of the car, not satisfied with the backup plan.

"This is great for you, but what about me? Your mistake has made getting back to Mexico very difficult for me. I will not pay for your mistake."

David walked up got in Francisco's face. Once again, all of them drew their weapons.

"That is the second time you've made a comment in the direction of not paying me. Now, I'm assuming you don't get your cut either until the girl is delivered."

"Girls," Francisco reminded him.

"Okay, *girls*. You see my point, asshole."

Francisco motioned for his men to lower their weapons.

"You are right, cowboy, I don't. But I did not agree to pay you two million for me to be involved in this end of the deal. If I hadn't received word that the CIA was coming for me in Mexico, I wouldn't have even taken the risk to deliver the girls this far. I never cross the border myself. But like you, I couldn't turn down this money."

David took a step back, and a worried look came over his face.

"Wait, wait, wait. CIA? You never said anything about the CIA being after you. You think we're playing games here?"

"Jesus, David," Jon started in, "this whole damn mission has gone to shit. Maybe we should just cut bait and get the hell out of here. Let El Guapo here worry about those girls."

David shook his head and walked a few feet away from the situation. Something was gnawing at the back of his brain, but he couldn't place it.

Francisco adjusted his pants by the belt.

"You leave now, you get nothing."

"Yeah?" David said. "And just what the hell do you get? Seems as though you need us a lot more than we need you."

"Then we can end this right now and see." Francisco didn't back down.

David turned toward Francisco to gauge his level of seriousness. The little man may have looked like an absolute fraud, but he didn't seem as though he was afraid. So he must just be stupid. A garage full of trained soldiers, and the pipsqueak and his three goons thought they were going to control how things would go. David meant it when he said he didn't need Francisco. Francisco had already made the rookie mistake of telling him where, when, and who he was taking the girl to. The more he thought about it, the more he liked the idea of taking Francisco's cut too.

But he had to be smart about it.

A man with an ego likes it to have it stroked.

Besides, there was something about the CIA comment that he wanted to know more about.

"Relax," David told Francisco. "You just threw me for a loop with this CIA business. No reason we can't finish what we set out to do."

David motioned for his men to put their guns down.

"You are not as dumb as you look," Francisco said, a cocky smile on his face.

That burned David up inside. But he took a deep breath and let it pass. Francisco motioned for his men to put their guns down as well.

"So, the CIA? How'd you know they were coming for you?"

"I've got eyes in places you have no idea about."

"That right?"

"That's right."

Then it hit David. The CIA comment was stuck in his craw because the CIA must be Xander King. It had to be. It was too much of a coincidence. His man in the tower at Burbank Airport had a friend who worked the air traffic tower in Mazatlán. He told him to report anything odd coming out of there. When a big jet flew in and its occupants got into a firefight, he called David earlier with that information. That's how David knew Xander was involved. Now that Francisco had mentioned the CIA coming after him in Mexico, two plus two equaled rich boy Xander King's jet was the one that flew in and got in the gunfight, so he must also be the CIA that was there to get Francisco.

"Yeah," said David. "I happen to have eyes in a few places myself. The name Xander King ring a bell?"

Francisco looked surprised.

"You know about Xander King?"

"I guess that means you do too." David read into Francisco's tone.

Francisco walked the ten feet that separated them. "You have a history with King?"

"Oh yeah, and not a good one either," David said.

"Then we have something in common. He is a skilled fighter. Are you worried he will interfere?"

"I know he will interfere, that's just what he does."

Francisco turned to his men, motioned for them to get the girls from the back of the Hummer, then turned back to David, wearing a confident smile.

"Let's finish what you came here to do."

"I don't think we are finished here, Francisco. If you know something about King, the CIA, and where they will be, you need to share it."

"Mr. Tarter, one thing you won't have to worry about tonight is Xander King. I've made certain of that."

35

Xander Tests His Faith in Humanity

Reign piled into the Tahoe, Kyle behind the wheel. They left José to explain to the police on the scene where the girls were, and about the pilot flying Francisco's chartered plane. Bob was handing off the girls to the FBI and taking care of the jet. Sam had just ended a call with Marv. The only lead they had was that a witness had called in and saw a Hummer driving wildly, heading east on Ocean Park Blvd.

"That has to be our man," Sam said. "All of you military types love your Humvees."

Xander couldn't deny that. He had one parked in his garage in Lexington at that very moment.

Kyle threw the truck into drive and sped out toward the airport exit. Zhanna was playing navigator in the passenger seat, pulling a map up on her phone.

"Turn right here. This is Ocean Park."

Kyle wheeled a right turn and they were on their way.

"What do you want me to do now? Just drive?"

"It's all you can do," Xander answered. "At least we're headed in their direction. Until Marv calls back, it's the best we've got."

Sam's phone began to ring.

"Marv?" Xander asked hopefully.

Sam shook her head.

"I don't recognize the number." She answered the call. "Hello?" She listened. "We don't have time for this right now. Xander will—" Sam was cut off, and she listened some more. "This had better be good," she said, then extended the phone to Xander. "It's for you."

Xander took the phone.

"Xander!" A female voice.

"Who is this?"

Xander noticed Sam shaking her head in the seat next to him.

"Gabriela. I have to see you."

"Gabriela? What happened to you back in Mex—"

"I don't have time to explain. Francisco had his men pick me up when I landed at LAX. They brought me to a hotel called Fairmont. I'm in room 736. They haven't hurt me, but I don't know what he'll do to me when he gets here. Please hurry, Xan—"

The line went dead.

"Gabriela. Gabriela!"

Xander handed the phone back to Sam, then tapped on Kyle's seat in front of him.

"Go to the Fairmont Hotel, now!"

"You can't be serious," Sam said.

"What do you mean? You heard her."

Jack spoke up from the back row. "I don't know about this, X. Lotta red flags."

On Zhanna's command, Kyle made a U-turn at the green light.

Xander turned to look at Sam and Jack.

"Yeah? Where the hell else are we going? Are we a patrol car?

We just going to drive around aimlessly? Searching for one Hummer in over a million cars? I mean, did you not hear her?"

"We heard her, Xander," Sam said. "And Jack is right, red flags everywhere. Why would we trust her?"

Xander looked baffled.

"Who said I trust her? Point is, we've got nothing else. Even if she is lying, we have nowhere else to go. Until Marv finds out where Francisco and Tarter are headed, we're just sitting here with our thumbs up our ass. But if we go check this out, it may lead to *something.* Maybe even right to Francisco."

Zhanna spoke up from the front.

"Does sound fishy, as you say, but Xander does have point. Maybe will lead to clue."

Sam was quiet for a moment.

"We are right on top of the Fairmont already, guys," Kyle said. "It wasn't far at all from the airport. What do you want to do?"

A couple of minutes later Xander and Sam were walking toward the entrance of the Fairmont Miramar Hotel. Darkness had begun to fall. The hotel was wrapped in an orange-and-purple glow that was highlighting the sky from the ocean just across the street. Sam had agreed that they would go in and check things out, at least until Marv called back. Kyle, Zhanna, and Jack were on standby in case things went sideways.

"What a cheesy line," Xander said, pointing to a black van just outside the hotel's entrance.

"Seriously? You're worried about marketing right now?" Sam, as usual, couldn't believe Xander and his ADD.

"I'm just saying, it's 2017. You can't do better than 'clean as a whistle'?"

Sam ignored his last ingenious thought completely.

"All right, you take the elevator, and I'll take the stairs. I'll make sure nothing looks out of place from that end. Just walk by the room, do not go in without me. Even if this isn't some sort of game Gabriela is playing, she already told us that there are men of Francisco's there."

"Just do a flyby, got it."

"Xander."

"I said I got it."

"You say that a lot, then come to find out, you do what you want anyway."

"Situations change, you know that. Anyway, we are all tied in through our earpieces, so you'll know what's happening."

"All right. And you'll hear if I get a call from Marv."

They nodded to each other, then split off. Sam toward the stairs, Xander for the elevator.

"I think it sounds like a dumb slogan too, Xander." Kyle came through over their earpieces.

"Oh, shut up, Kyle," Sam said.

Xander didn't respond, he just smiled as he pressed the button, calling the elevator. The door shut in front of him, and he was left alone to his thoughts, and some god-awful elevator music. Probably Kenny G. Xander knew that Sam didn't think this was a good idea. And even though he had been trained for war, and not covert investigations, he wasn't an idiot. He knew that there was a high likelihood this could be a setup. But he still thought it better than roaming around Santa Monica without a clue. At least here, if Gabriela was lying, if he could get his hands on her, he could probably make her talk.

"Anything unusual, Sammy," Xander asked.

"Nothing so far."

"No movement out here either," Kyle said from the truck.

The elevator approached the seventh floor. Xander's hand instinctively slid to his Glock at the small of his back. After his shower on the plane, he had changed into something more Southern California casual. Jack made fun of how tight his jeans and navy-blue V-neck T-shirt were, but Jack in his consummate giddyup attire could hardly judge fashion. Besides, Zhanna said she liked it.

The elevator dinged, and the doors slid open. Xander didn't move. He just listened. He heard some laughter echo down the hallway. Then quiet. He took a step forward and leaned out beyond the elevator frame, quickly scanning both sides of the hall. He saw no one. He noticed the sign on the wall across from him pointing out that room 736 was to his right. He pressed the "door open" button and held it for a moment while he considered his next move.

"Hallway is clear, Sam."

Xander heard nothing but silence in his earpiece.

"Sam?"

"Xander? Can you hear me?" Sam tried for the third time without a response. "Oh bugger off. Must be something in this bloody stairwell." Her voice echoed.

She picked up the pace, taking the stairwell two steps at a time now: then her phone rang. She stopped, and yet again it was an out-of-country number. But this time, she recognized it. Javier Romero. Seeing the number sent a chill down her spine. There was no way he could be calling with good news. She answered.

"Make it quick, Romero, I'm in the middle of running down your degenerate son."

"Samantha, you have to stop right now."

"Apologies, we are too far down the road for that."

"I'll tell you why you have to stop, but you have to promise not to kill my son. I'm not saying he isn't guilty, but he isn't the one in charge."

Sam froze midstride.

"You're talking about the American ex-military who is involved?"

"Again, I'll tell you, but you must promise not to kill my son."

This is where Sam and Xander were the most different. If Xander were on this call, he would absolutely promise not to kill Francisco, and he would mean it. His level of morality when it came to criminals was much higher than hers. Because she had been dealing with them far longer than Xander had. She decided long ago, after the first time she had been burned by a career baddie, that it would never happen again. But that didn't mean she wouldn't still make the promise. Regardless of how little she meant to keep it.

"All right, Romero. I'll do all I can to spare him if you tell me something I don't already know."

"That isn't a promise."

"All right, I promise."

"Gabriela Cisneros is the brains of the operation."

Sam's heart skipped a beat. Her lizard brain had sensed Gabriela was involved from the beginning. Now, here she was, separated from Xander as he walked right into a trap.

"Why wouldn't you tell us this at your mansion?" Sam asked him. Her voice was shaky as she began to sprint up the stairs.

"You know of her?"

"Unfortunately, yes. Why didn't you just tell us?"

"I didn't know," Romero said. "I told you I hadn't spoken with my son in over a year, and it's true. But after you left, I had to find out just how involved he was in this. Gabriela Cisneros is the daughter of Jorge Cisneros. One of the worst criminals in Mexico. He has been grooming her from birth to take over his empire. She must have seen weakness in my son and brought him in to use him."

"Why are you telling me this now?"

"To spare my son. And maybe if I can get him away from Gabriela, I can bring him back into my life."

Sam opened the door leading to the hallway on the seventh floor.

"I said I wouldn't kill him, Romero. I didn't say he would walk away a free man."

Sam ended the call and checked the room number on the first door. She was on the opposite side of the hotel from room 736. In front of her, the hallway broke off in a different direction so she couldn't see its end. As she was about to call for Xander, a door opened and a woman walked out with a child. At the same time two men came around the bend of the hallway, and judging by the hard look they had to them, they weren't there on vacation.

36

The Dynamic Duo Run Into Trouble

Xander was a lot of things, but one thing he certainly was not was a patient man. He knew Sam would be along in a matter of minutes, so he decided to clear the room himself; that way they could move on. Every second they didn't know where the young girl was, was a second they were closer to losing her forever.

After checking the part of the hall he could see, he walked casually out of the elevator toward room 736. It was a large hotel and somewhat oddly shaped, so the hall bent in a couple of different directions. There was no one in his section of the seventh floor. He walked right up to room 736, pulled his Glock, kicked in the door, ready to fire.

"Xander!" Gabriela called to him.

She was tied to a chair at the far end of the room. There was a lamp on, but where he stood at the entrance was fairly dark. He held up a finger telling her to wait, his pistol still at the ready. First he checked the closet on his left.

Clear.

"There's no one here," she told him.

He held his finger up once more, then pushed the bathroom door open on his right and stepped inside.

"Xander, there is no one here! Please hurry and untie me. They left to get Francisco!"

Xander heard her, but he didn't trust her, so he continued to check the shower. He found nothing. He walked back out, checked the rest of the room, and once satisfied they were alone, he tucked his gun in the back of his jeans.

"What happened in Mexico?"

Gabriela wasn't crying, but she did look disheveled.

"Xander, they will be back any second. Please, untie me and let's get out of here!"

"If they come in, I'll take care of them. For now, answer me, or I *will* leave you here."

Gabriela looked toward the door, then back to Xander.

"There was a flight leaving Mazatlán for LA. I didn't know if you would make it back to the airport alive or not when you left to go after the men in that van. I was afraid they would come for me, so I left. You have to understand."

"Why didn't you answer your phone when we called for you?"

"I was on the plane. What could I do?"

Her eyes were pleading with him to believe her. And she *was* tied to a chair. As he walked over to untie her, Sam finally came back into his ear.

"Xander, if you can hear me, it's a trap. Gabriela set us up!"

Immediately after he heard Sam's voice, he heard gunshots through the earpiece. Just as he went to retract his arms from Gabriela's, her facial expression changed, and before he knew it, she lunged at him, jamming a needle into his shoulder. He fell back onto the bed behind him, and she stayed with him, climbing on top.

Her hands weren't tied after all.

"You almost ruined this for me, Xander."

He reached for her throat, caught it, and began to squeeze. But she had already depressed the plunger. She fought his hand with both of hers, but after a couple of seconds, things began to blur.

Gabriela removed his hands from her throat and leaned into him, her mouth grazing his ear as she spoke. "Maybe I have a career in Hollywood after all. You bought every whimpering word I told you. You men are all the same."

Xander tried to fight to stay conscious, but there was nothing he could do. With a chorus of gunshots still ringing in his earpiece, everything went black.

Sam kicked in the hotel room door beside her, double-arm-tackled both the mother and the child, and dove inside the room, taking them both with her. She had gotten off a couple of shots to keep the men back, but they had been able to fire as well.

"Are you hit?" Sam asked the mother in between the small child's screams.

She pulled the mom to her feet and shuffled both of them into the bathroom. The mom couldn't speak, but she managed to shake her head. It was the face the mother made after shaking her head that worried Sam. She looked horrified, and she was staring at Sam's leg. When Sam looked down, she understood.

The adrenaline in her system had kept her from feeling the gunshot wound. Sam had been shot before. It was kind of an occupational hazard. But she wasn't sure she had ever seen that much of her own blood.

"Get in the bathtub, don't open the door, no matter what. If you have a phone, call the police."

Sam shut the bathroom door, then poked her head into the hallway. Gunshots blasted immediately; the men weren't far away. She fired a couple of warning shots in an attempt to at least slow them. She was in a spot now. She didn't want to draw the men into the room with the mother and child, but she couldn't get them to another room. A burning pain began to radiate from her left thigh, but she couldn't look at it. It would do her no good. She knew how bad it was already. No sense dwelling on it. She looked back inside the room and noticed there was an adjoining room door. She fired a couple more blind shots into the hallway, walked over to the adjoining door inside the room, and kicked it open with her good leg. She hurried back to the bathroom and ushered the mother and child over into the adjoining room.

"When you hear more than sixty seconds of silence after the next round of gunshots, get the hell out of the hotel. Do you understand?"

"Are you going to be okay?" the mother said, once again giving a horrified glance to Sam's blood-soaked leg.

"I've got a few friends close by. I'll be fine."

Sam shut the door, crouched behind the dresser, and waited.

"Kyle, if you can hear me, it has gone sideways in here. I can't get ahold of Xander. We've been drawn into a trap, and I've been shot."

"Sam! Are you all right?" She heard Kyle in her earpiece.

It was good to hear his voice. Calming. But judging by the ever-growing pool of blood at her left foot, she wasn't sure how to answer him.

"I've been properly nicked, I must say. But I'll be fine. I don't like not being able to hear Xander. Something is wrong. Worry about him first. We are on the—"

The first of the two men peeked inside the room. Sam shot toward his head, but he managed to dodge her bullet. Meanwhile, Sam wasn't feeling so good. Her body felt unnaturally weak. Her head was starting to spin. The men shot twice inside the room.

"Sam!" Kyle shouted.

"I'm all right."

One man charged the doorway. Sam shot his leg first, and

when he dropped, the next man had no cover. She shot him in the arm. Her head swam, but she shot around where she figured a bulletproof vest would be. She shot the first man in the top of the head, but the second gunman was still able to fire. Two bullets blasted into the dresser just in front of her face. A black circle began to encompass the right side of her vision. The darkness was closing in.

Come on, old girl, stay with it. You pass out, you're dead.

Two more shots hit the wall just above her head. Sam took a deep breath and did all she could to focus. She brought her pistol to eye level, and when she leaned out behind the dresser, she had perfectly placed the man's forehead in her sights. She pulled the trigger and fell to the ground. She hit the floor at about the same time as the gunman, now dead himself. The darkness moved over one eye completely.

"Sam!" Kyle continued to scream. "Sam, I'm coming! Just hold on!"

She wanted to answer him, but she couldn't spare the energy. If she was going to live through this, she was going to have to stop the blood from leaking out of her leg. She blinked her eyes several times, trying to clear the creeping blackness. It didn't work. She was incredibly light-headed. Like a worm, she wiggled on her stomach, turning toward the two fallen gunmen. She extended her left hand out in front of her, dug her fingernails into the carpet, and pulled with all her might. Her body inched across the floor.

"Sam! Talk to me! Are you there?"

She managed a moan, or at least she thought she had. She extended her right arm forward, dug her nails into the carpet, and pulled. Her breathing was much too heavy, her body drenched in sweat. The blackness was almost total. She reached out her hand and grasped for something, *anything*. The last man she had shot, when he fell to the ground, had rolled over the man on the floor in front of him. If he hadn't, Sam wouldn't have had a chance, because he would have been too far away from her. As it were, her hand scavenged his body and found what felt like the smooth leather of a belt. Or for her purposes, a tourniquet.

Come on! You've got to do this. You don't cut off the blood flow, you are dead. You are better than this. You will not die alone on the floor of a hotel room.

She continued her internal pep talk. It did nothing to keep the weakness from settling into her bones. Then her finger found a buckle. She felt a slight tingle of adrenaline at the discovery. She worked her fingers until the belt was undone, then pulled as hard as she could as she rolled over onto her back. The belt came free of the man. With the very last drops of her energy, and her consciousness, she managed to tie the belt above the wound in her thigh and collapsed onto her back. The darkness finally pulling her under.

37

A Dry Clean Getaway

The next twenty minutes of Kyle's life almost gave him a heart attack. Hearing Sam tell him she had been shot was hard. Hearing gunshots going off around her and not getting confirmation that she was okay after that nearly broke him. Not to mention how Xander had gone quiet. Once again it had become painfully obvious that he had not been properly trained for this sort of thing. Luckily, he had Zhanna and Jack. Zhanna took the lead as they hurried into the Fairmont Hotel. Jack broke off for just a second and informed the front desk that help was on the way and that they needed to evacuate the building. But it was too late for that. Someone had pulled the fire alarm.

Kyle heard Zhanna say that it was probably whoever was shooting at Sam who had pulled it. It would provide them some cover as they exited the hotel. She said soon the whole of Santa Monica was going to be on lockdown. After about another half hour, if anyone moved on the streets everyone would know it. She said that meant that Tarter, Gabriela, Francisco, or whoever the hell else was involved would be in a serious hurry to get where they were going.

Apparently they were, because they were nowhere to be found. By the time the three of them made it to the seventh floor, there was no sign of any of them. Not Xander King, not Sam Harrison, and not even one of the bad guys. Only two dead men lying on top of each other in a room where the door had been kicked in. But Kyle did find something. And it was the reason the last twenty minutes had gone from bad to horrific.

Just beyond the two dead men were two pools of blood and a generous smear of it in between. Lying just above the last puddle was a gun.

Sam's gun.

"Where the hell is she, Zhanna? Jack?"

Panic had a tight hold on Kyle's voice. They didn't have an answer for Kyle. The three of them searched the adjoining room and found nothing. Kyle's phone began to ring. It was Marv. Kyle hit speaker and handed the phone to Zhanna. He wasn't sure he would be able to retain what Marv was saying.

"Marv, Xander and Sam are gone."

"Zhanna? What do you mean, *gone*?" Marv's voice was worried.

"I mean *gone*. Nyet. They came into hotel to find Gabriela. Now they are both missing."

"Gabriela?" Marv didn't know that name.

"She is girlfriend of Francisco Romero. Said she was being held hostage here at Fairmont hotel. Apparently she was lying."

"Damn it. Wait, what? I thought you were looking for David Tarter?"

"We were, but you had no info, so Xander moved on."

"How could they be missing?"

"We heard gunshots. We heard Sam trying to tell Xander about a trap, that Gabriela was in charge."

"A woman named Gabriela is in charge? And you said she is Romero's girlfriend?"

"This is what Xander said. Marv, we need to know what to do next. Xander, Sam, and girl are all missing. What do you know? Did you find this Tarter's Hummer?"

"Better than that. You won't believe this, but David Tarter's brother called the police. Said Tarter killed his own sister—foster sister. But he let his brother, Tommy, go. Tommy was so pissed that he ratted his brother out. Talk about a family feud."

Jack spoke up. "Marv, we ain't got time for the long version. Our friends are in trouble."

"Right. Tommy called the police and spilled everything. Apparently the way they are moving the girl is in one of three identical vans."

"Now how the hell are we supposed to know where they are? Must be a million vans in this city."

"Well, Tommy said the vans all have a dry cleaning logo. Black vans with a big white whistle on the side. We find those vans, I bet we find Xander and Sam too."

Marv's words felt like a slap in the face to Kyle, and it snapped him out of his trance.

"Clean as a whistle," he said out loud.

"What's that, son? You okay?" Jack asked Kyle.

"When Xander was on the way in to the hotel earlier. He said it was a dumb slogan and Sam got mad at him for caring. He was laughing at the van, said something like, 'It's 2017 and you can't do better than "clean as a whistle"?'"

"That's right, I remember," Jack said.

"One of the vans was here, Marv. Right down at the front entrance," Kyle shouted.

Kyle grabbed the phone and bolted for the door. Zhanna and Jack hurried behind him.

"I'm heading out front now. Get word to the police not to let that van leave!"

"Will do," Marv said. "And we'll get the word out to all of our eyes to find those vans. We find the vans, we find Xander and Sam."

Kyle ended the call. That elevator ride down was the longest minute of his life. As soon as the doors dinged open, he sprinted for the front entrance. He skidded to a stop just outside the door, but there was no van to be found. Police cars were everywhere, and every cop there turned their guns on Kyle.

"Now hold on now!" Jack caught up. Sam had given everyone their own CIA credentials. Jack flashed his to the police. "Anyone see a black van here with a whistle on the side of it?"

The police moved forward, but none of them had seen anything. Kyle knew Xander was walking in the front of the hotel when he made the comment about the slogan on the van, but he couldn't remember if he had seen it himself on the way in or not. His mind was on Sam and Xander at the time, so it didn't compute. After asking the police several times, one of the members of the valet stepped up.

"I saw the van you're talking about leave from around the back earlier. It was just before the police arrived. I was around back smoking when it pulled up."

"What did you see?" Kyle asked the young man.

"A few guys in black were carrying out a couple of huge laundry bags. They seemed heavy. I just figured they were full of clothes or towels. I didn't know. The black they were wearing matched the black van so I just figured—"

"Can you remember anything else?" Kyle interrupted, desperately searching for something they could use.

"Just that there was this real pretty girl with them. At first I thought it was Jennifer Lopez."

"Gabriela," Kyle said to Jack and Zhanna. Then he turned back to the valet. "Did you see which way they went? Did they say anything?"

"The big guy told some skinny Mexican man in a white suit

that everything was in place. I just thought the guy in the suit was the owner and the guy was telling him the job was done."

It sounded like Tarter was with Francisco and Gabriela already.

Kyle ignored the young man, turning back to Zhanna and Jack.

"If we don't find that van, like now, they're both going to be dead."

Kyle's phone was ringing again. Marv.

"Marv, please tell me you have something!"

"I just might. I just remembered something. Were Xander and Sam wearing the earpieces I supplied you with?"

"Yeah, but what does that—"

"I put GPS trackers in them. I'll pull the coordinates and send them to you immediately. Be ready to get on the road ASAP."

"Marv, you're a genius!

38

Everything's Not Lost

First, he began to regain his sense of smell. But Xander didn't dare make a move or even think about opening his eyes. His brain snapped back instantly to Gabriela stabbing him in the shoulder with the needle, so he knew, since he was still alive, that he had been taken. Only one thing registered to his sense of smell, and that was the unmistakable scent of blood. He didn't feel any painful spots on his own body, so that meant that someone else was in there with him. Either already dead or close to it. The faint smell of rubbing alcohol then began to announce itself. This told him that someone had been doctored. But he didn't dare open his eyes. Not until he could be sure no one was watching him. He needed more information. Then he could find an advantage.

He felt ropes around his wrists and he was sitting up, so he knew he was tied to a chair. He thought of Sam, hoping she was okay. He wiggled his right ear, and as he suspected, his earpiece was gone. David must already be involved, because he doubted

Gabriela knew enough to look for it. Then again, he had underestimated her for the last time. There wasn't a heavy light penetrating his eyelids, so he knew that wherever he was, it was mostly dark. Just as he was about to take a peek at his surroundings, a door slammed somewhere above him, and he could hear the muffled sounds of a man and a woman in what sounded like a heated argument.

The next thing he heard sent chills down his spine. No more than a couple of feet to his left, a young woman's voice shouted into the room.

"Help me! Please, someone help me!"

This gave Xander several bits of information. The first being that he wasn't too late. The girl he was trying to save was left beside him. Second, the room wasn't very big, because her voice didn't echo. And lastly, the argument didn't skip a beat upstairs, so whoever was up there was fully aware of the situation below them. Therefore, once Xander figured a way out of his restraints, no one up there was safe.

It also made him even more certain that David was directly involved. The only reason he would put Xander in the same room as the girl would be to rub it in his face. Xander knew that once David learned he was involved, it would change his behavior. He would want revenge, and he would want it to be painful. Since Xander stopped him from ruining a woman's life in Afghanistan, it made sense to him that David, being the sick bastard that he was, would want to create a scene where he was successful this time in doing what he wanted with a woman. Or a girl in this case.

The girl continued to shout, and because no one had tried to quiet the girl, Xander thought the probability was good that he could get away with a peek at the room. It was imperative that whoever was involved in holding them down there believe that he was still out of it. Their lives depended on it. One millimeter at a time, he lifted his left eyelid. It also registered to him that the smell of blood must be coming from the girl, but hopefully she wasn't too terribly hurt.

His eyes found an empty basement directly in front of him. To his left was a flight of stairs leading up to the only light source in the room, which he assumed was coming from underneath the door at the top. He slowly moved his head to the left, and there was the girl, shouting toward the stairs. Her hands were also tied behind her back. Beyond her, something was lying on the ground in the corner. Xander opened his right eye, blinked away the blur, and that something turned into a silhouette of someone.

Sam.

He couldn't see very well, but the bottoms of her shoes were the most lit, and he could tell those silver, ski-boot-like clips on her boots anywhere. A silent prayer went up that it wasn't her blood he smelled and that she was, at the very least, alive. As the girl continued to shout, he worked his wrists for the first time. The ropes didn't give an inch. The shouting continued upstairs and then the door opened. Their voices were no longer muffled. He rested his head back down on his right shoulder, exactly where it was when he woke up.

"This is an unnecessary risk, and we aren't going to keep them alive just so you can have revenge!"

Xander recognized the angry woman's voice immediately.

Gabriela.

"News flash, bitch, your end of the deal is complete. So you and your Mexican *Miami Vice*–looking boyfriend better move on. This no longer has anything to do with you!"

David Tarter.

"Please get me out of here! I promise I won't say a word to anyone!" The girl continued to plead.

Then there was silence.

A light came on in the room. The stairs began to moan under the weight of someone walking down. Hearing David's voice made Xander's heart rate quicken.

"He's still out," he heard David say. "But it won't last much longer. You two get the hell out of here, this is my show now."

The stairs groaned; David was going back up.

"No! Please." Sobs from the girl. "Please just let me out of here. Please!"

Xander's heart squeezed and his stomach clenched hearing the fear in the innocent girl's cry.

"We are not leaving until you make the exchange, and you are going to do it right now!" Gabriela must have been at the top of the stairs.

David said, "For the last time, your part in this is finished. Xander is going to watch this girl get handed off to some creep. And he is going to know that there is nothing he could do to stop it. Then I'll make him watch his gimpy sidekick die right in front of him."

That confirmed beyond doubt that it was Sam lying in the corner. And it confirmed that it indeed was her blood. But they had kept her alive just so Xander could watch her die.

Xander had Tarter pegged exactly.

"You are a fool," Gabriela said.

He heard a couple more footsteps, then the door once again shut. Over the sounds of the girl crying, Xander could hear one more muffled shout, and it was a man's voice. Then he heard two consecutive gunshots, and almost simultaneously two bodies hit the floor. He knew that David had just executed both Francisco and Gabriela. And he knew that if he wasn't able to get this girl next to him free, he and Sam were going to be next.

That was not an option.

39

Sometimes a Happy Ending Is Hard to Imagine

"I have located them," Marv told Kyle over the phone.

"The vans?"

"Xander and Sam. I've located their GPS coordinates through their earpieces. Good news is that they are together. They aren't far from you, but I can send the police over to check it out if you want."

"No," Kyle said quickly. "I have Jack and Zhanna with me. We'll go to them."

"Sending the coordinates to your phone now. Just copy and paste them into your maps app."

"Got it."

Kyle ended the call, and the three of them jumped into the Tahoe. The map said they were only half a mile from where Marv said they would find Xander and Sam. Now that Kyle had half a second to process, his heart was heavy. Not only was his best friend in possibly the worst trouble Kyle had seen him in, but now, so too was his woman. He had of course always cared about Sam, but over the last five months, they had become all but inseparable. They had downplayed to Xander how serious their relationship was. For the first time in his life, Kyle was sincerely in love. And now the two people he loved most in the world were in real trouble.

"I'm gonna kill this son of a bitch, David Tarter, when I find him. With my bare hands," Kyle told Jack and Zhanna as he threw the truck into drive.

"I love your enthusiasm, son," Jack said. "But let's not get ahead of ourselves. That boy's an ex-SEAL. Probably tougher than a pine knot."

"I don't care. Either way, he's a dead man."

———

Xander opened his eyes once again. This time, he had intent.

"Don't scream, okay?" he said to the crying girl beside him.

She jumped in her seat, gasping in fright, but managed to do as he asked.

"It's okay, I'm going to find a way out of here."

The girl stifled a cry.

"But how? We're all tied up."

"I promise I'll get us out. I don't know if you were with them in Mexico, but we saved all the other girls that were in that van with you."

Through the small trickle of light that was coming from the door up the stairs, Xander could see her eyes light up.

"You did?" She realized she said it a little too loud, so she said it again in a whisper. "You did?"

"We did. And I'm going to get you out of here too. I just need you to tell me everything you know—"

"Did that man just kill those two people upstairs?"

"I think he did."

"Good," she said. "That man in the suit is the one who brought me here."

It sank in how terrible this situation had become. Xander knew it was bad, but for a teenager to be happy someone was dead, things were off-the-charts terrible.

"I don't blame you for being happy about that. But I need you to stay focused, okay?"

"Okay." The girl nodded, eager to hear what he had to say.

"Did you see anything that might help us when you were on the way in?"

"There are about eight or nine guys who all have the same look as that man who just came down the stairs. Is that what you mean?"

As the girl talked to him, Xander was trying to figure a way out of there.

"Yes, that's perfect. So they didn't blindfold you?"

"I think they were supposed to, but they were really worried about you and that lady over there in the corner."

Xander's stomach dropped.

"Is she alive?"

"Yes. They were fixing something on her leg. The man in charge, they call him David, said he wanted her alive . . ."

The girl trailed off. Xander already knew why.

"So I could watch her die, right?"

"R-right. I'm sorry," she told him. And her tone told him she really meant it.

"I'm sorry you are involved in this sweetheart. But I can tell you, they already made their biggest mistake."

"They did, how's that?" she said.

"They should have never let me live."

Kyle swerved onto a side street. The closer they got to Xander and Sam's location, the harder his heart pounded.

"Should be right up here on right," Zhanna told him.

Zhanna press-checked her Glock; it was ready to go. Jack had already made sure his Colt Python was ready to strike.

"Right here!" Zhanna shouted.

Kyle jerked the steering wheel to the right, the truck skidded to a stop, and all three of them jumped out of the car, pointing their guns at a massive dumpster.

"No. No, no, no, no!" Kyle was overcome. The only thing he could see in his mind at that moment was Xander and Sam piled on top of each other inside that dumpster.

Dead.

"Don't panic now, Kyle. Not yet." Jack said.

Jack took the lead. He had seen enough dead bodies in his time, he thought he may as well spare Kyle seeing his friends first. With his Colt Python extended in front of him, he grabbed the large plastic cap, tossed it back, and it clanged against the back of the dumpster on the other side. The light fixed to the side of the building they were behind shined a blueish light down over the three of them. Kyle was in agony as he watched. There were a lot of scenarios running through his head, and not one of them had a happy ending.

Jack leaned over the edge of the dumpster, his pistol pointing down inside.

"Well, there ain't no bodies. So that's good. I can't see anything else."

Kyle breathed a sigh of relief, but the reality that Xander and Sam were still missing swooped right in to steal his joy. He took out his phone and turned on the flashlight. He walked over and shined it inside.

"See anything?" Zhanna asked.

"Looks like something in the corner. Hold this."

Kyle handed his gun and phone to Zhanna, then hopped up and

over the rim of the dumpster. He bent down in the corner, and his hand found two earpieces and a piece of paper. He held them up to Jack and Zhanna.

"Well, what's it say?" Jack asked.

"I can't," Kyle said. Then he handed the paper to him.

Jack read aloud. "If you ever want to see your friends alive again, come to Anderson Automotive. Come alone. And bring Xander's checkbook."

Kyle's heart sank. He knew from what Xander said about Tarter that he would never let them out of there alive. No matter how much money Xander had.

40

Teamwork Makes the Dream Work

While Xander was questioning the girl, they heard some footsteps upstairs, then a couple of doors shutting at the front of the house.

"Did you see anything else? Anything that might help me know where we are?" Xander asked her. He knew they were running out of time. They heard more and more footfalls upstairs. He figured they would be coming back down for the girl soon.

"I did. We are right across the street from the Santa Monica Pier. My mom took me there just a couple of weeks ago, and we rode on that famous Ferris wheel. Those men tried to cover my eyes, but I knew I had to try to find some sort of reference point if I made it out of here."

"Fantastic. You did great. What's your name?"

Xander wanted her to remain calm. And he thought he saw an opportunity to get her free.

"Carrie. They tried to take my sister when they got me. But she got away. The other girl reminds me a lot of her."

Other girl?

"What other girl, Carrie? It isn't just you?"

"No, they brought two of us on the plane. They already took her somewhere else."

That news broke Xander's focus. He turned his head from Carrie. He didn't know if she could see him in the dark, but if she could, he didn't want to upset her by showing his emotion.

"She's younger than me. Is she going to be okay?"

Xander knew the answer was most likely a no.

"We'll find her too. Don't worry. Let's concentrate on getting you out of here first."

"Who are you? The police?" she asked him.

"Something like that. Now, you ready to get out of here?"

"Yes, please!"

Xander had noticed a few things while he kept Carrie talking. One, there was a small window behind her. One of those that opened outward on a horizontal axis. Xander would never fit through it, but Carrie could. And hopefully Sam could as well. Two, David had tied Xander's arms behind his back and his feet to each leg of his chair. He also had tied him to the pipes on the back of the wall, so Xander was completely immobile. However, they did not tie Carrie's legs. Instead, they tied her left hand down behind her to the left back leg of the chair. And did the same to her right hand on the right side. This helped to keep her from working her hands together to get free, but it also left Xander an opening.

"Okay, good. Now, I can't move, but you can. But listen, before you do, we have to do this quietly. So go slow."

"Okay."

"Use your feet to scoot your chair this way. Just try to be as quiet as you can."

The footsteps were still moving along the floor above them. And now Xander could faintly hear a conversation. Time was almost up. But he didn't hurry Carrie. He couldn't afford her making a mistake.

If she tipped over, they were sunk. She wouldn't be able to right herself or get her arms free. Carrie pushed against the floor, and the wooden chair moved. It also made a fairly loud scooting sound.

"Sorry!" Carrie whispered.

"It's okay, you're doing fine. Just keep your balance. I know it's hard, but I need you to pick up the pace a little. But if you feel wobbly, stop."

Carrie only nodded. She was concentrating on her feet. She moved them again, this time more smoothly. The chair moved a few more inches.

"That's good," Xander coached her. "Keep coming."

She continued to move along the floor, keeping the noise to a minimum. She was almost there.

"You're doing great. Now, scream at them upstairs, like you were before. Can you make it sound real?"

She nodded. "Please! Someone help me! I just want to go home!"

"Watch out, Jennifer Lawrence," Xander praised. She was very convincing.

He wasn't sure, but he thought he saw a smile.

She scooted the rest of the way, and now she was right beside him.

"Please!" She sobbed. "I want to go home!"

"Good," he whispered. "Now, you see that knot in the rope on the left side of my leg? I know it's dark."

"I see it. But I can't untie it."

"I don't think you'll have to. It isn't very well done. I think if you kick it, just right, you'll be able to unravel it a bit, and we can go from there."

"I can do that. I'm a black belt in karate. Well, I was when I was eleven."

"Perfect. You'll be able to do it easily then."

Xander was trying to keep his voice calm, but he knew time

was up. And if David or any of his men came down there right then, they were all dead.

The stakes couldn't possibly be higher, and he was left to rely on a teenager. But so far she was proving to be very resourceful.

"Just try to hit the very end of it."

"What if I kick you?" Carrie asked.

"I think I can take it, so don't worry about it. Just keep your eye on the spot, and drive your foot right down on top of it."

She lifted her right leg, kicked downward, and hit right on the spot.

"Good one!" Xander whispered.

"But it didn't work!" A bit of panic seeped into her voice.

Then the door upstairs opened.

His attempt was too little too late.

He failed her.

"What do you mean? I'm going to check on them like Tarter said!" a man shouted from the top of the stairs.

There was a pause.

Xander began to sweat as adrenaline poured into his system. He wanted to do what he always did and smash out of his restraints, escaping with brute force and stopping these men from their mission. But he couldn't find enough wiggle room inside the ropes to manage enough momentum. He could hear Carrie laboring for air. She was terrified. He wanted to console her, but he couldn't.

"I'll just be a second!" the man shouted again. He sounded irritated.

This was it. This young woman's life was going to be ruined. He was right here, right beside her, and he couldn't help her. There was nothing he could do but wait for death. He knew they would make him watch as they delivered Carrie to her fate. His stomach turned and he almost vomited.

"Oh, for shit's sake, Jerry. Do I have to do everything?" the man shouted again. Then the door slammed shut.

They had one last chance.

"Okay, Carrie, this is it. I need you to kick like your life depends on it. Because it does."

Carrie didn't say a word, and she didn't hesitate. She began to kick wildly at the knot on the rope holding Xander's leg. She kicked and kicked until finally a piece of the rope came loose, and a loop fell over it.

"You did it!" Xander said. "I still can't get free, one more move. You can do it. Now, scoot toward me and take the dangling piece between your shoes and pull. You can do it. Then I'll get us out of here."

As she scooted over and attempted to get the end of the rope in between the tips of her shoes, she was skeptical. "How will getting one foot loose get you completely free? We don't have time to do the other leg, do we?"

"No, but you get this done, I have another idea that will be faster."

She yanked away at the rope with her feet, and sure enough, the rope fell to the ground and Xander wiggled his left leg free.

"Great job, Carrie. Almost finished. Just scoot up a couple of feet, just out in front of me."

She didn't question him. She just shuffled the chair forward as he asked.

"Now, when I break the leg of your chair, you'll be able to slip your rope free from the broken end of the leg, but it's going to collapse backward. It might hurt a little, but you'll be okay."

"Break my arm if you have to, just get us out of here."

Xander liked this girl. He could tell she was smart—and tough. Reminded him of Sam.

"No need for that. But listen, this might be loud, so as fast as you can, untie your other arm, then get to work on mine. Don't worry about anything else but that. You might hear them coming, but no matter what, you can't stop untying me. Got it?"

"Got it."

"Here we go."

Xander pulled up his leg, jammed his foot down just below her tied hand, and the leg snapped perfectly. The chair collapsed back like he said it would, and she didn't make a sound. But the chair did. The footsteps he heard above him as he was kicking stopped.

They had heard the chair break.

"Okay, nice and steady, but fast. They're coming," Xander told Carrie.

Carrie didn't say a word, and she showed zero fear. She freed her other hand, then moved around behind him and began working on his knot. She had been through a lot already in the last two days. Ironically, all of that had prepared her for this. Without it, she may have been too frightened to get it done. But her fear tolerance was at an all-time high. At this point, this was almost par for the disastrous course.

The footsteps that had stopped were now moving again, only faster. Coming from the back left of the house and walking straight for the door to the basement.

"How's it coming?" Xander said.

"Almost there—"

The door crashed inward at the top of the stairs.

"Got it!" Carrie shouted.

"What the hell is going on down there?" They heard the man's voice first, then his boots thumping down the stairs.

Xander pulled his hands free, snapped the leg of the chair that was fixed to his right leg, took the broken leg in his hand, grabbed Carrie by the shirt, and threw her toward the wall in front of them. Unfortunately, it was away from the window he needed to get her through, but he didn't have a choice, he just had to get her out of harm's way. He dove forward as he saw the end of the man's gun raise toward him, and slid on his stomach behind the wall and into the corner where Sam was lying, all while gunshots echoed in the small basement. Bullets ricocheted off the concrete block wall, and

Carrie couldn't contain her frightened screams, matching the decibel level of the gunfire.

Xander scrambled to his feet, jumped forward to put his back to the wall in front of him, and when the man wielded his gun around the corner, Xander smashed down on his arms, swinging the chair leg down like a hammer. As soon as he hit the man's arms, a spray of bullets bounced off the concrete floor and against the walls. Xander swung the chair leg and pummeled the man in the throat. Then he pulled back his makeshift weapon again and smashed the man in the forehead. As his victim fell to the floor, Sam woke up.

"Xander? Is that you?"

Xander's spirits rose when her heard Sam's voice. He quickly bent down, felt for her arms, and untied her from a pipe along the wall.

"It's me, Sam. Just stay right there. I'm getting Carrie out of here, then you!"

Xander ran to the other side of the basement toward the screaming Carrie. Above them now was a chorus of shouts and banging footfalls as the men scrambled to come down and deal with the noises they heard. His hands found Carrie in the dark. He lifted her off her feet and carried her over to the small window by the ceiling.

"Remember that Ferris wheel?" he asked her.

"Yeah, at the pier."

"That's right, run right toward that Ferris wheel. There is a small police station on the pier. Find it, and tell them who you are. They will already know what is going on. Go now, and don't look back, you hear me?"

"Yes, I hear you. But what if they find me before I get there?"

They were at the back wall now, and Xander popped the window outward. He knew the police would have evacuated the area by the beach by now. They would have started that process as soon as the gunshots happened at the hotel just a couple of blocks away. It was possible she would run into one of David's men on the way, but there was no other choice.

"Sweetheart, if you run, I know you'll make it to the police station. Don't stop for anyone, no matter what."

The footsteps had reached the stairs behind them. Time was up.

"Just run for the Ferris wheel, you'll run right into the police station!"

Xander lifted Carrie up and pushed her through the window just as gunshots erupted behind him. His body tensed, waiting to feel them enter somewhere in his skin. But no bullets made it to him. He turned and looked down. Sam had managed to work her way over to the man Xander knocked out, grabbed his gun, and was firing at the men trying to enter the basement at the top of the stairs. Once again, she had Xander's back.

"What about you! I don't want to leave you!" Carrie shouted back through the window to Xander.

Xander's heart nearly burst.

"Just run, I'll be fine. I promise. I'll see you soon. Run!"

Carrie hesitated for another moment, then finally turned, and Xander watched her tennis shoes disappear from sight.

41

It's Hard to Keep a Good Man Down
(in the basement)

Xander turned and dove for the unconscious man. He knew that after the man had sprayed bullets, and now with Sam dispensing more from that gun at a rapid pace, the magazine had to be near empty.

His hand found a spare magazine clipped to the man's belt.

Click.

Sam shot the last bullet, ejected the magazine, and reached her hand back over her head, where Xander placed a fresh magazine. As if they were in an ER and Doctor Sam had shouted, "Scalpel," to Nurse King. She slammed the magazine in place just as two men were headed down the stairs. One managed to slide back out the door, but the other managed to get filled with holes.

"How bad are you hurt?" Xander said.

"Not sure, but bad enough to have no idea where we are or how we got here."

"Join the club. Gabriela drugged me when I tried to help her. You were right." The words tasted like worms on Xander's tongue.

"What?" Sam turned toward him with an exaggerated look of shock. "You mean you were fooled, by a pretty woman?"

"All right. Anyway. Can you walk?"

Sam shot a couple more warning bullets up the stairs.

"Not sure, really."

Xander moved over behind her, pulled her to her feet from under her arms, and caught her as she wobbled. Sam made an audible wince. That meant it was bad. She had the pain tolerance of a rhino. She handed Xander the gun and took a few steps. They were wobbly.

"There's nowhere for you to go, so make it easy on yourself and give up!" a man shouted down the stairs.

Sam took a couple more steps, and she seemed to be getting the hang of it again.

"Okay, you got me. I give up!" Xander shouted back up the stairs.

Xander could hear the mumblings of a brief conversation at the top of the stairs.

"That's right. Now throw the gun down."

Xander only had the broken chair leg close to him, so he gave it a shot. He threw it down on the ground as hard as he could. He glanced up and saw Sam shaking her head at him. Xander just shrugged his shoulders, as if to say, "It was worth a shot."

"Good, now put your hands on your head."

No way. Had they really bought it?

"Okay, hands on head!" Xander answered. His finger wrapped gently around the trigger of the AR-15.

He knew it wasn't David Tarter, or even Jonathan Haag, at the top of the stairs. Neither of them would have bought the fact that Xander would just give up. Nor would they have remotely believed a chair leg was an AR-15 hitting concrete. David must have had to scramble and get some less than talented soldiers to fill in at the last minute. The men who were once again trying to decide what to do must have been left to hold the fort until Tarter and Haag delivered the other girl. Xander was going to take full advantage.

"I'm all right, Xander," Sam whispered. "Someone stitched me up."

One of the men jumped inside the door, and Xander laid him out with a quick burst of bullets that hit somewhere around his chest. He fell forward, but not all the way down the stairs as Xander had hoped. They were lucky to have the one gun; he supposed two would have been asking too much.

Xander nodded toward the back wall, then whispered, "You think you can fit through that window? No way I can. But if you can, and then come around the back of the house behind them, we might be able to get out of this."

"I can make it. I'll go in through the back and meet you upstairs."

"Okay, King. Very funny," a different man called down the stairs. "That worked on Finnigan, but it won't work on me."

"Come on," Xander said, trying to stall while Sam made it out. "I swear, this time I really will put the gun down."

The man answered by tossing a canister of tear gas down the stairs. It clanged down, rolled onto the basement floor, and began to hiss. Xander walked over to Sam, helped her up on the chair, pushed her through the window, and handed her the gun.

"I'll find another on the stairs. See you in a minute."

Sam nodded and hobbled out of sight. Xander put his mouth to the window and took the deepest breath he could manage. He turned and moved quickly through the gas; it had only made it waist high, so his eyes were unaffected. But he had to get out of there, gun or no gun. He bent down and picked up the broken chair leg, holding it by the bottom, with the jagged broken end out in front. He rushed up the stairs. Before he could get to the man he shot a moment ago and get his gun, the other man stepped inside and raised his weapon. Xander had no choice but to dive for him. He slapped up at the barrel of the AR-15 as he landed on his stomach atop the dead gunman. Bullets blasted into the ceiling above them, and Xander jammed the splintered end of the chair leg into the man's inner thigh. He then reached up, grabbed the barrel of the gun, and yanked backward as hard as he could. The man was already off balance from the blow to his leg, so he easily toppled forward and rolled end over end down the stairs.

Xander looked up at the doorway, and he was staring down the barrel of shotgun. The next thing Xander heard was a trail of gunfire from the back of the house, and the man holding the shotgun on him dropped out of site.

Sam.

Xander jumped to his feet, picked up the gun from the man he'd shot a few minutes ago, and after he performed a press check on it, Sam stepped in front of the doorway.

Xander smiled. "You know, I really don't get what Kyle sees in you."

Sam answered by putting one more bullet in the man with the shotgun, ending the moans of pain.

"How's the leg?"

"It's been better. Let's clear this house and go get the girl."

Xander nodded.

When he entered the hallway of the house, not only did he have to step over the dead man with the shotgun—he took the shotgun with him—but he also had to step over Gabriela and Francisco as well. Their lifeless bodies stared off into the ether. Their last act as humans to help enslave young women, thwarted. If there was a hell, Xander believed that their actions had bought them both one-way tickets. As he and Sam moved on, he nevertheless couldn't help but think their deaths would somehow come back to haunt him.

Xander followed behind his hobbled partner. Though he knew she was in pain, you would never be able to tell it by the way she soldiered on. She was as tough, or tougher, than any man he had ever fought alongside—including battle hardened Navy SEALs. In just a matter of minutes, they had cleared the house. The rest of the men, if there were any, must have escorted David and Jon. Xander and Sam came back down from clearing the upstairs and stood looking out the front window in the foyer. The lights of the Ferris wheel sparkled in the distance.

"I've got to go find Carrie and make sure she's okay. I told her to wait for me at the police station on the pier."

"Smart. Who knows how many tentacles David has out around here. You go to her, and I'll find a phone. As soon as I can get ahold of Kyle, we'll be back for you and we'll go find Tarter."

"Okay. After I know she's safe, I'll come back to the Shore Hotel. It should be just around the corner from here."

Sam stepped forward and gave Xander a hug.

"Be careful. Who knows if he is watching. Hurry and get to the hotel. No getting sidetracked. I'll make sure it's clear for you to come back to. I would imagine it's possible that I'll find more of his men there if it's that close to here."

Xander nodded.

"That's why I didn't send Carrie there, or anywhere else. I couldn't take that chance."

"All right. I'll see you in a few."

Sam walked down the hall and out the back door. Xander opened the front door and scanned the area right outside. It was eerily quiet. The only sounds were police sirens in the distance. Everyone else was either evacuated or holed up in their houses. Xander walked down the front stairs toward Ocean Avenue, the lights of the pier just on the other side. And hopefully, the girl he had sent there in haste.

42

Gone Fishing

Xander crossed the empty street and made his way toward the arch that announced to everyone that they had made it to the Santa Monica Pier. Usually at this time of night, the pier would be bustling: tourists jockeying for position, vendors selling cheap trinkets, and the smell of hot dogs, churros, and body odor hanging in the air. But not tonight. Xander only found one thing as he walked toward the pier, and he didn't like the look of it one bit. Up ahead, there were two black vans, still running, pulled in sideways like they'd arrived in a hurry. He stalked up behind the radiating red taillights, holding his gun at the ready, but both vans were empty. He checked the side of the van, and it looked as if something had recently been removed. There was a large square, still sticky from whatever had clung to it before. Someone was in a hurry, and judging by the missing logo, they hadn't wanted to stand out either.

There was zero movement ahead of him on the pier. The parking lot on his left was mostly empty. All the lights of the pier were still on display against the black backdrop of night, but no children were playing, and no music was playing across the speaker system. The only sounds Xander heard were the waves coming to shore and the occasional call of a seagull. Remaining crouched, Xander moved forward. He had hoped to see movement at least around the police station, but again there was nothing. He imagined most of them were out setting a perimeter with road-blocks. He didn't know if lack of commotion was a good or a bad thing when it came to the two running vans.

A bright sign for Bubba Gump Shrimp flashed on his right, and he could see the entrance to the police station on his left. There was a light on inside, but again no movement. He sprinted the twenty feet to the other side of the pier, the police station just in front of him now. He crouched and tuned his ears to see if he could gather anything at all. He could see the front desk of the police station through the window, and now he knew something was wrong. There was no one there. Someone was always there.

He moved the ten feet in front of him, AR-15 at the ready, and glanced inside the station. When he found nothing, he slowly opened the glass door and stepped inside.

Silence.

He moved toward the front desk, and there on the other side, on the floor, was a man in uniform surrounded by a puddle of blood. Xander turned and went right back out the door. There was no need to investigate further. Carrie wasn't going to be there. She was in trouble. He ran to the edge of the station building and bent his head around the edge, looking down the long walkway of the pier. Down just past where the roller coaster would be on the left, a shadow moved across an opening between vendor stands. And then another.

They were looking for Carrie.

They must have seen her crossing the street earlier.

Xander surged forward, stopping for a moment behind Pier Burger, then continuing to the end of the patio outside the arcade. He could hear the music from the idle games inside. It gave him an eerie feeling being out there in the dark as these grown men were chasing after Carrie. He felt like he had been dropped right into a horror movie scene. All that was missing was some sort of mechanical clown laughing at him. That thought gave him an idea.

Xander was outnumbered, and outgunned, so he needed to level the playing field. He needed to cut the power to the pier. If there was complete darkness, it would be easier for him to move in unseen. It would also be easier for Carrie to stay hidden. He turned and backtracked to the police station. It made sense to him that they would want the power close to the station if there was an emergency. He was right. On the back side of the building, there were four massive power boxes. Xander moved in, went to pull the first lever, but of course it was locked.

Sirens began to wail off in the distance. Sam must have called in reinforcements. This was actually a bad thing. Xander felt like this might hurry David, causing him to make a rash decision. These types of situations were very delicate, and SWAT teams weren't normally known for their delicate touch.

Xander looked around at the surrounding vendors but saw nothing that would help him bust the locks on the power levers. No matter what he did now, it was going to make a noise. And they were going to know someone was moving on them anyway once the power shut off. So Xander glanced down at the twelve-gauge shotgun strapped around his shoulder and did what any red-blooded American man would do in that situation.

Blow shit up.

He took five steps back from the power boxes, shouldered the AR-15, took the shotgun in his hands, and racked the slide.

Boom. Boom. Boom. Boom.

Four shots later, the power all around the pier shut off, leaving him in almost total darkness. Xander dropped the spent shotgun and readied the AR-15.

Once again, Xander was about to ruin David Tarter and Jonathan Haag's fun.

43

Tell Me Something I Don't Know

The black Tahoe screeched to a stop, and before it could settle, Kyle was already out of the driver's side and running around the front end.

"Sam! Sam, you're okay!"

Kyle ran up to her, grabbed her, and lifted her in a bear hug. He immediately put her down gently when she audibly winced. He was frantic.

"Are you okay? Sorry, I didn't know . . . your leg! Were you shot? I was afraid that was your blood in the hotel room. What—"

"Kyle, please. Calm down. I'm all right. Just not as mobile as I would like to be."

"Okay. Good." Kyle was relieved. "Where's X?"

Sam nodded in the direction of the pier across the street, when suddenly they heard four loud bangs and all the lights went out.

"What the hell is he doing over there?"

"He somehow got us out of a basement—"

Kyle broke in. "Us? You mean, you and him?"

"And the young girl."

"You found her?"

"Yes, Kyle. But this will have to wait. Xander is over there right now. He was going to get her at the police station, but judging by the gunshots and loss of power, he must have run into a complication."

"Okay," Kyle said. "David just sent us on a wild-goose chase to some car repair shop. The place was empty when we got there. If you hadn't called, we'd still be wandering the streets with no direction."

Zhanna walked up. "But now we are here. Let's get over to pier and help Xander."

"Right," Sam said. She moved into mission-control mode. "Zhanna, you and Kyle take some weapons and get over there. Jack, you and I will go to the top of this hotel. Since I won't be much help for Xander on the ground, I'll keep you safe while you get their back with your sniper rifle. Remember what Xander said, Kyle. If Tarter and some of his men are down there, they could be well trained like Xander. So be careful. And Xander is down there as well, so don't go in half-cocked and shoot him. Got it?"

"Got it."

"All right, go on then. Let's end this thing before the girl gets hurt. If we're not already too late."

Kyle's phone began to ring.

"It's Marv, you want it?"

Sam took the phone from him.

"Marv, please tell me you found Tarter."

"Sam! You're okay!"

"Marv."

"No, we haven't. But my team has been combing security cameras and they found two of the vans we were looking for. They stopped behind a strip mall and removed the logos. But we tracked them through various cameras and they stopped at the Santa Monica Pier. We could only see their backs as they got out of the vans, but we think it is David and his men."

"Yeah, we were afraid of that."

"You saw the power go out?" Marv said.

"Just now."

"Well, that was Xander."

"Marv, I'm going to need you to tell me something I don't know."

"There are seven men on the pier. And they are heavily armed."

"How heavily."

"One of them has a rocket launcher."

"Christ." Sam took the phone from her ear. "Jack, get to the roof ASAP. Xander is down there in a war zone."

Jack moved immediately, his bagged sniper rifle over his shoulder.

"That's not all, Sam."

"Let me guess, the men are after the girl. Right, Xander freed her just a few minutes ago from the basement we were thrown into. Like I said, tell me something I don't know."

"The last camera that picked her up had her running out of the police station. So the last we saw her, she was safe."

"But Xander isn't. We're on it."

"Wait, Sam," Marv said. "There's one more thing. There were two girls brought in from Mexico on Francisco's plane."

"Two? Where is the other? We only found one."

"They already delivered her. We were too late."

Sam let that settle in for a moment. A young girl had just been sold to a wealthy man as a sex slave. This would break Xander's heart. And even though it wasn't his fault, he would consider it as happening on his watch. But now wasn't the time to dwell on that.

Xander and the girl they *did* know about were in danger. And Sam wasn't going to let anything happen to them.

"Find out what you can about the man they sold her to, Marv. We'll deal with him later. Right now, get men to the pier."

"They're already on their way."

44

Identity Thief

Xander remained crouched beside the now-ruined electrical boxes. It was nearly pitch black around the corner where the pier jutted out over the water. Only the light casting from the city behind him allowed for some visibility. It surprised him when the lights also went out on the Ferris wheel. He had heard somewhere that it was the world's only solar-powered wheel. It must have had some sort of fail-safe that shuts it down when the power goes out. It was a bit of a blessing, as it would allow him to stay more easily in the shadows. His body wanted to go right then and jump right into the fray, but he had to start thinking like Tarter. Tactically, they were similarly trained. The split-off would be that David was also a sociopath, so Xander would have to work accordingly.

If he were Tarter and he heard gunshots that shut down the power, he would send a scout. Depending on how many men he had with him, maybe two scouts. Xander was already at a massive disadvantage in the situation, but not knowing how many men there were was almost crippling. This would mean he would have to be patient, and for Xander patience was not a virtue.

As he waited, crouched to one knee, hiding behind a temporary wall of one of the vendors—hot dogs, by the smell of it—the sirens were closing in. While he would gladly have welcomed backup, he needed his people. They would show the finesse that this situation needed. Xander duckwalked over to the other side of the vendor stand and took a look behind him back toward Santa Monica. The police cars, several of them, had made it to the mouth of the pier. If he could, he would radio to them to stay back, but he had no way of doing so.

It was then that something screamed through the air beside him, and a second later, the entrance to the pier exploded in a fiery blaze. The sound that traveled by him was unmistakable. It was a rocket, launched by one of David's crew. And it did its job of making sure the police would have to take the long route along the beach to reach him. Another rocket screamed past Xander's position, and this time it was much worse. The rocket blasted into the police cruiser at the front, sending off a chain reaction of explosions. Tarter had zero morality. He cared nothing about his fellow man. Not even men who served like he had. Especially since his little operation was burnt. He was now a wild animal backed into a corner. He would be willing to do anything to get out.

It was time Xander adopted some of David Tarter's morality.

It was time to get dirty.

Xander turned back to the other side of the hot dog stand, and sure enough, he caught a glimpse of a shadow moving in between the buildings on the shore side of the pier.

The scout.

Xander moved quickly down the pier, and just as he got to the arcade, a man in tactical gear and a black baseball cap rushed right by him. He was too focused on where he was going and didn't see Xander. Xander mirrored his footsteps and fell in behind him. He took three longer and quicker strides, and before the man could register someone behind him, Xander jumped forward and wrapped the shoulder strap of his AR-15 around the man's neck, then pulled him down on top of him as he fell to his back. He wrapped his legs around the man's waist, holding him in place, then slid his arm under the man's chin. The rear naked choke was a silent killer, and silence was paramount to keeping his position on the pier a secret from Tarter and the rest of his men.

Xander squeezed like an anaconda. The man was large, but position and technique were all that mattered in jujitsu. He choked the man unconscious, then, with a violent twist of his neck, made sure the man wouldn't be coming back to haunt him. To Xander's delight, the man had an extra magazine for the AR-15 and a tactical knife. A Ka-Bar, to be specific. Xander knew it well. The knife was a staple with his brothers in the marines. He unstrapped the sheath and fastened it to his own belt. Now he could kill silently if the opportunity arose.

He could hear more police pulling up to the fiery scene behind him. He needed Sam. Together it would be tough to bring these guys down. Without her, Xander was staring at odds that weren't in his favor. But he couldn't let that stop him. Because if his odds were bad, Carrie's odds of surviving these men without him were insurmountable. The last thing he did before moving on was take the dead man's earpiece and his hat. If Vegas were watching, they would have upped his odds a bit with that move.

With the knife strapped to his side and the semiautomatic rifle in his hands, he moved forward. He could hear a helicopter in the distance. But he knew they wouldn't engage. By now Marv would have been able to inform everyone what was going on out there. That there was a girl in danger. SWAT would be moving onto the beach soon, then climbing in behind him onto the pier. Tarter would be ready for them. Xander's only hope was that Tarter wouldn't be ready for him.

Xander moved around the winding metal of the roller coaster's frame. Up ahead of him was the iconic Ferris wheel. Beyond that the pier narrowed on his right and extended out over the ocean, the harbor office and a large restaurant the only things at its end. Since he couldn't see anyone at the moment, he figured they were searching for her there. Getting there for Xander would be the most dangerous part. The section of the pier that led to that end gave him nowhere to hide, no buildings for cover. If he were Tarter, he would most certainly have had someone watching.

"What do you see, Thompson?" a man's voice came through his commandeered earpiece.

The man he'd just killed—Thompson—was a big man, and he looked dumb. So Xander did the best big dumb guy voice he could muster. "All clear. Heading back."

"Roger."

The man in the earpiece bought it. He now had a clear run at getting across the empty section of the pier. However, he knew that nothing short of war waited on the other side.

45

A Real Kick in the Teeth

Kyle pulled Zhanna back away from the blazing fire.

"Are you okay? Zhanna, are you all right?"

He pulled her into his lap. She was dazed, but she seemed to be coming around.

Sam came in through his earpiece. "Are the two of you all right?"

"Barely. If that rocket, or missile, or whatever the hell it was would have come a second later, we'd be dead." Kyle sat Zhanna up and held her there. "You okay?"

"I think so," Zhanna finally responded. "What the hell happened?"

"Marv said they had a rocket launcher, I guess they decided to use it."

Kyle stood and helped Zhanna to her feet. The fire at the mouth of the pier continued to blaze, and the police cars to their left were in shambles. Kyle's ears were ringing from the explosion. More police cars were coming down the street, so he pulled Zhanna toward the stairs down to the beach. He had left his CIA credentials back in the truck, and he didn't have time to explain to the police just what in the hell he and a beautiful Russian were doing at the scene of a domestic terrorist attack. With weapons.

Kyle had been to the Santa Monica Pier several times, so he knew there was an alternate set of stairs on the sides that they could use to get back onto the pier. He pointed this out to Zhanna, and the two of them resumed making their way to Xander.

"There goes Xander, right there," Sam pointed out.

She was crouched beside Jack on the roof of the Shore Hotel looking through a spotting scope.

"You sure about that?" Jack peered through the sniper rifle's scope. "He wasn't wearin' a hat earlier."

"That's him. I can tell by the way he runs."

"The two of you is thick as thieves, huh?"

"We are," she answered. Then she moved her scope from Xander running along the pier, up in front of him to the second level of the restaurant. "There is a man on the—"

"I see him," Jack broke in. "He's got a gun, but I don't—"

"Take him out!"

"Now hang on, he ain't gonna use it. Not yet anyway."

"He thinks it's his own man." Sam followed what Jack was saying.

"That's right. Ole X must have taken that hat off one of their men. Good thinkin'."

"Shoot him anyway, Jack. Xander thinks he is on his own right now. Let's send him a message letting him know that he's not."

Xander pulled the cap down low over his eyes and jogged for the end of the pier. If whoever just checked in over the earpiece didn't like what he saw, there was no way around it: Xander knew he was a dead man. About halfway across the empty stretch of planked wood, the ocean now under him, he heard a crack from somewhere behind him. Instinct kicked in, and even though it would have been too late, he dove to the ground. An automatic response to the sound of a rifle being shot. But a smile quickly grew across his face when he looked up and saw a man drop from the second story of the restaurant.

He wasn't alone after all.

Xander jumped to his feet and sprinted for the restaurant ahead of him on his right. After stepping around the man Jack just took out, he sidled up to the wall, next to one of the many oversized windows in the restaurant. The windows were of no help to Xander. He couldn't see a thing inside. But he knew if someone was in there, they could easily see him. A cool ocean breeze blew across his face. With his back to the wall he looked up in the direction of where the sniper rifle must have fired from. He knew Jack was watching, so with his fingers held up against the dark wood of the building behind him, he counted down.

3 . . .

2 . . .

1 . . .

Xander opened the door of the restaurant, and just to his left a bullet shattered a window and the shadow of a man fell to the floor. He knew Jack would have his night-vision scope on, and clearly it was working. Another man in the lower level heard the crash of broken glass, and when his shadow passed in front of a window at the back of the restaurant, Xander squeezed the trigger on the AR-15, and the flashes from the muzzle showed a man dropping to the ground.

"What the hell is going on over there?" A man's voice came through Xander's earpiece.

David Tarter.

Xander did his best to clear the bottom floor of the restaurant, but there were a lot of places to hide. Booths, tables, a bar—men could be anywhere.

"Rodgers, you listening to me? What is going on over there?"

It was Xander's turn to speak.

"Rodgers isn't feeling so hot. He'll have to get back to you on that one, boss."

"King," Tarter said with disdain. "You just don't know how to mind your own business, do you?"

Xander moved through the swinging door into the kitchen and gave it a once-over. All was empty.

"What the hell are you doing, Tarter? Everyone knows you're an asshole, but trafficking young girls? That's low, even for a dirtbag like you."

"Oh yeah? We all can't be choir boys and live off Daddy's money, King. Speaking of daddies, I heard your old man murdered your mommy. That must have been a real kick in the teeth."

Xander stopped dead in his tracks. He didn't need motivation to save Carrie and take out Tarter, but hearing David taunt him with the murder of his own mother made his eyes glaze over. That primal feeling that came over him back on that mountain in Sinaloa burned up the back of his spine. He tapped the release button on his rifle, ejecting the magazine from its well. He felt for the top round with his index finger as he popped in a fresh mag, struck the bolt release with the palm of his left hand, and walked back out into the dining room, heading straight for the stairs.

Ready to hunt.

"Did you happen to hear how that story ended, Tarter?"

Silence.

Xander ascended the stairs.

"They say those who don't learn from history are doomed to repeat it."

"Keep talking, King. I can't wait to shut your smart-ass mouth, once and for all."

Xander turned the corner and sprayed the man coming for him with a string of bullets. His heart rate was steady, his breathing was normal, but his senses were tingling. He felt like a man in his element. For whatever reason, he was meant to do this. Mentally and physically, he could feel that now, more than ever, that he was uniquely qualified to be the man who fought for others. Now that he was no longer just fighting for himself, that much was clear.

This was his calling.

"Men much better than you have been trying for years to shut me up, Tarter. Good luck."

46

Someone Order a Pizza?

Xander stepped over the man he'd filled with bullets and continued down the aisle between the tables on his left and booths on his right. Out of the corner of his eye, the fire from the pier drew his attention for a split second, and it was long enough for him to feel someone wrap their arms around him, tackling him to the ground. The man landed on him with force and raised up to punch him. Xander dodged his head left as a shadow of an arm came at his head. The man punched the tile floor and cried out in pain. Using that miss, Xander bridged his hips as he trapped the man's arm and rolled over on top of him. A classic jujitsu sweep.

"Always use your elbows, that way you don't break your hand."

The words were automatic for Xander as he dropped an elbow onto the man's forehead. But at this point in the fight with Tarter's men, unconscious wasn't good enough. He slid his thumb across the snap and pulled the Ka-Bar knife from its sheath. This man was aiding the sale of a girl into slavery. That made it easy to slide the knife into his throat. As blood flowed from the dead man, the tat of a semiautomatic rifle sounded off behind him, and bullets clanged into the tables along the wall in front of him.

Xander rolled to his right, under a four-top table which he tipped over to create a shield. More shots were fired, definitely from more than one gun. He was pinned down. He reached his gun over the table and sprayed some bullets just to back them off for a second. He heard one of the guns shooting at him click—an empty magazine. Xander rose to one knee to fire, but before he could get off a shot, he heard a quick BOOM-BOOM-BOOM-BOOM!

Shotgun blasts.

The two shadows at the far end of the dining room dropped out of sight, and someone walked in from the right side of the room.

"Someone order a pizza?"

Kyle Hamilton.

Xander jumped to his feet.

"Kyle?"

"And Zhanna. Are you all right?" she said as she walked around the corner behind Kyle.

Xander felt a wave of relief wash over him as he ran over and gave them a hug.

"How'd you get up here?"

"The deck goes all the way down out there," Kyle explained. "We saw gunshots flashing in the upstairs window. We were just hoping we made it in time. They blew up the entire entrance to the pier. Have you found the girl?"

"Not yet, she must be hiding in the office next door." Xander jogged over to the two gunmen Kyle had just mowed down. Neither of them was Tarter. "Tarter is still alive, we have to hurry. You two make sure we cleared this building. I'm going to get David."

"That's it? You're not going to even acknowledge my pizza line?" Kyle asked.

"Let's just say it wasn't as bad as Yahtzee. So there's that."

Xander was referencing a moment in Paris when Kyle shouted Yahtzee to distract a gunman from surprising Xander. The pizza line was an attempt to wash that embarrassing moment away. It didn't work.

"I'll never live that down," Kyle said, disappointed.

As soon as the last word left Kyle's lips, the three of them could hear the faint hum of a motor in the distance. It was getting closer to them, and it was coming fast. Then Xander heard David's voice in his ear.

"A SEAL always leaves himself an out."

Two things registered immediately. One, Tarter was about to make a run for it. Two, that was a boat's motor that they heard, and it was already much louder than before, so it was really moving. Xander glanced out the window facing Santa Monica: SWAT was coming up the side steps of the pier in the distance. Then he turned 180 degrees and looked out at the darkness of the ocean beyond the window. He wasn't close enough to see the pier below them, but he could feel it in his bones that David was making a run for the end of it, and that boat they could hear was his exit plan.

"New plan," Xander said as he opened the door on the city side of the restaurant—the only side with a way down. "I'm still going after David, but you two make sure SWAT doesn't kill me before I get to him."

Xander didn't wait for a response; he opened the door to the deck, jumped the eight steps to the first landing, turned and jumped the last eight to the bottom. As he turned the corner for the edge of the pier, he raised his gun and wrapped his finger around the trigger. The rail was about fifty yards from him, and thanks to the soft light of the fingernail moon, he could see David pulling himself up to the top of the rail. Without hesitation, Xander squeezed the trigger, but as he heard his own gun fire, he watched David drop out of sight to the water below. Simultaneously, he could hear the boat, and see its light coming in from the right as it slowed to pick Tarter from the water.

Xander broke into a dead sprint. If that boat pulled away, there was a chance he would never see David Tarter again. Xander wasn't OCD, he didn't have to have everything perfect, but there was no way he would be able to leave this thing open-ended. It would haunt him until the day he died. And he was through with things from his past keeping him awake at night and driving every decision he made by day. He had no idea what he would be getting into once he jumped over that rail, but not knowing the future didn't really matter.

It never had, and it never would.

47

A *Hell* of a View

The passenger car wobbled again as another strong ocean breeze swept through. Carrie had never been afraid of heights, but this was beginning to scare her. She only jumped on the Ferris wheel because the men were right behind her inside the police station. She was going to run for one of the buildings at the end of the pier, but when she heard the gunshots from inside the police station, she panicked and jumped in the first cart that came around low enough for her to get into. They had almost seen her when her tub came back around to the bottom. She thought for sure that they had her, but the two men were too focused on combing through the vendor stands to look in the Ferris wheel. Every time the wheel made a full rotation, she thought they would surely find her. But then she heard more gunshots, and just at the peak of the wheel's rotation, the power shut down, and there she was, stuck more than a hundred feet in the air. Apparently, right above a full-on war zone.

All she heard from the time the power went off were explosions, sirens, and gunfire. Was all of this really for her? Had her hero in the basement managed to get out? Was he looking for her?

For over a half hour, she had managed to keep her curiosity from getting the best of her. But now that the gunfire had slowed and she could hear a motor coming in her direction, she couldn't help but look. Inch by inch, she peeked her head above the top of the cart she'd been cowering in. The first thing she saw was a massive fire at the edge of the pier and what looked like dozens of cop cars, all flashing their blue and red lights. She raised up a little more, and she could see a group of what looked to be policemen moving onto the pier from the stairway going up the side. That brought some relief, but she still had no way down. The power could be out for a while. As she moved her left leg around so she could check the other end of the pier, where she heard the motor coming from, the cart creaked loudly as it wobbled back and forth. Her stomach dropped and she froze her movements. Without the Ferris wheel in its normal steady rotating motion, it seemed the cart was much more vulnerable to movement.

A fear of heights was quickly settling in.

She moved more slowly this time. Then she raised her head to peek at the end of the pier. The source of the motor's sound became visible. A boat was approaching the end of the pier, and it was moving fast. She heard a couple of shots from what looked like the restaurant where she and her mom had eaten last time they were there. She squinted trying to focus on where the shots had come from, but she couldn't quite see. She raised up a bit further, the cart wobbling in the wake of her shaky legs. The boat was coming to a stop at the end of the pier when she could have sworn she saw someone dive face-first right over the rail. When she leaned out just a little farther, right above her head something slammed into the metal that fastened her cart to the rest of the wheel. It startled her, and when she fell back onto the floor of the cart, she could swear there was a hole in the white painted metal that wasn't there before.

The thing that scared her most was that it looked an awful lot like a bullet hole.

48

All Aboard

Xander planted his right foot and launched himself forward, flying over the top rail at the end of the pier. Looking before he leaped would have been ideal, but there had been no time for that. Halfway down the twenty-foot drop he heard the throttle being pushed, and the three large engines fixed to the back of the massive center-console Boston Whaler roared to life, surging the boat forward. As Xander fell, he reached out with both hands, bracing for impact at the back of the boat. But the boat was power-ful, and it moved just enough that when he hit the water where the boat used to be, his hand was lucky to find the cleat at the far-right side of the back of the boat. In rapid succession, his body hit the cold water of the Pacific Ocean, his shoulder was almost jerked from its socket, and he drank about a gallon of sea water. He was lucky it wasn't worse. If the boat had moved a couple of inches to the right before he dove into the water, instead of hitting the right end of the boat his arms could very well have landed right in the middle of the spinning blades of the motor just to his left. As it were, he found himself holding on for dear life, being dragged through the water by the powerful speedboat.

When the boat jerked him forward, his AR-15 was torn from his shoulder. The water washing over him at that point was enough to drown him. If he didn't pull himself up onto the boat now, before it got up to top speed, there would be no way to hang on. As the boat hit a wave, it actually helped him swing his right arm forward, and he was able to catch the bottom part of the rail just above his left hand. The force of the pull was unbelievable. The roar of the engines was deafening. The water drowning his face inhibited him from taking a breath, and after the run and jump that put him in his current position, he had very little air to spare. He was going to have to let go.

He pulled once again with all his might, but his forearms and shoulders were on fire. He barely even budged. And it was only getting more difficult as the boat gained speed. Like a bodybuilder pushing up the last rep of an impossibly heavy bench press, his arms were failing him. He wasn't holding on longer than humanly possible because he needed to find Carrie. Most likely, she was now safe. And it wasn't because he had any sort of vendetta against Tarter. It was because of what Carrie had said down in that basement that kept him holding on against all hope.

They brought two of us on the plane. They already took her somewhere else.

There was a girl somewhere at that very moment going through the most terrifying experience of her life. She had already been kidnapped by strange men. Torn from her family. Hog-tied, gagged, thrown around in a van and then a plane. Only to be taken to some monster who now could do whatever he wanted to her, most likely with no one having any idea where she was.

No one but David.

Xander's hands squeezed once more, harder, when all they wanted to do was let go. He tensed every muscle in his body. He had to hang on. If he could manage to keep hold of the back of the rail, maybe the boat would hit another wave just right and he could—

The nose of the boat pitched upward, hard, momentarily suspending the water's violent push against Xander's body. And because he had adjusted his grip, he was ready. He jerked with his arms in a rowing motion, and his body pulled from the water and slammed against the back of the boat. When the engine's propellers once again found purchase in the water, the boat jerked forward and Xander scrambled, barely able to grab a different rail, one that separated the engine reservoir from the far back seats of the boat. The small reservoir that he had pulled himself into was just wide enough for his body. Though he had managed to pull himself up, one wrong move at the speed they were traveling and it would be all for naught. He could see the back of two men's heads just over the rise of the stern. They were standing at the center console. Two walkways wrapped around the outside of that center console and opened up to a seating area at the front of the boat. There was another man sitting there at the bow.

With his body almost entirely spent, he pulled himself to his knees. He barely had the strength to maintain an upright position against the bounce of the boat on the water. But if he could maintain the element of surprise, his lack of strength wouldn't matter as much. The man on the left was a lot larger than the man steering the boat. Xander knew that it was David. He took two deep breaths, desperately fighting against complete fatigue, and brought himself up to a crouching position.

The wind was whipping into him, pushing him, doing its best to topple him off the back of that boat. He steadied himself with two hands, holding onto the backs of the seats in front of him, then finally pulled himself up to his feet.

It was now or never.

Just before he went to run at Tarter from behind, his hand found an empty sheath where it meant to find the Ka-Bar knife.

The ocean had claimed it as well. But there was no time for it to matter. He knew he wouldn't be able to hold Tarter with his arms; they were burnt, and David would still be fresh. His only chance would be to use the only parts of his body that had any strength left. In the battle to get himself up on the boat, his legs for the most part had been innocent bystanders. That was how he would have to do his damage.

Xander pushed forward over the seats and jumped on David's back. Because David wasn't expecting it, Xander was able to wrap his left leg around David's waist like a belt; then he closed his right leg over his own left ankle, and as they fell to the left walkway of the boat, he had David in a body triangle. The most effective way to hold someone in place from behind. Xander also managed to slip his arm under David's chin, catching him in a rear naked choke. If Xander had been fresh, there would have been no way for David to fight him, but as Xander squeezed, he could tell the pressure he was applying wasn't near his best.

David began to thrash around violently. He was able to get a good push off the side of the boat with his left arm, rolling Xander onto his back. David went with him because Xander's lock with his legs was inescapable. Over the roar of the boat's engine, Xander heard a man shout—most likely the driver—but couldn't make out what he said. The driver didn't so much as slow the boat, however, because he likely knew that if he did, the police would easily catch them. David continued to fight Xander's hands, doing everything he could to keep from being choked. Xander saw that the driver of the boat must have been shouting at the third man to get his attention. It worked because a large man stepped into sight. He had a gun pointed toward them, but he wouldn't be able to shoot. The boat was all over the place, and he couldn't risk shooting his boss.

"Let him go!" the man shouted.

Because he couldn't risk shooting it, Xander knew the man would have to let go of the gun and get down there to help his boss. He also knew that if he let go of the body lock he had on David, he was in trouble.

This was going to get tricky.

Xander let go of the choke and began to launch elbows downward on the top of David's head.

"Don't just stand there, get him!" David shouted to the big man as he gasped for air.

The man did as he was told and slung his gun over his shoulder. Xander squeezed even tighter with his legs, putting extreme pressure on David's midsection. If nothing else, it would make it harder for him to breathe. It was all Xander had at the moment. The big man dropped to his knees beside them so he could get a good shot at Xander. He threw his lunch-pail-sized fist down on Xander's head. The lights around the bottom of the boat allowed Xander to see the fist in time to shift his head to the right. It sounded like a baseball bat when it struck the floor beside his ear.

Xander couldn't punch the big man, so while he continued to hold David with his legs, he did the only thing he could and reached his right hand between the man's legs until he found his groin, then used everything he had left in his grip to squeeze it like a vise. The man let out a roar of pain. Xander simultaneously hammered the side of David's head with his left fist. David finally caught his hand and held it in place. Xander was now completely vulnerable.

The man slammed both of his hands down on Xander's arm, breaking the grip on his groin. He just couldn't hold on. He knew what was coming, and there was nothing he could do about it. He felt a heavy blow to his head, and purple stars burst in front of his eyes. On pure instinct, Xander managed to push off the big man with his right hand, scooting himself over just enough that the second fist barely missed his head. If that second attempt would have made contact, it would have been lights out.

49

King's Reign

The position Xander was in wasn't working. He couldn't win the fight from his back. Not against two of them. He was going to have to let go of the body lock. He waited for just the right moment, right when the big man was once again drawing back his fist, and pulled his right leg off his left, brought it forward, hard, and caught the big man in the jaw. The man fell back, hitting his head against the rail, and dropped to the ground. At the same time, David felt the body lock release and turned into Xander, who was now in the worst possible position.

Without any hesitation David threw his first elbow, fast, right at Xander's forehead. David was smart. He knew that elbows did more damage than fists when it came to soft tissue. Xander managed to get both of his forearms in front of his face in a defensive boxing position, and they absorbed the blow of the oncoming elbow. Another one rained down right behind it, then another.

"I'm gonna kill you, King! You son of a bitch!" David screamed as he kept pounding.

The blows hurt, but not like they would if they were bouncing off his head. Xander needed to turn this around, and fast. If the big guy woke up right now, it was over. He was going to have to use David's aggression against him. One of the most important things in a fight is staying in control. Right now, David was angry, and it was showing in the way his weight was going off balance after each elbow he threw. Much like when Xander lost control in Paris and almost got himself killed by Akram Khatib.

Xander waited until David was in another full downward swing; then he violently bucked his hips upward. That motion, coupled with David's overextending momentum, threw him forward just enough for Xander to slide out the back door between David's legs. Both men scrambled to their feet at the same time. Both men were laboring for breath, and both were off balance from the motion of the boat. In his right peripheral vision Xander saw the driver of the boat swinging a fire extinguisher at his head. Xander jerked back, landing on his back. The momentum of the swing carried the man toward the side of the boat, and Xander was kind enough to help him on over the edge with a hard kick in the ass. As the man flew overboard, Xander jumped to his feet and grabbed the fire extinguisher from the floor of the boat. He tossed it at David, who was charging at him, and it did the job of slowing him down by forcing him to dodge it. This gave him just enough time to reach for the controls and pull the throttle back to neutral, pitching the nose of the boat forward, sending David onto his back. The boat came to a stop, and for the first time, Xander had solid footing.

Both he and David located the big man's gun at the same time, and they both hurried for the left side of the boat. They reached the gun simultaneously, both wrapping their hands around each end of it. Unfortunately for Xander, he was on the business end of it and had to let go when David pulled the trigger. Bullets clapped into the back seats, and the loud report echoed over the water. David couldn't point the gun at Xander because it was still strapped around the big man's arm and neck, so Xander took advantage and head-butted David in the nose. The sickening pop of the cartridge snapping sounded loudly, and blood gushed from David's nostrils.

David wasn't at all deterred. He rolled to his left, into the open space around the front of the center console, and Xander immediately rushed him, tackling him onto the wraparound cushion behind him. Xander bounced up, then crammed a knee into David's midsection and delivered an elbow to the side of his head. Xander turned to find the big man disoriented but rising to his feet. Xander crossed the open space between them, front-kicked the gun from his hands, then torqued his waist, pulling an overhand right above his head and whipping it down to meet the man's jaw. The man dropped to his knees and the boat wobbled under his weight.

Another important rule in a fight, especially with multiple attackers, is never turn your back on anyone if you can help it. On that tiny boat, it simply couldn't be helped. And Xander paid for it. David had been able to get up faster than Xander had hoped, and Xander felt a thump on the back of his head. Those purple spots returned, and Xander dropped to a knee. He felt the bottom of a boot connect with the middle of his back, and before he could retaliate, he was on his stomach, lying face to belt with the big man he'd just put down. His head was swimming. His eyes found the shiny buckle on the big man's belt, and it helped him uncross his eyes and focus. As David turned him over, out of the corner of his eye, Xander noticed something else on that same belt. And though he could have been imagining it, he swore he heard a helicopter in the distance.

"This is the last time you fuck me over, King."

Through blurred vision, Xander saw David standing over him. His arms were raised above his head. Xander blinked, then saw the red fire extinguisher suspended there in David's hands.

"This time tomorrow, I'll be sipping mai tais on the beach

while some dude is stuffing that little girl like a Thanksgiving turkey."

David kicked Xander in the ribs. Pain seared all the way down his right side.

"Say hello to your mommy for me."

He saw David's arms jerk; the fire extinguisher was coming. Xander shot his hand toward the big man's belt, extracting his tactical knife, and as David brought the extinguisher down, Xander shifted onto his side. The fire extinguisher slammed into the floor of the boat, just as Xander slammed the blade of the knife into the side of David's stomach. David's face was one of shock. He hadn't expected Xander to have the knife. The fire extinguisher fell from his hands and clanked against the floor of the boat.

Xander extracted the blade from David's stomach as he brought himself up to his knees. He punched him hard in the knife wound, and David's legs buckled from the pain, dropping him to his knees as well. David made a move to grab for Xander's arm but he was too weak to stop him. Xander slammed the knife into the side of David's neck, and fell forward with David as he fell on his back.

Xander held the knife there for a moment. Partially to relish the fact that he had won the battle. Partially because he was too exhausted to move.

Xander watched as David was bleeding out. While he waited, and while David couldn't talk back, Xander wanted to make sure he heard Xander's smart-ass mouth one last time.

"Remember what I told you about history?" Xander whispered in his ear.

David responded with a blood-gurgling moan. Xander finally let go and labored to his knees. Defying his body's need to collapse, Xander scooted forward and lifted the seat cushion on a section of the sofa. Inside, he found what he was looking for, and he tied the big man to the rail of the boat. Everything inside him wanted to kill him too, but they needed the man to wake up and spill any information he had about where the girl might be. With David bleeding out below him and Gabriela and Francisco already dead, there was no one else around to offer any information.

Then it hit him: nowhere in all the chaos back on the pier had Xander seen David Tarter's beloved sidekick.

Jonathan Haag was still alive.

50

Target Practice

All of Santa Monica was in a panic. Police had done their best to evacuate the area around the pier and to keep those who wouldn't leave inside their homes. The fire at the entrance to the pier was still blazing, and the normally busy street that ran directly behind it was empty, save for cops. Jonathan pulled back the bolt on his M24 sniper rifle and slammed in a new round. As he peered down the scope at the shifting Ferris wheel cart, he felt sick to his stomach.

"How the hell did I end up here?" he said to himself.

If he was any kind of shot at all, the poor girl would already be dead, and he would be on his way out of town. But shooting a sniper rifle at long distance had never been his strong suit. And being years removed since the last time he had even shot one made it worse. Somewhere in the back of his mind, he supposed the fact that he really didn't want to kill the girl was playing a part in him missing the shot. But he really had no choice. Other than David's brother, Tommy, she was the only person who could link him to the crime. And Jonathan could handle Tommy.

Sure, Jonathan knew that Xander would assume he and David were in it together, because he knew they always were. But he wouldn't have proof. Jonathan squeezed the trigger on the silenced sniper rifle once again, and once again he missed the cart entirely. The cart was moving, it was breezy, and it was a long way from where he stood in the room at the top of the Shutters on the Beach Hotel. But it was as close as he could get and still be out of the fray.

He was lucky to have a shot at her at all. David had told him to be ready to come and get them. That he would be the last line of defense if for some reason they couldn't get to the boat, which was the other backup plan. When they saw the girl make a run for it from the house to the pier, they didn't really have time to solidify anything spectacular. And now it was just in a scan of the pier with his sniper rifle that he had been lucky enough to spot the girl. He hadn't heard from David in over a half hour, so he had to assume the worst. Especially since the power at the pier had gone down.

Once again, he pulled back the bolt, then slid it back into place, chambering a round. David had really left him in a spot with this one. But this was nothing new. He had been following David around from the time they were teenagers, and it had always left him in trouble. Not this kind of trouble, but never a good place. He didn't know why he let him drag him into things like where he was in that moment. But, good or bad, Jonathan never really had anybody else in his life that he could count on.

Besides, this wasn't about that now. This was about the rest of his life. And if this girl lived to tell, he would be thrown in jail forever. He looked back through the scope and once again found the cart. All he had to do was put a few holes in it; one of them would easily kill her. He had to adjust a little more for the wind. He dialed in the scope once more, determined to put an end to this nightmare.

51

Even Wackos Can Be Lovable

The engines on the boat were still idling in the water. And before he could get back to the console to radio for help, or drive the boat back to the pier himself, the sound Xander thought he had heard earlier was suddenly coming right for him. He was forced to assume the worst, because so far that was all that had happened. The thought of another fight drained even more of his already depleted energy. But this was always the point in a soldier's life that separated him from everyone else. He had been trained to shut off the part of his body that said "stop" and keep on going.

As the helicopter approached, Xander turned back to the big man on the floor of the boat and pulled the AR-15 strap up over his head. When he turned back around, the helicopter was right in front of him. As Xander raised the AR-15, he pictured Jonathan Haag doing the same from the opening in the side of the chopper. A bright light flipped on, momentarily blinding him. He ducked behind the center console and once again raised the gun to defend himself. That was when a familiar voice came over the loud speaker, one Xander hadn't heard in a while, but that goofy man's Ukrainian accent was unmistakable.

"Jack says boss need help. Viktor jump in helicopter to come help. Looks like you already take care of bad guy. Did they not know that boss is good at killing bad guy?"

Viktor.

The tension fell from Xander's shoulders. The weight of the evening finally gave way, and a smile grew across his face.

"I send down ladder. Boss lady says there is still work for boss man to do."

Xander knew he meant Sam, but he couldn't fathom what could possibly be left. Unless Haag had Carrie. Xander pulled himself to a standing position, and when the rope ladder fell from the helicopter, he climbed up.

"The news must not be too bad from Sam," Xander said as he pulled himself inside and got his first glimpse of Viktor. Same crazy disheveled hair, same wide goofy-ass smile. "If it was, I'm assuming you wouldn't be wearing that familiar shit-eatin' grin."

Xander walked over and wrapped his arm around Viktor. Viktor let go of the controls to embrace him, and the front of the helicopter pitched forward. He quickly let go of Xander and scrambled to level it out. Xander just shook his head.

"Sorry, boss, there is no pause button on real helicopter."

"Just give me your phone, you crazy son of a bitch. Sam say what the problem was?"

"She does not like Viktor, so I don't get extra information."

Xander nodded as he dialed Jack's phone. He knew Sam's phone was still lost somewhere with his own.

Jack answered. "Hey, Vik, tell me he's all right."

"Hey Jack, it's Xander. I'm fine. Tarter is out of the picture."

"X! Damn good to hear your voice, and even better to hear you ended that bastard. Never had a doubt. Sam will be glad to hear you're okay."

"What's the problem back there? Viktor said that Sam told him I had more work to do."

"You do, but it ain't what you think. Kyle and Zhanna was talkin' with SWAT when they heard the girl scream. You won't believe this, but she's stuck at the top of the Ferris wheel. Sam hoped if Viktor found you, and you were okay, that you'd be able to drop down and get her."

Xander was relieved to hear that Carrie was okay. Finally, some good luck. If her cart would have been at the bottom of the Ferris wheel's cycle when the power went out, she would be dead right now.

"So you're telling me that Sam trusts Viktor to hold the helicopter steady over the Ferris wheel long enough for me to get Carrie out of there? No way. Coast Guard can handle that one. It will be much safer. Plus, I'm not sure at this point I could even lift her into the helicopter."

Xander of course was exaggerating a bit, but his arms were about as dead as he could ever remember them being in all the time he had been a soldier.

"Xander, hang on just a sec," Jack said. Then Xander heard him talking to Kyle. "Do what? I'm talking to Xander now. Yeah, he's okay. I'll tell him. Get that girl out of there, Kyle!" Then Jack's voice came back to the phone. "Xander, you gotta get over to that Ferris wheel now. There ain't no time to wait for the Coast Guard."

Xander's heart jumped into his throat.

"Someone is shooting at that poor girl. Has been for a minute, Kyle said, but they just figured it out."

"A sniper?" Xander said.

"Well, I don't know. You figure a sniper'd be able to hit her already. But you'd better hurry if you're close."

"I'm on my way. Tell Kyle to let SWAT know we're coming."

Xander ended the call. From somewhere in the bottomless pit

of his brain, he remembered Jonathan always scoring low on the sniper tests. It had to be him. He was trying to cover his tracks.

"I don't like that look, boss. Every time Xander King get look like that on face, Viktor get shot at."

"Sorry to tell you, Viktor, this time is no different. Take us back to the Ferris wheel, you're going to help me save a young woman's life."

Viktor bounced in his seat with excitement and steered the helicopter back toward the pier.

"I love when boss let Viktor help save people."

Xander shook his head. He couldn't believe his life was once again in the hands of that lovable wacko.

52

Holding On for Dear Life

A large crowd of first responders, SWAT members, and EMTs had gathered on the pier, but most looked to be steering clear of the Ferris wheel. Who could blame them when someone was firing at it from a distance? Xander knew he couldn't worry about the bullets that would be coming his way as he helped Carrie to safety. He had no choice but to hope that Jonathan was as bad as he remembered. So far, if she hadn't been hit yet, chances were that he had only gotten worse.

"Bring us down as close as you can to the very top, Vik. Even though I am saying it, it goes without saying that you have to be steady."

"I have been lots of practice, boss. Only one customer so far at helicopter tour company is suing."

"A real shot of confidence," Xander said.

"I know, right!?"

Xander could see in his eyes that he actually believed it was a good thing.

Viktor slowed the helicopter over the top cart on the wheel. Though Xander didn't have a lot of confidence in Viktor keeping the copter steady, he could tell that he had improved.

"Right here, Vik!" Xander shouted back as he made sure the rope ladder was still secure.

He looked down over the edge, but due to the construction of the Ferris wheel carts—they were like saucers on the bottom, but over each of them was a metal awning, fashioned like an umbrella —he couldn't see if Carrie was there, much less if she was still alive. While the awning would make it easier for him to step down if needed, it completely blocked his view from above. If Carrie was still alive, he imagined she was most likely frantically waving her arms at the moment, screaming for help.

Something smacked loudly against the back end of the chopper.

"I think that was bullet, boss! Might want to hurry!"

Thanks, Viktor.

Though Haag wasn't a great shot, the helicopter was big enough for a novice to hit. As Xander put his first foot out over the edge, he hoped that Haag didn't get lucky. And as it normally did in situations like this, his mind flashed through dozens of missions where he had stepped off a helicopter into far worse situations than this. But that didn't make it any less dangerous, because the cargo he was determined to retrieve this time was much more precious.

As he climbed down toward the top of the cart below him, a quick glance told him that there were a lot of hotels Haag could be firing from. But the boys in blue would find him. He could see the lights of their cars searching for him now. Even if Haag was successful in what he was trying to do, Xander knew it would all be for naught. The LAPD would never let him get away.

Another bullet clanked off the thick white railing just outside the cart Xander was aiming for. Haag was getting closer. Xander hurried his pace, his arms feeling the fatigue as he steadied on the rope ladder. The umbrella top of the cart was just below him now, about five feet. But he was out of ladder. The jump down wouldn't be a problem; it was getting back to the rope that made him nervous. A stiff breeze moved through just as Xander was about to jump, blowing him out away from the cart. Viktor really was doing an amazing job, and he didn't even have a spotter telling him left, right, up, or down. And right on cue, Viktor waited out the breeze and floated Xander right back where he was. Xander jumped and landed on top of the cart.

The cart shook violently back and forth, but immediately his question of whether or not Carrie was in there, and alive, was answered with an ear-piercing scream. Xander leaned over the edge.

"It's okay, Carrie," he shouted. "It's me. From the basement. Are you hurt?"

Looking down at the fear on her face as she huddled in fetal position was heartbreaking. But Xander had to get her out of there. The wind that the helicopter's rotors were creating was violently swaying the cart now.

"I'm okay!" Carrie screamed.

Xander could barely hear her over the noise of the chopper.

"But I can't move! Someone is shooting at me!"

"I know, Carrie, but I need you to get up now and take my hand!"

Xander reached down over the edge of the metal umbrella. Carrie didn't move.

"I can't! He'll shoot me!"

This time a bullet ricocheted off the metal not two inches from Xander's leg.

"Carrie, I need you to trust me! I got you out of that basement, didn't I?"

She still didn't move.

"Didn't I?" Xander shouted again.

Another bullet cracked metal, this time only a couple of inches from Carrie's head. Xander watched as she eyed the bullet hole in horror, then she jumped to her feet.

"That's it, just grab my hand!"

She did.

Xander squeezed her hand with his left as he gorilla-gripped the edge of the metal umbrella with his right. He had no leverage, and he had nothing to secure himself with; this was going to have to be all arm. He decided since he was weak that faster was a better plan, so he jerked her upward as he rolled to his back. As soon as her chest was above the lip of the cart's cover, he wrapped his right arm around her waist and pulled her on top of him.

He got her out of the cart.

Before her mind could register a measure of safety, Xander scooped her up with him and then bent back down on a knee.

"Grab hold of my back, and don't let go!"

By now, Carrie had learned not to question the man who kept saving her, so she jumped on and squeezed her legs around his waist and her arms around his neck.

"Hang on tight!"

Xander didn't give her much time to squeeze before he reached for the bottom rung of the ladder. He was going to have to pull all of their weight up the first few rungs, all arms. It was not going to be easy, and the longer he waited, the harder he figured it would be.

So he didn't wait.

As soon as the breeze brought the ladder to where he thought was the closest it was going to get to him, he reached out for it. At the same time, a bullet crashed through the windshield of the helicopter and Viktor must have been startled because it moved out away from the Ferris wheel. But Xander had already leaned for the ladder. There was no turning back. With the tip of his shoe that was still touching the top of the metal umbrella, watching the ladder move away, he gave as much extra push as he could. It was enough to get his left hand to the ladder, but the way his body jerked when his grip caught their weight, it shook loose Carrie's grip, and she slid down his right shoulder.

Xander felt her lose her grip around his neck, and in reflex, he shot his free hand down to her leg that was wrapped around his waist. He caught her leg at the knee, and he dug his fingertips into her leg as he squeezed. When he looked down, the 150-foot drop beyond her dangling dark hair seemed to morph into a thousand. She screamed in terror, and probably in pain. Xander would break her leg in half before he let go of her. But after the night he'd had, his mind was more powerful than his grip. And slowly, her jeans began to slide through his fingers.

When you've seen as many things as Xander had seen in war, been through as many horrifying missions, filled with death, betrayal, and death-defying stunts, you'd think you would've felt every sort of fear a human can feel. But feeling this innocent young girl literally slipping through his fingers made Xander terrified in a way he never thought possible. Her leg was like sand: the harder he squeezed, the faster she fell. At the last second, he caught her shoe, and he thanked God for a brief moment that she had tied it tight. But that didn't help him get her out of this.

Xander's left hand felt like it was melting into the bottom rung of the ladder. He knew Viktor couldn't see him, and that he couldn't step away from the controls for a second to check on him. He knew he would hold it as steady as he could until he saw Xander come up from that ladder. But there was no way that was going to happen. It was impossible for him to pull Carrie up now and then pull himself up too. And anyway, his grip on her shoe was failing him.

A flood of emotions ran all through Xander's system—pain, fear, anger—and when the helicopter began to lower slowly and in fact get closer to the Ferris wheel, you could add shocked to that list. He instinctively looked up, but of course there was nothing to see but the belly of the helicopter. It was when he looked back down that his entire emotional axis shifted yet again. Somehow, Kyle Hamilton had managed to crawl up the Ferris wheel and make his way out to the passenger car that was smack in the middle of its downward trek—the cart at the outermost point of the wheel. Later he would let Xander know that there was a ladder that ran up the middle of the wheel, and that it was only shimmying out on the crossbar the last fifty feet or so that had been tricky. But all Xander knew in that moment was that his friend had just magically appeared in the outermost cart, and somehow Viktor was able to see him. And although this gave Xander new life, it couldn't give him a new grip, and he was losing Carrie fast.

53

Fueled by the Fire

A few feet lower, and Xander finally understood how Viktor was able to navigate where he was going. Kyle was leaning out from the cart, a cell phone to his ear. Xander couldn't hear him, but he knew Kyle was talking to Viktor; it was the only thing that made sense. They were still too far away from the wheel, because they had to be; otherwise, the rotors spinning atop the helicopter would hit the side of the wheel. But it didn't matter anyway; he couldn't hold on to her any longer.

As Carrie screamed, so too did everything inside Xander. His lungs, his muscles, his heart.

"I can't hold her!" he shouted. Emotion and strain distorted his voice.

He didn't know why he said it, but maybe he was hoping someone in another realm would hear him and help him.

Then he remembered the moment he had in front of the mirror back on the plane. He didn't need to call on someone from another realm to help him. All he needed to do was reach inside those flames that burned deep inside him. The fire that he realized was there for moments just like this one.

"Swing the ladder!" Kyle shouted up at him.

"I can't hold her!"

Xander squeezed her shoe. At least he thought he did. He could no longer actually feel his arm below the elbow.

"Fight it, X! Swing the ladder and drop her! I'll catch her!"

Xander looked back up at his hand on the ladder; it was bright white. All the blood had drained from it. He looked back down at Carrie, then beyond her to Kyle. Though he didn't at all like what Kyle was asking of him, it was the only chance he had of saving her. She was about to fall either way; he might as well give her a chance. No part of his body wanted to move, but he pulled strength from that burning fire and lifted both legs out in front of him, then swung them as hard as he could backward, then immediately forward again. As he went to kick back one last time, he finally lost his grip on her.

"No!" Xander shouted.

"Aaaah!" Carrie screamed as she dropped.

"I got you!" Kyle shouted as he caught her.

The swinging motion had been enough. Kyle's words at just the right moment had saved her life. Xander watched as Kyle pulled her inside the cart. She was safe. As he reached up and hooked his elbow around the bottom rung to give his hands a break, it occurred to Xander that he hadn't heard another bullet come near them. The police must have closed in on Haag and either captured him or at least caused him to make a run for it.

"She's okay, X! I got her!" he heard Kyle call up to him.

He took his words in and slowly began to pull himself up. He couldn't bear to look down again. Not even one more time. He made it up to the entrance of the helicopter and collapsed onto its floor.

He had given everything his body had been capable of giving.

And it had been enough.

54

The Cable Guy

The sun was high in the sky as Xander and Sam rolled down Sunset Boulevard through Beverly Hills, California. Their windows were rolled down, and they were letting the warm breeze wash over them. On the radio Chris Stapleton was telling everyone how his lady was as smooth as Tennessee whiskey, and traffic wasn't even all that bad, considering they were in Los Angeles. It had been quite the week since they managed to shut down Francisco's entire human trafficking operation. Or Gabriela's. It was still unclear who had really been pulling the strings. Sam told Xander that Javier Romero had said it was Gabriela. And it didn't seem too far-fetched to them because, as it turned out, she indeed was the daughter of one of the highest-ranking bosses in the Sinaloa Cartel.

The CIA told Reign that they had heard rumblings from some of their contacts in Mexico that retaliation plans for the deaths of Gabriela and Francisco were being made. But until anything actually happened, Xander wasn't going to let any of those rumors bother him. Not today anyway, he was in too good of a mood.

Carrie was home recovering with her family. Xander had in fact broken her leg in two places while he was trying to hold on to her. When he went to visit her, his apology for breaking her leg was met with a hug. "My leg will heal," Carrie had said. "And thanks to you and your team, I'll be back to normal in no time."

The police had indeed apprehended Jonathan Haag. He of course told them that it was all David. Xander knew that he was telling the truth, but being guilty by association, combined with the fact that he was instrumental in helping David with his plans, was going to win him a lot of years behind bars.

"You look ridiculous, Xander," Sam told him from the passenger seat.

"And you don't?"

"They are never going to believe that you're the cable guy. Not a chance. Look at you."

Xander toggled the rearview mirror downward and took in his red polo shirt with the cable company logo on it.

"What? It's not that bad."

"Not that bad," Sam shifted in her seat to get a better look at him. "You look like you raided an eleven-year-old's Halloween costume drawer. Seriously, how did you fit into that shirt?"

Xander looked again. It *was* a little small, but he didn't let on that he agreed.

"Oh yeah, Sam. 'Cause eleven-year-olds dream all year of dressing up like a cable guy on Halloween."

"Doesn't change the fact that you look ridiculous."

"Maybe." He gave an inch. "But at least I still look good."

"And I don't?"

"No, Sam, that shirt is so big you're swimming in it."

"Ask your best friend if I look good in it. I barely got it back on before you showed up in this van."

A wry smile grew across her face.

"You and Kyle are disgusting."

"Just because you're going through a dry spell doesn't mean you should take it out on us."

Xander changed the subject. "Are we getting close, or not?"

"Yes, Mr. Sensitive, there is our turn right there."

Xander ignored Sam's jab about being sensitive and pulled up to the gate. He pressed the call button on the box, and a voice came through asking who was there.

"Cable guy," Xander said. Then he turned to Sam and whispered, "I always wanted to say that."

Sam, in typical Sam fashion, just rolled her eyes.

The gate opened to a beautifully landscaped driveway, and Xander pulled the mock cable company van forward.

"You know you can't kill him, right?"

Xander didn't answer.

"Xander, I'm serious. The only reason the FBI let us run your little charade here is because Director Hartsfield called in a personal favor. But she promised you wouldn't kill him. That's the only reason they're letting you do this."

"Pretty awesome, right? Remember when Charlize Theron did it in *The Italian Job*?"

"No, but are you wearing the same shirt she was?"

Xander put the van in park just a few steps from the front door.

"I'm not going to let you ruin this for me. I get it, the shirt is small, move on."

Sam laughed. Then she patted him on the arm.

"You really are a rare breed, Alexander King. How such an amazing soldier, so big and so strong, can be such an absolute child will always baffle me."

"Whatever. Just stay here. I'll be back in a minute."

"Xander," Sam said in a more serious tone. "Seriously, you can't kill him."

Xander shut the door and walked toward the front of the house. The "him" Sam kept referring to was Tony Sanders. An old, rich, and completely horrible excuse for a human being. And apparently, a man who thought himself completely above the law. Last night, CIA Director Hartsfield called Sam to inform her that the other girl—Ashley Thompson—who had been taken along with Carrie, had managed to escape Tony's home in Beverly Hills. The police and the FBI were already on their way to his house when Xander convinced them to let him finish what he started. Because of Director Hartsfield's rank, and because the FBI had already heard about Xander's heroics at the Santa Monica Pier, they gave the okay as long as they could keep surveillance on the house, and as long as Xander promised not to kill him.

Xander walked up to the front door and rang the doorbell. A few seconds later, a total sleazeball answered the door in a tacky maroon silk robe, a hand full of gold rings, and a gold rope chain that dangled an emerald-eyed panther's head down into his disgustingly hairy chest.

"'Bout time you got here, cable's been out all night. Get your ass in here and fix it. I got shit to do."

Tony took a puff of his cigarette, blew a cloud of smoke out his mouth into Xander's face, then turned around and walked back into the house.

Xander turned around and looked back at Sam. Due to the glare the sun created on the windshield, he couldn't actually see her, but he imagined she was giving some sort of signal not to kill him. Sam, if nothing else, always had been predictable.

The problem Xander was having was that Tony committed one of the cardinal sins of fighting: he turned his back on his opponent. What kind of man would Xander be if he didn't teach him a lesson?

Xander smiled to himself, turned back to the house, and practically floated through the front door with only one thought on his mind.

No kind of man at all.

ACKNOWLEDGMENTS

First and foremost, I want to thank you, the reader. I love what I do, and no matter how many people help me along the way, none of it would be possible if you weren't turning the pages.

To my family and friends. Every creative person is neurotic as hell about their creations, and I just want to thank you for always helping to keep my head on straight. And for indulging all of my ridiculous ideas.

To my editor, Deb Hall. Thank you for continuing to turn my poorly constructed sentences into a readable story. You are great at what you do, and my work is better for it.

To Team X, my advanced reader team. You are my megaphone in helping spread the word about each new novel I release. You all have become friends, and I thank you for catching those last few sneaky typos, and always letting me know when something isn't good enough. Xander appreciates you, and so do I. (Sam couldn't care less)

I would also like to thank the men and women in the military that do what Xander and his team do, in real life: protect us from the evil in the world. Thankfully what I write is fictional, but we know that your sacrifices are not. That includes police officers, EMT's, and anyone else that keeps our asses safe.

And finally, to the man/woman who invented pizza. You have contributed more to the happiness of mankind than any other human in the history of time. I think I speak for all of us: thank you.

ABOUT THE AUTHOR

Bradley Wright is an emerging author of action-thrillers. King's Reign is his fourth novel. Bradley lives with his family in Lexington, Kentucky. He has always been a fan of great stories, whether it be a song, a movie, a novel, or a binge-worthy television series. Bradley loves interacting with readers on Facebook, Twitter, and via email.

Join the online family:

www.bradleywrightauthor.com
info@bradleywrightauthor.com

Made in the USA
Las Vegas, NV
13 July 2021